Reviews of The Abdication

"As a discerning reader not easily impressed by genre fiction, The Abdication came as a long-desired, pleasant surprise. The novel is worthy not just to be read but for a compelling discussion afterward. Tula, a young woman, is the protagonist whose journey of self-discovery leaves the reader questioning free will, self-determination and the forces guiding fate. The novel is a journey of destiny, wisdom, and the abdication of a higher purpose."
Vincent Triola.

"A thoroughly enjoyable and compelling read – fast paced, full of adventure, it kept me seeking the answers to finding what was next. I especially related to the main character, who never gave up on her quest."
Mary McGrane.

"The characters draw you in, keeping you intrigued until the end. It's a novel you won't want to finish so you can stay in Tula's world a little longer. If you enjoy mystery, philosophy and action, then read The Abdication."
Sarah Byard.

"I thoroughly enjoyed this absorbing, multi-layered novel, which follows the story of Tula, a determined seeker of truth and destiny. There are adventures, heartbreak, spiritual truths, and science fantasy in this book. I loved the anagrams and the allegories, and I particularly loved the ending."
Jennifer's Reviews.

JUSTIN NEWLAND is an author of historical fantasy and secret history thrillers – that's history with a supernatural twist. His historical novels feature known events and real people from history which are re-told and examined through the lens of the supernatural.

His novels speculate on the human condition and explore the fundamental questions of our existence. As a species, as Homo sapiens sapiens – that's man the twice-wise – how are we doing so far? Where is mankind's spiritual home? What does it look or feel like? Would we recognise it if we saw it?

Undeterred by the award of a Doctorate in Mathematics from Imperial College, London, he found his way to the creative keyboard and conceived his debut novel, The Genes of Isis (Matador, 2018), an epic fantasy set under Ancient Egyptian skies. His second novel, a supernatural thriller entitled The Old Dragon's Head (Matador, 2018), is set in Ming Dynasty China. His third novel, The Coronation (Matador, 2019), speculates on the genesis of the most important event of the modern world – the Industrial Revolution.

His stories add a touch of the supernatural to history and deal with the themes of war, religion, evolution and the human's place in the universe.

He was born three days before the end of 1953 and holds a Ph.D. in Mathematics. He lives with his partner in plain sight of the Mendip Hills in Somerset, England.

THE
ABDICATION

JUSTIN NEWLAND

Matador
9 Priory Business Park,
Wistow Road, Kibworth Beauchamp,
Leicestershire. LE8 0RX
Tel: 0116 279 2299
Email: books@troubador.co.uk
Web: www.troubador.co.uk/matador
Twitter: @matadorbooks

ISBN 978 1800463 950
British Library Cataloguing in Publication Data.
A catalogue record for this book is available from the British Library.

Printed and bound in Great Britain by 4edge Limited
Typeset in 10.75pt Adobe Garamond Pro by Troubador Publishing Ltd, Leicester, UK

Matador is an imprint of Troubador Publishing Ltd

To the Trio.
Because the best debts are those which can never be repaid.

When a man loses his way, he feels desperate.
When a nation abandons its purpose, it slides into anarchy.
When Homo sapiens shuns its nature as the wise, the kind and the humane, it
can only be called…
The Abdication.

CHAPTER 1

The Welcome Boulder

Tula's swollen ankle ached as she trudged up the mountain. It had moaned incessantly, ever since she had left her home in the city before embarking on this journey. Then again, it had always hurt. Perhaps since birth: she could never remember that far back. She had complained to her parents, who could not afford to get it seen by the doctor.

A gust of wind whipped up particles of sand which spiralled in the fractious air ahead of her. She squinted and pulled her keffiyeh up to cover her nose. At this altitude, the air was a thin gruel, offering paltry nourishment. Her gut was rumbling, but that was nothing new. She had walked uphill all afternoon from Seliga in the valley below and now she was gasping for breath. Her backpack seemed to weigh as much as that boulder up ahead. A vulture circled effortlessly in the azure blue sky. There was another one above the next valley, griffon vultures searching for prey; so long as they left her alone.

Wisps of straw-coloured grass sprouted beside the graves of an unkempt cemetery. The top of the surrounding low stone wall was speckled with reddish spots, like splashes of copper rain. A few of the gravestones had fallen over and kissed the parched earth. This was the summit of a mountain and even the grand old yew trees huddled in one side of the cemetery were bending to the east, bowing to the omnipotent goddess of the winds in her distant unseen shrine.

Between the cemetery and the town lay a vibrant carpet of blue thorns; large cones of tiny blue flowers surrounded by a spiky, electric-blue collar.

Up ahead were the town walls, shimmering in the waves of heat rising from the scorched land. Finally, her journey's end was in sight. On the side of the road just outside the town's South Gate was the Welcome Boulder. It towered above her, which was not that difficult because in the city she was constantly mocked as the shortest amongst her peers. Most of the boulder was coated in that brownish-red dust. Towards the top of it was the immortal sign that declared the town's identity:

Welcome to Topeth.
The First Free Town and
'The Top' Town of all.

Long before her arrival, her parents and teachers had fired her imagination with their stories about Topeth. As the sign proudly declared, it was once 'The Top' town, not only because it was perched precariously on the highest mountain in the range, but also because it was the living exemplar of humanity's stumbling progress. Many years before, that epic story had featured Herman, the First Man. It told how he had ushered in a brilliant new freedom for mankind – hence the First Free Town. Yet, after that early spring advance, there was now a torrid decline in which mankind's development resembled a crumpled, fading autumnal leaf.

Many people asked whether their forefathers had used that freedom wisely. Some answered with a resounding 'Yes', but Tula had doubts. That was why she was in Topeth; to find out for herself.

On either side of the entrance road was a row of tall, spiky cacti, standing like pale, bloated fish out of water.

To the west of the town was a large area of open ground. Huge scars pitted the land which was dotted with peaked mounds of reddened earth. A gnarled ghost haunted the land. Crouched amidst its shadow lands were rickety sheds and wooden shacks, all dowsed in the same brown-red dust. Even the town's walls were tainted in the same hue. This was the infamous Topeth open cast copper mine.

In these dangerous times, many towns shut their gates well before sundown. Thankfully, the main gates to Topeth were still open.

An old man sat cross-legged with his back against one of the gate posts, whittling a long, rod-like piece of wood and chewing on a wedge of tobacco. What an obnoxious substance. Yellow pouting lips glared at her from within a grey, untended beard. On his head, he wore a scruffy, black and white chequered keffiyeh.

"Who's there?" He completed the question by spitting prodigiously onto the earth.

"Me, I'm Tula. And you are?"

"Can't you see I'm blind or are you as well?" The man was gruff. He faced her. Empty sockets peered into the void.

"No, I mean yes. I'm sorry, I didn't notice. I'm exhausted. It's been a long day."

"Don't recognise your voice. You new here?"

"Yes, sir. I've just arrived."

"Got your pass?"

A blind man was asking her for a pass to travel. That she had not expected. She pulled out a wrinkled piece of paper from her knapsack and hesitated, not knowing what to do with it.

"Give it here," he demanded. "I may be blind, but do you think I can't see right through you?"

"No, sir. I'm sure you can. It's just that…" She gave him the travel permit.

He held it to his cheek. He rubbed it first against his left cheek, then against his right, and nodded to himself, as if reading its contents with inner eyes. She gazed at him wide-eyed.

He handed it back to her. "Go on. All in order here."

"What did you just do?"

"When I hold something against my cheeks, I get pictures in my mind."

"I never knew that was even possible. What did you see?"

"I saw a fair-haired young woman with blue eyes, sparkling like rays of sunlight dancing on a flowing river. I saw a smile that warms the day, a pretty face. Your fringe and pale skin and freckles will drive the young men crazy."

"That's kind of you to say," she said, failing to hide a blush. "May I ask you something?"

"Carry on. You're good at asking questions."

No one was going to intimidate her. No one. She swallowed hard. "What are you carving?"

He sheathed the whittling knife and lifted himself from the ground with the agility of a mountain ibex. The name tag dangling around his neck read 'Vitus'.

"So, you're Vi-tus, are you?"

"You can read as well?"

"Tell me, what do you do here?"

"What do you think? I'm the guard and customs officer for South Gate. And like it or not, you'd better show me some respect 'cos round these parts, my little brother's a very important person."

"Who's that then?"

"You'll find out soon enough."

With one hand, he leaned against the sturdy wooden gate post. With the other, he moved his palm across the surface of the post until he found a marking in the wood. A series of peculiar, random scratches covered the gate post. No, on second glance, they resembled an elaborate engraving. The markings were akin to rods of lightning, some long, others short. They zig-zagged vertically up and down the wooden post. Vitus ran his index finger up one of the lightning rods until he reached a sign. Two words were engraved on it:

Via Angelica.

"It means the Way of Angels," he said.

"It's an evocative name. But it's completely wrong for this street ahead of me," she said. "There are piles of rubbish. There are tufts of grass growing out of the curbs. The cobblestones are uneven. It's more like a river than a road, it's got so many waves. Not very Via Angelica, if you ask me."

"It's true," he moaned. "Things ain't what they used to be around here. Back in my day, it wasn't like this at all."

"So I've heard," she murmured. "And what about those broken columns at the summit of that hill?"

"What hill?"

"I'm sorry. I forgot."

Vitus frowned, his face morphing into what resembled a dried prune.

"It looks like the wreckage of a stone temple," she explained.

"That'll be the old Acropolis. Been there a long time, it has. And you're right, it's a wreck. It's no longer used, nor is it needed."

Despite its derelict appearance, she was drawn to the place, but for the moment she had other plans.

Vitus returned to his whittling. He was etching a series of vertical lines, similar to the lightning rods on the gate posts.

"Now I see what you're carving," she said.

"Lightning's powerful. Power's what you need in this world, eh, don't you think, lass?"

"That reminds me. I've got my own lightning rods here."

She delved into her bag and pulled out a semi-circular metal coin. She gave it to him, and he moved his finger up and down the tiny lightning rods inscribed on it.

"Don't see many of these broken coins."

"How come?"

"See, some years back, they experimented with a different alloy, only to find it was poor quality. Where'd you get yours from, eh?"

"It's a keepsake. I've had it as long as I can remember."

"In Topeth, it's a religious item, a sigil," Vitus said, making admiring noises. "What happened to the other half?"

"Don't know," she shrugged. "I keep it on me all the time because it stops bad things happening."

"That's what a sigil is for." Vitus handed it to her.

"What do you mean?"

Further explanation did not follow. He was an awkward cuss. If everyone in Topeth was like Vitus, it was going to be hard work to uncover the truth.

"Can I enter now?"

"I already said you can. What are you after in Topeth?"

"Angels, sir. I've come to find them."

"Good luck with that. They're long gone."

"What do you think happened to them?"

"Once, the angels provided the power – the lightning source – not anymore. The devils have taken over, they have. Now, they occupy the bridge."

"Is that right? I'm still going to try to see the angels," she said.

"Lass, you're trying me. The wings of dusk are beating slowly now, can't you hear them? I need to be closing these 'ere gates, 'cos they won't close themselves, you know."

As he shut the gates, the metal hinges screeched so much it set her teeth on edge. She grabbed her backpack and limped into town.

Vitus yelled after her, "Hey! Lass, come back here, will you?"

She trudged back to see what he wanted.

He grabbed the walking stick he had been whittling and lifted it into the air. "Here. It's finished. You need it. Take it."

"But how did you know?"

He gave her a wicked, beguiling grin and flicked his ear. "I may not see it, but I can sure as hell hear it. You got a slight limp."

His hearing was acute. The sounds of the differences in her steps must have been subtle, yet Vitus had detected them. Like a bat, the man must have echolocation.

"Why, thank you, sir," she said and dabbed his hand. His leathery skin was rough to the touch.

"I'll tell you what else I knows about you. You're a leftie," he chuckled.

"Leftie?"

"Left-handed. Always think lefties make for stubborn, awkward, defiant folk. That you, Tula?"

5

"You'll find out, soon enough," she said and strolled into town, accompanied by ribbons of early evening shadows. Golden sunlight splashed onto the rooftops of dilapidated houses. The firm grip of the walking stick gave her a refreshing surge of strength. While the straps of her knapsack rubbed hard into her shoulders, at least the stifling heat was waning.

Disturbing a brown rat, she jumped in fear. She ended up wrapped around some railings of what turned out to be an old school. Its windows were boarded up and the playground was covered in tufts of grass interspersed with more of those blue thorns.

Further on, the entrance gate to a stonemason's yard hung precariously off its hinges. The notice 'Closed for Business' was plastered on an apothecary's shop front. Outside his empty premises, an innkeeper stood, arms folded, eyes downcast. He smelled of stale beer. Strands of paper soiled the cracked gutter in the middle of the street. At the end of the alley, she was greeted by a lone olive tree with its gnarled bark. No one was there to hold out its branch to her. This was not the welcome she had expected from 'The Top' town.

At this late hour, the birds' vigour was in decline, cloaking their songs with faded evening softness. Tula was tired, but not beaten. Each day, she had walked and climbed in pursuit of her destiny. It nagged at her like a dog biting at her ankle. In the city, an inner voice had urged her to leave her home. She could never remember being little. It was as if her early childhood had never existed, and the voice badgered her to find out about it. It had propelled her across the plains, over fast-flowing rivers, through mountain passes and along deep valleys and, on this day, into Topeth.

The reddish dust had settled on the leaves of the trees and, over the years, turned the flat roofs of the houses a dark mustard brown. A warm breeze gusted through the town, stirring up more clouds of the dust into the atmosphere. From somewhere in the middle of the town came the distant sounds of raised voices and metal clanging against metal. Perhaps the market traders were closing for business. Behind her, an old man was talking to two donkeys as if they were his children.

Ahead in a narrow alley, a woman was striding towards her. She wore a scarf over her head, out of which burst sunlit curls of auburn hair. Her emerald green eyes scanned the alley with lightning speed. With high cheekbones and a tall, thin neck, she moved with the grace and elegance of a swan.

"Abel, where are you? Abel," she was calling.

When the woman saw Tula, she asked, "My son, Abel. He's lost. Have you seen him? He's seventeen, yes, about your age, but he gets confused. It's not his fault and he's missing. I'm so worried about him. Tell me you've seen him, please."

"I'm afraid not," Tula said.

The woman was frantic as she rushed off down the alley.

"Who shall I say is looking for him?" Tula shouted after her.

"His mother, Sarah," the woman yelled back, before questioning the old man with his donkeys and disappearing down the alley.

Tula waited for him. From an early age in the city, she had discovered she possessed an acute sense of smell, such that she could detect the subtle vibrations of a person's essence, the aggregation of all the person's thoughts and actions, which often made for quite a concoction. Some folks had an acrid, bitter smell. Old folks often wore a musty, well-used odour. This old fellow whiffed of donkey. But there was another smell about him; it was putrid, like rotting flower petals. He smelled of death. She was not sure if it was his imminent demise or that of someone close to him. There were no clues in his lean, gaunt face.

He touched his large-brimmed straw hat like it was a forelock. "I'm Zach. This is Betty and this here is Bethany."

"Nice to meet you and your lovely ladies."

The older of the two donkeys sidled up to her, bending her donkey head at an angle as if inviting her to stroke her, which Tula did.

"Well, Bethany's taken to you," Zach said.

"She has, hasn't she?"

"That's strange."

"What's strange?" she asked, as Bethany nuzzled her snout against her hand.

"She only ever does that to people she knows. You been here before?"

"No, I haven't," Tula said.

"They're more important to the people of Topeth than you can imagine."

"Why's that then?"

"Water; it's the water. See, they work the pumps. Without my two ladies and the team of other donkeys, the town would not exist. We'd have no water and that would be no good."

"I'm Tula and I'm pleased to meet you. Can I ask you; the woman who was here a moment ago, Sarah, did she ask you about Abel?"

"She did, lass. Abel, well, the poor lad's not all there in the head."

The alley filled with the clamour of shouts and yells. A man rushed past them, hotly pursued by a uniformed guard. Ahead of them, a gunshot rang

7

out, scattering a flock of starlings into the air above the town. Tula took a sharp in-breath and edged towards the noise. Poking her nose around the corner into the market square, the scene was chaos. About sixty people were swarming around the Bell Tower. The crowd was chucking rotten vegetables and hurling obscenities at the harassed guards, who held the mob at bay with brute strength and batons. An officer in a white kaftan seated on a horse patrolled the line of guards, brandishing a pistol above his head.

"Keep in line. Don't fall back," he was shouting.

Zach edged along next to her. Betty brayed. Bethany snorted. They liked it less than she did.

"What on earth's going on here?" Tula asked.

"You're not local, are you?" the old man said. "If you were, you'd know about the copper mine. The burnt sienna dust is from the open copper workings – you must have seen it. It's a pall of death sitting over our town and our lives. It's in the fetid air we breathe. The people of Topeth are sick and dying. I'd say they've reached the end of their tether."

"That's awful."

Another troop of guards rushed to thicken the line, as more townsfolk streamed into the square, which was quickly descending from mayhem to madness.

Zach was not one to loiter. "My family has suffered a sad bereavement. I must get home. Please, excuse me."

"I'm so sorry. Yes, of course." So, the smell – she had been right.

He tried to lead the donkeys down the alley, but Bethany refused to leave Tula's side. After much cajoling involving bribery with a carrot, Zach persuaded the donkey to follow him and Tula was on her own again.

The mob pelted the guards with small stones, vegetables, twigs, olives and anything they could lay their hands on.

The walls of the square resounded with a single, hostile cry: "Every breath, nearer to death!"

It arose from the front of the crowd. Tula climbed on top of a nearby barrel and clung on to the wall for safety – even at this low level, her fear of heights made her head spin. She could see the culprit now. At the head of the mob, between them and the line of guards, was a tall, wiry young man, fist beating the air into submission, leading the belligerent chant.

"Every breath, nearer to death! Every breath, nearer to death!"

Next to the mob leader was a man dressed in a black robe with a black hood drawn over his head. He was odd. Odd enough to make Tula stand on tiptoe to peer over the heads of the crowd. Despite the hood, she glimpsed his face, a stark picture of grief, frozen in time, his stare haunting. And wait. He carried something in his arms. In bleached swaddling clothes. White against black. A child. No. It could not be a child. Lord! It was. A dead child. He cradled the lifeless thing in his arms with such tenderness it made her gasp.

Inconsolable with grief, the hooded man yelled at the guards, "She's dead. You've killed her."

His words echoed into the mountain air, rebounded off the walls of the ravine and rose like incense to the Creator above.

To the crowd's refrain of "Every breath, nearer to death," the mob leader grabbed a stone and flung it over the heads of the guards. It crashed into a window, smashing it into a thousand shards, raising a celebratory cheer from his compatriots. Spurred on, the rioters filled the evening air with more righteous indignation and pieces of aerial vegetable matter.

Zach had shown her the way of safety and this fight was not hers. Frightened and worried, she wanted to get out of Topeth as soon as she could. Her goal was to reach Unity on the other side of the ravine bridge. With the town in upheaval, this was the ideal moment. The alley behind her had filled with townsfolk, pressing to get into the market square. There was no way back. How to get to the bridge?

A horse-drawn wagon lurched out of a side alley, spilling more guards into the market square. The rioters pressed forward but failed to breach the reinforced line of guards. The square was heaving with horses and wagons, choking with gun smoke. The guards pushed back and clubbed their way into the mob. Men and women lay prostrate, blood pouring from their wounds.

Clouds of dust were kicked up by the horses and the people. The smell was odious. With the market square in a violent uproar, she backed along the boundary wall until she reached the side alley from which the wagon had emerged.

Another horse-drawn wagon raced up the hill. It was heading straight for her until she dived out of the way, the horses' hooves thundering inches away from her head. The man in black with the dead child passed her on the other side of the street and headed down the hill. She hauled herself out of the gutter, brushed herself down and waited until the coast was clear. Grabbing her walking stick, she headed downhill towards a wooden gate; the sign said Bridge Gate. It was open. She needed no second invitation to leave.

With the tumult behind her, Tula sneaked through the gate. Away from the riot, she heaved a sigh of relief. Ahead was the yawning ravine;

it plunged into the depths as if a giant had gouged a huge wedge out of the earth and flung it away in disgust. The valley floor was down below in a world of its own. As the evening cooled, tentacles of mist rose from the abyss. The huge, near-vertical crags of rock gave the area a primordial feel, as if this was the beginning of time, not the end of it.

In this primal landscape there, at last, was the bridge.

CHAPTER 2

The Devils' Bridge

Emerging for their night foraging, a colony of fruit bats glided and spun through the twilight shadows. Tula's antipathy for bats, their clumsy flight and shrill cries, induced almost as much terror as her fear of heights. She limped on, scanning the path for guards. Thank goodness, there were none. Still patrolling the riot, she assumed. The bridge was swaying back and forth, yet there was not a breath of wind. That was odd. There was no one she could see. Perhaps an animal had strayed onto it.

The hour was late, and dusk was descending like a shroud over the gorge. She peered across the bridge to glimpse the town of Unity, nestling behind the boulders and crags. Silhouettes of the roofs of the houses shimmered in the ebbing heat. The twin spires of the Cathedral punctured the sky.

So far in Topeth, she had met a blind man, an anxious mother, and an old man with two jennies, one of whom seemed to know her. Once Tula was across the bridge, they would all forget she had ever been in the town. Her destiny was in Unity. The angels were there. That was the legend. Even if no one else did, she believed it was true. She was determined to find them.

A narrow path snaking down the steep slope linked the town to the bridge. Fearing the guards' return, she hurried along the winding, uneven path. It was fine for mountain goats, but with her bad ankle and her walking stick, she was nowhere near as fleet of foot as they.

The bridge had a quietening effect, like a warm homecoming after a long absence. Ever since she had heard about the abandoned town of Unity, she had wanted to visit the place for herself. Within touching distance, she felt a keen sense of belonging, even though she had never been near it – until now.

A solitary wicker lantern sat in a cradle, shedding a pale light over a crescent-shaped area covered in flagstones that had been carved out of the side of the mountain. In the middle of it were the bridge pillars and a small wooden shack.

The bridge itself was a slender rope structure slung across the open chasm. Narrow matting formed the bridge deck wide enough for one person to cross. At least there were hand ropes. At the Topeth end, it was attached to two thick, green-coloured pillars. Fingers of mist rose out of the ravine, obscuring the Unity end of the bridge. The structure reminded her of a long, thin hammock tied between two pairs of massive tree trunks.

By the bridge entrance was a large sign:

'THE DEVILS' BRIDGE.
DO NOT CROSS.
IGNORE THIS WARNING AT YOUR PERIL.'

It was true. She had heard rumours about the bridge, about how predatory devils prowled the dip in the centre of the rope bridge. It was forbidden to cross it.

How ridiculous. These views were deluded. Ever since she was a little girl, arranging her coloured stones and drawing her pictures, she had known, in every fibre of her being, that life was a gift, rarer than starlight, more beautiful than the dawn. Being a special gift, it called for a response, a celebration, and one that she tried to enact through every part of her life. It was not so much what she did that mattered, but what she would not do. Then, the angels could act through her in whatever way they saw fit. She would never consciously hurt herself or another. The angels would be confident she would not abuse their divine powers, corrupt them or use them for personal gain or material profit.

From behind the guard's hut came a rustling noise. Someone was about to jump her. Her heart raced and she froze.

"Who's there?" she whispered.

Meow. It was a cat: a tabby.

"You beautiful thing." Tula stroked the agile feline while she rubbed against her ankles.

"Tabby, I have to leave you now. I'm going to cross the bridge."

The cat meowed in agreement. Alerted by a noise near the hut, the creature darted off across the flagstones.

A shoulder-high wooden gate protected the entrance to the bridge. Fortunately, someone had left the key in the lock. She turned it, only to find the gate was already unlocked. Tucking the key in her pocket for safekeeping, she opened the gate.

The rope bridge was about one hundred steps. She steeled herself and tried not to look down. She was already feeling giddy. To defy her vertigo, she was going to have to ignore her moistening palms and dry, hoarse throat.

In the dusk, a shadow hovered on the bridge. Someone was on it. She was not the only one prepared to ignore the warning not to cross the bridge. From the silhouette, she could tell it was a man. In the sunken middle part, he was partially hidden from her line of sight. He was bent over, perhaps examining an object. Dressed in a black robe, he did not seem to have noticed her. When he stood up, he appeared to be carrying a parcel. No, that was the child.

Her mouth dropped open. She recognised him; he had been at the riot and had passed her on the road near Bridge Gate. What on earth was he doing? She was about to call out to him when he crouched down again and squeezed himself between a pair of vertical guide ropes. For a moment, he perched on the edge, like a bird of prey about to alight into the enclosing darkness.

The world stopped spinning and ground to a halt. In that stark hiatus, the angels held their breath. The man swayed back and forth as if he was resisting some unseen power. Behind him, there appeared to be a dark-winged entity urging him to jump and end it all. Or were they filaments of mist outlined in the dusk? It was difficult to tell.

Slowly, his body tipped forward until it reached the point of no return. Losing his balance, he fell off the bridge and spun into the arms of the gaping abyss, still clutching the dead child to his chest.

Birds can fly. Angels can fly. A man cannot.

No cry was made. No prayer was heard. No mourning song was sung. He made a soft whistling sound as he plummeted through the unforgiving air. Soon, he was out of sight, brutally ejected out of this world. The bridge rocked from side to side, a silent witness to this nameless tragedy.

Her hands were icy and her feelings, numb. She dared not accept what her eyes had seen.

Man and child, child and man; both were propelled into the next world. Not naturally – after a long sigh – but in a rupture, a terrible end that tore at the very fabric of life itself. Gripping the edge of the bridge gate, the blood drained from her hands and face. She swallowed her vomit and grimaced at the acidic taste in her mouth.

A pistol shot rang out. The booming sound rebounded off the mountainside opposite her, the echo blasting her ears again and again like a thousand and one trumpets. The mists in her mind dissolved and she snapped out of her nightmare.

"Stop! Don't step on the bridge!" The commanding voice came from the snake path.

Her head spinning, she turned, lost her balance and fell backwards onto the flagstones.

A horse walked onto the flagstones. She recognised the rider – he was the officer in a shining white kaftan from the riot. He dismounted, tethered his horse and pointed the pistol unerringly at her head. He was tall, thickset, with hunched shoulders. Deep furrows like crags ran across his forehead. His blue eyes had lost their youthful sparkle.

"Don't shoot!"

"Stand up. Step away from the bridge," he shouted.

For once, she did as she was told. He did have a pistol.

"That notice is clear," he said.

"I-I—"

"I haven't got time for this," he interrupted. "What's your name?"

"T-Tula, sir."

"Tula, eh? Who are you? What are you doing here?"

"Just arrived from the city, sir. But the man. You must have seen him."

"Seen who?" he said, peering along the bridge. "Listen, if you'd taken one more step, I'd have been peeling bits of you off the valley floor. Saved you from certain death, I did."

She rolled her eyes and murmured, "Did you? But, what about the man?"

"What man?"

"He fell from the bridge," Tula said.

"What? Say that again."

"I saw him with my own eyes. He leapt into the clouds." Tula's pained expression seemed to convince him of her honesty.

The officer puffed out his cheeks and let them out slowly. His face wore a mask of absolute dread. "No, no, no. It can't be happening again."

"What's happening again?"

"Never you mind." The officer shoved his pistol into his belt and added, "What exactly did you see?"

"In the dusk, all I could make out was a ghostly silhouette – and the man dressed in black. I saw him at the riot. And… and I think…" She covered her face with her hands and stifled a tear. When she recovered, she said, "He carried a child in his arms."

14

"Oh, no," the officer hissed.

"What is it?"

"I know who it was. It was Jevros. His baby girl just died. She had been struggling to breathe."

"It must have been awful for him," she murmured.

"That's what the devils are like. They drift across from Unity onto the Devils' Bridge."

"Devils? What are you talking about? I-I thought Unity was where the angels lived."

"That's a myth," the man said. "Across the bridge, there are only devils. Trespass on *their* bridge and they'll whisper crazed thoughts in your ear. They'll persuade you that you're an angel and that you can fly. Well, you can't. No one can."

"Not even poor Jevros."

"He is, I mean – he was – the town's doctor and an exceptional one at that," the man said. "Another life sacrificed to the devils. After the last time, I prayed – well, we all prayed – it would never happen again, yet it has. I'd hoped we'd kept them to the temples and towers of Unity, but no, they've crept back onto the bridge. If they cross it, they'll possess us all and who knows what'll happen then. We have to keep the devils out of Topeth and out of our lives. Hell, that was why we put the gate there."

"The gate?"

"Yeah, this gate," he said. "It's always locked. But today it's not. How did that happen?"

"That's how I found it."

In the twilight, a lantern bobbed and swayed along the snake path. Someone else was coming from the town.

The officer with Tula issued the customary challenge. "Halt. Who goes there?"

"Geb, it's me, Musa," came the reply.

The hackles on Tula's neck rose as she watched a man dressed in a white kaftan stride onto the flagstones. With a pistol shoved into one side of his belt and a curved dagger in the other, he stared at her wide-eyed as if *she* was one of those devils. Young and slight of build, his dark eyes flitted from side to side. His jagged movements betrayed a man afraid that one of those sinister devils was about to lure *him* to his death.

If he was nervous, she was near-terrified. A young woman, eighteen years of age, she was on her own at dusk in a strange town. Her company was the ghost of a suicide and two armed strangers.

"What's 'appening 'ere, sir?" Musa asked.

15

"It's Jevros – and his baby girl." Geb pointed ruefully at the gaping chasm.

"Oh no," Musa said. "So sad. I 'eard the news of his child's death just this mornin'."

"Mmm, as did the damn rioters," Geb replied.

"It ain't no good," Musa said. "He loved his baby girl more than life itself. And after she died, I never thought them devils would go after a man in grief."

"Nor me, but that's exactly what they've done," Geb said. "From now on, we'd better keep our eyes peeled."

"You see it happen, sir?" Musa asked.

"No, no I didn't," Geb replied. "But this young woman, Tula, yes, that's her name. She saw it all – she spun me quite a yarn about it."

Too upset to respond to his innuendo, Tula swallowed her emotion.

"I saw her by the entrance, about to walk onto the bridge," Geb said. "I found the gate flung wide open. Why wasn't it locked? And where's the damn key?"

"Mine's right 'ere, sir," Musa said, holding up an old, metal key. "Must have been the doctor's. He had a key, didn't he?"

"Yes, he did," Geb murmured. "Where is it now? And who on earth was meant to be on duty here?"

Musa's cheek twitched as if he was expecting a reprimand. "That would be me and Kalim, sir. But you needed us to help at the riot."

"Mmm, so I did." Geb puffed out his cheeks. "Then what are you doing here?"

"I come back 'cos of that." Musa pointed to the skies above the ravine.

"What? There's nothing there but a few clouds and the evening star," Geb said.

"Exactly. The vulture's gone. And you know what that means," Musa said.

"Yeah, it's found prey," Geb said. He scratched his cheek and stared up at the empty skies. "Then find Rufus. He'll be at the Copper Company's offices. Get him to go to Seliga. And don't take no for an answer. Tell him to arrange a search party to look for Jevros and his baby girl in the river and to be quick about it. We need those bodies back in one piece, otherwise the townsfolk will be up in arms again. And damn it, he was a good man. Let's get them back here and bury them with full honours."

"Yes, sir," Musa said.

Geb went on. "While he's down in the valley, tell Rufus to give a message to his master. I suppose we'd better inform Damien of these dreadful incidents."

"'Course, I'll do that."

"And I want guards stationed at the flashpoints; the market square and all roads in and out of Topeth. I want no repetition of this evening's riot. And while you're going that way, escort this young woman into town."

"Yes, sir. What about Irit? Shall I go tell her the bad news?" Musa asked.

"Mmm, a baby lost and now a husband, too." Geb sniffed the evening air. "No, you carry on. I don't relish breaking the sad news to her. But I'll go and see her. Besides, before I leave, I want to lock the bridge gate and make sure no other interlopers are hanging around here. Well, what are you waiting for?"

"Sir," Musa replied.

Lifting his lantern, he smiled at her and said, "Come on, Miss. Let's get you into town. Follow me, will you?"

She liked his easy, friendly manner. It made her feel safe. She picked up her walking stick and limped along behind him. She had a good feeling about him.

As they walked up the snake path, hundreds and thousands of starlings swooped around the bridge in an incredible susurration, a giddy, swirling dance to the dying embers of the day. There may have been devils on the bridge, but there were none that she could see.

CHAPTER 3

The Missing Daughter

Tula followed Musa until he stopped at the entrance to an alley by the side of the market square. The rioters had dispersed. A man was lighting the wicker lanterns on cradles perched around the square, bringing light to the darkness and hope to despair. Near the Bell Tower, another man was handing out spades and brooms from the back of a donkey cart.

"Now, Miss," Musa said. "I got to go find Rufus and then get to my post. But before that, I want to see you're safe and well tonight."

On her journey here, she had slept in many towns. In the absence of a deserted house, a stable or a barn, she would slide into a deserted soldier's hut or, as a last resort, sleep curled up in a shop front. Tonight, she feared exposure in such a lawless, desperate place.

Warmed by his offer of help, she replied, "Thank you, Musa. I don't have much money. Where can I stay tonight?"

"I wish I could help, Miss, I really do," he said. "'Cos of the riot, all us guards got a double shift. And you shouldn't be out at night, no, that's not right at all, not a pretty, young girl like you."

She blushed deeply and, to hide it, pretended to look for something in her knapsack.

"But look, you could try the Miners' Inn. It's cheap. It fits the bill. It's just down here," he added, pointing to the alley.

"Oh, Musa. Thank you so much. I'll not forget your kindness."

"I hope to see you again soon and now I'll be takin' my leave."

"Until the next time," she murmured.

"Oh, I'm already lookin' forward to it. Keep safe out there, Miss Tula," he said with a beguiling wink and marched off across the market square. She was impressed; he had even remembered her name.

The crows' evening squawks seemed louder and their cries eerier than before. From around the corner, she caught the whiff of a vagabond. Another shuffled by her, his eyes shifty, his back hunched, his clothes tattered. She was a stranger in their eyes, as they were in hers. At the far end of the square, two guards were rounding up the strays.

Her quest to meet the angels in Unity had brought her this far and she was not going to abandon it. She refused to believe the prevailing dogma about the bridge devils. Despite that, Jevros's death had chilled her to the bone. As had the shocking news that he had carried his dead child to his grave.

Tula was so near and yet so far from realising her dream. She shoved her hands in her pockets and found the bridge key. She had forgotten it was there. So, even at this late hour, she could sneak down the snake path, unlock the gate and skip over the bridge. She quivered at the prospect of passing the lowest point in the bridge arc from where Jevros had launched himself into the skies. Or had something launched him? Whatever had despatched Jevros might be waiting for her, lurking in the gloom, marauding amidst an airy expanse of nothing.

And Geb had said it was the doctor's key. A dead man's key. She banished that line of thought. Intending to return the key in the morning, she put it back in her pocket. Until she could cross the bridge – safely and preferably in daylight – she would stay in Topeth.

Stalking the market square was a sense of doom that chilled her to the bone. Her breathing was laboured, and the plaintive cries of the rioters resounded in her ears. The air was shot with the smell of vegetable matter thrown by the rioters. Some workers were sweeping up shards of glass and stones. Another group struggled by the light of a lantern to board up the broken windows. Guards cleaned up the rotten vegetables, cursing at the stench.

To one side of the square, a beacon was swinging in the late evening breeze, casting a gloom between the narrow walls of the alley. That was where Musa had pointed. She poked her nose down the alley. Goosebumps rose on her arms. Up ahead, two people flitted between the shadows. With her back to the wall, she edged through the darkness, trying to keep out of their sight. She had to be careful because her knapsack and swollen ankle would prevent a quick escape.

Two young men were shouting at another young man, who was cowering in the shadowy corner of a shop entrance.

"Stupid dolt, you're the thickest boy in Topeth," one of the young men cried, shaking his fist at the cornered lad, who hid his face behind his hands.

Without a moment's hesitation, she confronted them.

"Hey, you lads! What do you think you're doing?" She puffed out her chest. Or at least what little there was of it.

The two lurched at her. She backed against the alley wall. Nowhere else to go. No one around. Her heart thumped inside her chest. When she needed protection, where was Musa?

"Yeah? Who's askin'?" one snarled.

"I am." She mustered every shred of defiance.

"What you gonna do about it, little cub?" said the other. He was the same young man who had led the mob in the market square.

Despite trembling legs, she forced herself to stand tall. "Leave him alone."

"What we gonna do with 'er, Taurus?" the first one asked.

Taurus snapped at his friend, "Shut it, will you? Now she knows me name."

Her throat dried and her palms moistened. On her journey, she had encountered some awkward moments, but none as threatening as this.

"Get on with you!" she yelled.

They both stood stock still, mouths open.

She had them on the run. "I mean it," she added, brandishing her walking stick.

"Oh, watch out, she's got... a walking stick," Taurus said. He sniggered, chuckled, and then doubled over, howling with laughter.

She hissed with fury and was about to give him a wallop when, opposite them, a door flung open, spilling a tranche of light into the alley. A group of men lurched out of an inn, howling, punching the air, singing a bawdy melody. Taurus and his mate were as surprised as she was. With their false courage punctured, the two of them ran off into the gathering dusk.

Turning the air blue with their song, the men lumbered down the alley, barely giving her, or the young men, a second glance. For probably the only time in her life, she mouthed a prayer of thanks to an unruly bunch of drunks. As she closed the inn door, she read a notice above the lintel:

Welcome to the Miners' Inn.

After a deep breath, she went to tend to the stricken young man.

"Are you hurt?" she asked.

With his head between his knees, his chest and shoulders were heaving. In his lap was a long, thin bag, about the length of his forearm. She crouched down and touched his hand. It was freezing. He glanced up at her, his eyes two deep pools of fear.

"You don't need to worry about them anymore. They've gone," she whispered.

Clutching his bag, the lad stood up. His face was as round as the moon, with chubby cheeks, wispy brown hair and eyes to match.

"Hello, I'm Tula."

No reply.

"What's your name?"

"Ab-Ab." The syllable stuck in his throat.

"Sorry. Say it again, please."

"Ab-el."

"So, you're Abel. Your mum's looking for you."

"Mama, looking for me." His eyes flitted nervously up and down the alley.

"Let's get you home."

"Home." He stood up and forced a smile. "Abel go home."

He stared ahead and broke into a fast walk. With her ankle hurting, she struggled to keep up.

"Wait for me."

The young man stopped a stone's throw ahead of her. Beneath a lantern in a cradle, he was examining whatever was in his bag and seemed to be muttering to himself.

"What have you got there, Abel?"

"M-my friend," he said, meek as a wren.

"What's that, then?"

Slowly, he opened the flap on the bag to reveal a long, flat rock, about the shape and size of a man's foot, on which clung a small, bearded reptile.

"M-meet Miriam. My chameleon and her heat rock," he said with a warming smile.

"Hello, Miriam," Tula said, gritting her teeth. She was sure about one thing: chameleons, like snakes, made her skin crawl.

This one, Miriam, had some white patches on her skin, set against its black and green colouring. Miriam moved in that strange slow-motion way and stared at her with her huge, round eyes. Tula had encountered them along the way. She would prod a stick at one to see if it was alive. Only to discover that it was the skin that the reptile had shed.

She had seen enough. "Close the flap on the bag, there's a good lad. Now, let's get you both home."

He nodded and they set off through deserted streets. Familiar with the town, he seemed to glide through the dimly lit back alleys and by-roads. Once again, he got too far ahead of her. She almost lost sight of him and had to call to him. He slowed down, waited for her to catch up, then moved off at speed. Eventually, they reached a crossroads where two guards stopped them. One of them she recognised.

"Musa!" she cried.

"Miss Tula," Musa said, lifting his torch, its flames casting a light on their faces. "Why aren't you at the Miners' Inn? And what you doin' here with young Abel?"

"I found him in an alley."

"With Miriam," Abel chimed.

"Abel, we've searched everywhere for you. Where have you been?" The other guard's gleaming white kaftan matched his crisp delivery.

"Kalim," Abel said to him. "I'm here. I've been here all along."

"So, you have, Abel," he chuckled. "Now come with me and I'll escort you home. Would you like that?" Kalim was a slight man, with a pointed chin, black hair, pencil moustache, wide brown eyes and a reassuring smile. Tucked loosely into the belt around his waist was a curved dagger in a bejewelled sheath.

"Mmm, yes, I would. Can Miss Tula come as well? I want her to."

"Of course she can," Kalim said.

While Musa remained at the crossroads, she and Abel followed Kalim until they reached a narrow, paved street. His burning wicker torch lifted the evening gloom. Up above them, in clear, cloudless skies, a three-quarter moon was passing due south. They arrived outside a large, stone house.

Abel turned to her and said that immortal word, "Home."

No sooner had Kalim knocked on the front door than a woman burst out of the house. Sarah swept past Kalim. With a grateful tear in her eye, she threw her arms around her son and clung on as if she was never going to let him go.

While they embraced, Tula felt a twinge of regret. In the city, she had never bonded with her mother, who never gave grand displays of affection. Tula was often left alone because her mother spent much of her time caring for the children at the local orphanage where she worked. Tula's father was a carpenter. When he had finished with his mortise and tenon joints, he was often to be found downing ale at the local inn.

"Tula saved me, Mama." Abel wiped away his tears with the back of his hand.

"You're Tula?" Sarah asked.

"Yes, that's me."

"We met earlier… In the alley, wasn't it?"

Tula nodded.

"Yes, and Miss Tula, I like her. She beat off the Taurus," Abel said.

"You mean Taurus," Sarah murmured.

"Mmm, he was one of the bullies," Abel said.

"You knew them?" Tula asked.

Abel nodded.

"My dear, you've been in the wars protecting my son. I thank you from the bottom of my heart," Sarah said.

"I'm glad I've been able to help."

The silhouette of a tall man with hunched shoulders appeared in the doorway.

"Geb!" Tula exclaimed.

"Tula," Geb replied, and then asked the young man, "What happened, son?"

"Your *son*? Abel is… your son?" Tula asked.

"Yes. And Sarah is my wife."

"We found Abel on the main road junction, sir," Kalim said to Geb. "This young woman was bringing him home."

"I see," Geb said. "You did well. How's the town, now?"

"All quiet, sir," Kalim replied.

Geb nodded with satisfaction. "Keep it that way."

"Dear," Sarah interrupted, "the lads were bullying our son and this young lady rescued him. But have you two met before?"

"Yes, earlier this evening," Geb said. "She was about to trespass on the bridge and – there was the other matter."

"The other matter? You mean Jevros?" Sarah replied. "Tula, you witnessed his fall! That must have been awful."

Tula swallowed the emotion that welled in her chest.

"Come, my dear." Sarah put her arm around her. "It's forbidden to step on the bridge. That could easily have been you. Something terrible could have happened. Just as it did to our Abel."

"We're not going to talk about that," Geb said, a heavy note of reprimand in his voice.

"Why not?" Sarah turned to her husband, eyes glaring like scythes. "It's common knowledge. When he was a child, Abel strayed onto the bridge with his sister and, well, let's just say it was quite traumatic for him."

"I said, enough of that," Geb repeated, clenching his fists by his side.

Feeling she had overstayed her welcome, Tula shifted her feet. "It's dark and I need somewhere to stay. I'm going back to the Miners' Inn."

"Tula stay here." Abel touched her with affection on the shoulder and lowered his head apologetically.

"Abel's right," Sarah said. "The streets are unruly. That inn is full of out-of-work miners and definitely no place for a young lady like you." Turning to Geb, Sarah asked, "She can stay, can't she, dear?"

"After what she's endured and as thanks for finding Abel, yes, she can stay," Geb said.

"Thank you, I appreciate it." Tula heaved a sigh of relief.

"As long as you behave yourself in my house." Geb could not resist a reprimand.

Abel broke into a smile, held her by the hand and led her over the threshold.

"Kalim, return to your post," Geb said.

Kalim saluted and set off into the night.

Inside, the house was as pure and virginal as sunlight, not a bit of fluff anywhere. Tula imagined Sarah chasing the specks of dust, berating them like unwelcome intruders until they ran out of the house, screaming for help. The obedient wooden furniture was neatly arranged in the small rooms. Sarah showed her into the dining room where the long table was already laid for three until she added a place for her opposite Abel. Hung on the wall behind Geb's table place was his portrait. Seated on a chair with a high back, he was both imposing and dignified, with a white keffiyeh head-dress with black cord and chain of office.

Sarah served grilled trout, which Tula assumed had been brought up the mountain road from Seliga on the valley floor. Sarah was kind enough to share half of hers with Tula. The smell of the fish and the freshly ground almond sauce was like manna from heaven. After scratching around for crumbs for the past few days, Tula was salivating well before the plate landed in front of her. The taste of the first morsel danced around her mouth. For a poor thin city girl accustomed to being the last to be fed at the table, this was a welcome feast.

When they finished, she and Abel sat at the table while Sarah cleared away the dishes. Geb helped his wife in the kitchen. The door was slightly ajar, enough for Tula to overhear their conversation against the background of clinking plates and glasses.

"What's this white stuff doing on the kitchen floor?" Geb was asking.

"It's Miriam," Sarah replied. "She's nearly a year old and she's starting to shed her first skin."

"That's what the boy needs to do; shed his baby skin and grow up. It's long overdue."

"We both know that. We both pray for that. But I'm the one who chased around town after him all afternoon."

"Well, maybe you should keep a closer eye on my son. Luckily, my guards found him; I dread to think what might have happened to him in that alley. I don't want him getting mixed up with that hooligan Taurus. He and his mob are inciting the townsfolk."

"It wasn't your guards who rescued him, it was Tula. If only you'd been able to help earlier on…"

"Yes, well, earlier this evening, I happened to be busy in the market square and then at the bridge. And I've just returned from Irit's, where I had the unpleasant task of breaking the tragic news of her husband's death to her."

"I'll go and comfort her first thing in the morning," Sarah said. "But that's you all over. Work, work, work; it's always your excuse. I thought I married a man, but it turns out I married an institution."

"You knew who I was when you married me," Geb said. "Just try and care for our son, will you?"

"I don't believe you," Sarah tutted. "You want me to care for him. Look how you cared for our daughter."

"That again?"

"Yes, that again. Remember, on that day, you said you'd take care of her."

"I've apologised a thousand times. But you're like a ghost haunting my every turn. Are you ever going to let me forget?"

"I'll stop when you change."

"I can't change who and what I am."

"Yes, you're Commander Geb, the officer in charge of the Topeth guard and distant relation to the First Man!"

"Keep your voice down, will you?" Geb asked.

Trying not to overhear their argument, while being intensely drawn to it, Tula moved uncomfortably on her chair. To distract herself, she rubbed her sore ankle and ran her finger up and down the lightning rods on her walking stick. Then she watched Abel, who was blithely fashioning the napkin into a paper tiger.

She yawned as Sarah and Geb emerged from the kitchen.

"Ready for bed?" Sarah asked.

Tula nodded.

"Follow me," Sarah said and led her upstairs. On the way, they passed a room with a solitary candle and the door ajar. Without thinking, Tula wandered into it. The room was small but cosy. She plonked her knapsack and walking stick on the floor. Even though the bed was a child's size, it was still big enough for her. In one corner, a handful of dolls with pink dresses and matching bonnets were enjoying afternoon tea. In another, papers covered with a child's scribbles were strewn about the floor like autumn leaves. Inside the door, a small mound of coloured glass marbles mingled with pebbles and stones.

"My dear," Sarah said, poking her nose round the door. "Please, your room's next door."

Realising her mistake, Tula stood up. "I'm so sorry. Was this her room?"

Sarah nodded, a look of quiet resignation on her face. "You must have overheard our conversation. I apologise for that. But yes, so now you know we have a missing daughter. This was – is – her room. We left it as it was."

"Of course," Tula said. The room wore this musty, unused smell, a shrine to unrequited love.

"Your room is over here. I hope you sleep well."

"Thank you, I'm sure I will." Tula closed the door. The night-time breeze through the open window was warm on her face. She could hear a distant screeching sound. The roof hatch in the ceiling was slightly ajar to air the room. When she closed the hatch and the window, the sounds faded and she limped over to her bed.

As soon as her head rested on the pillow, the night wrapped her in its silent embrace, and she slept.

CHAPTER 4

Opal's Grotto

Abel skipped all the way over to the other side of the bridge. It was such a long way across that he was soon out of sight, obscured by the mists.

Next thing, he fell to the ground near one of the big pillars, his body trembling as though it was cold yet the day was warm. Hovering over him was a pale-yellow cloud that glowed with a peculiar flickering light, flames of living fire. Like the burning bush, they were flames that burned but did not scald. It settled above him, wrapping him in its healing wings. After a while, its lithe flames retreated into the embrace of the air from which they had come.

Abel lay still on the ground.

Tula opened her eyes. Her head was pounding. Sunlight burst through the flimsy curtains into an unfamiliar room.

It was a dream, only a dream.

She had seen him. She had seen Abel – on the bridge.

Outside, the sun was rising over the flat, bleached, stone roofs of the houses of Topeth. Finding her one change of clothes, she tidied her hair and headed downstairs.

Sarah was waiting, her emerald green eyes sparkling. Abel shuffled nervously back and forth behind his mother. His eyes lit up when he saw Tula.

"Before breakfast, can I show you my garden?" Sarah asked.

"I'd like that."

"Come on, Abel, you can come too," Sarah said and took her son by the hand.

Sarah's garden was laid out with bedding plants hugging one side of a single stone path down the middle. A rose bed with petals of a rich yellow and ochre, full with aroma, adorned the other side. There was shade from the incessant sun provided by a couple of elegant Mount Tabor oaks. The earth was moist, so she must have already been out watering the plants. The path was swept clean, with not a mote of earth to be seen. Every plant seemed obedient to the wishes of their demanding mistress. The order, the fragrances and the layout; this was the garden of someone who had been rocked by the storms of chaos in their life and was desperate to claw back some order and sanity. Soon enough, Tula found out the source of Sarah's deep anxiety.

At the far end of the garden, tucked behind a small laurel hedge, was a concealed grotto, in which sat a white marble sculpture of a seraph, the height of a small child.

Sarah swallowed a lump in her throat. "I often come here, to be with her, to think of her, to cherish her. It's a special place for me, for my family and, well, you've been in her room, I thought you'd like to see this."

She and Sarah sat on a wooden bench facing the statue.

Tula read the engraving on the base of the plinth:

To our beautiful daughter, Opal.
Wherever she is, may she be happy and loved.
Whatever she does, may she be found,
And come home to us, safe and sound.

Sarah welled up. "This is my angel, my Opal, my missing daughter. It breaks my heart to talk about her."

"I understand. Memories can be both rich and painful."

"I know you're new here and after the way you helped Abel with those bullies, I feel I can trust you," Sarah said. "I'd like to tell you about Opal's story."

Tula touched Sarah's hand and smiled.

Abel wandered off to look for Miriam and found her perched on a low branch. He sat with his back to one of the oak trees, an expression of childish delight on his boyish lips, gazing intently as Miriam crawled along the branch and extended her long tongue to catch a passing fly. Since the day before, the chameleon seemed to have more white blotches on her skin.

"The story begins with the founding of Topeth, nearly a millennium ago," Sarah said. "In those days, Unity was blessed by a glory of angels, entities invisible to the naked eye. Some called them agents of the Creator. People went freely back and forth across the bridge, which was called Via Angelica."

"Wait, I saw that name in town. Yes – it was on the two pillars at South Gate."

"They made the original bridge pillars out of wood. Later, after the discovery of metal ores in the area, they were replaced by metal ones – copper on our side, zinc on the Unity side. The wooden ones were reused as the pillars for South Gate."

"Why was that?"

"I suppose someone thought the metal pillars would be stronger and last longer than wooden ones."

"Nothing is simple in this place," Tula said. "The elders in the city where I lived have this idyllic view of Topeth as a golden niche, a haven from the war on the plains and a sanctuary of angelic peace. But yesterday, I walked into a riot and witnessed a truly awful suicide."

"I don't know if Topeth will ever be that place of safety again. The landscape's scarred with open cast mines. All the seams have been worked through – there's barely enough copper left in the earth to make a plate. A few of the miners hang around here drinking and gambling, and well, you probably know what else miners get up to. You ran into some last night. I wish they'd all go away and leave us in peace. The women just want our town back, a place to bring up our children in peace, but it's a ruin and so are our lives. We've suffered too many nightmares. A young child has died. And it destroyed Jevros. We're tired and angry – and tired of being angry. You've seen what it's done to us. We're desperate. I'm desperate."

"If it's that bad, why not follow a fresh trail?"

"Is that what you're doing here?"

"I've come to look for the angels and, well, I'm also here to prove something to myself. See, at home, my mother called me this nickname."

"What was it?"

"Little Tulip Seed."

"Did she, now?" Sarah said with a knowing smile.

"So, you understand what she was suggesting?"

"I do," Sarah said. "But do tell me in your own words."

"My mother was a gardener like you and planted rows of vegetables and flower beds in the orphanage garden. She knew that a tulip that grew from a bulb flowered in the same year, whereas a tulip grown from seed took years to flower. By calling me 'Little Tulip Seed', my mother implied that I was a late developer. I wanted to prove her wrong. That's why I'm here."

Sarah nodded.

"So what about you and Geb? You're both young enough to start again and lay down roots."

"I stay here because of Opal, my missing daughter." Sarah let out a long, gentle sigh.

"It's a lovely name." In the city, Tula would often stand outside a jewellery store, nose against the window, admiring the opal rings and necklaces, entranced by the opalescent play of light on the semi-precious stone.

"So, you see, I can never move away. How would it be for her, for Opal, if she came back and I wasn't here to embrace her, to welcome her into the bosom of the family? Imagine that. No, I couldn't live with myself. I can't allow that to happen. I'm her mother. I'll wait for her until I die. That's what I'll do. I'll never forget her. That's why I'm rooted here."

Sarah tilted her head and, with sublime tenderness, rubbed the back of her hand against the cheek of the seraphic statue of her daughter.

"This is her grotto, her memorial. And I'm certain that she's still with us. We'll find her, eventually. I know it, I feel it in my bones."

Tula wondered whether Sarah's hopes were real, so she asked, "Have you looked for her?"

"Of course. At first, Geb sent out search party after search party. Now, after so many years, they've stopped looking altogether. But I pray every day for her to come home."

Abel wandered over to where they were sitting. Nearby, he found a compost heap of cut grass and dead flowers. He lay on his stomach watching a trail of black ants carrying flies back to their nest.

Sarah tucked her locks inside her headscarf. "Twelve years ago, Opal was six; Abel was five. Opal strayed onto the bridge and wandered into Unity. Abel was on the flagstones at the Topeth end of the bridge, which was when that tyrant Damien found them."

"I've heard that name before."

"Well, Damien is Vitus's younger brother. Damien took over the running of the Topeth Copper Company when Vitus was blinded in a freak mining accident."

"So, what happened next at the bridge?"

"According to Damien, he finds Abel at the bridgehead and spots Opal playing in the middle of the bridge."

"But that's forbidden. I found that out last night."

"Yes, and there's a heavy punishment for anyone who trespasses on it. Damien took little Opal to the market square to pronounce sentence. I knelt before him and begged Wincorn for mercy."

"Wincorn, who's he?"

"The ultimate authority around here; the High Priest."

"Then?"

Sarah shook her head with rue. "Then, Damien and Wincorn were

30

like statues with hearts of stone. They showed no mercy and pronounced sentence!"

"What was it?"

Sarah's stare was so cold it chilled the embers of Tula's soul.

"Death."

"Death? What, kill a six-year-old girl?"

Sarah nodded.

"That's barbaric!"

"And not just any death, but death by passing through the fire."

"What happened to her?"

"Damien's guards, those other beasts Rufus and Silus, put her in that cockroach-infested prison. Rufus was going to tattoo her. The trauma must have been terrible for her," Sarah said, her chest heaving as the nightmare flooded back.

"That's terrible. I thought you said Opal was – is – still alive. So how did…?"

"Wait, there's more. The next morning, Geb and I – we left Abel at home – headed off to the Temple of Moloch, the execution site. We were expecting the absolute worst, only to hear that Opal was no longer in custody."

"She'd escaped?"

"Well, at first, we didn't know what had happened. Soon after, news filtered through from Copper Gate, the town's west gate. In the middle of the night, three people had departed. They were Enoch, his wife, Ruth, and our blessed little girl, Opal." Sarah clenched her fists.

Tula frowned. "Who were these people, Enoch and Ruth?"

"Enoch was the prison warden guarding Opal. Ruth was his wife. It turned out that they had freed Opal and escaped from Topeth with her. I'll never forget that moment when we heard the news. Both Geb and I sank to our knees in prayer. They had saved her from a terrible death. To this day, I celebrate their names, although in Topeth they are wanted criminals, like our Opal. And on that night, I didn't just lose my daughter, I lost my son too. You've seen him yourself. Abel's never been the same since. He's like a tightly coiled-up spring, all his emotions buried deep inside. I want my Opal back. I want my Abel back too. Is that too much to ask of the Creator?"

"No, I don't think so."

Sarah dried her eyes.

Tula's inner voice whispered:

"One day, he'll walk into this garden and he'll be Abel again, fully restored."

Wait, how do I know that's true?

"It will come to pass."

You'd better be right. Because I don't want to give Sarah any false hope.

"Have a little trust."

Tula took a deep breath and, her voice breaking with emotion, said, "One day, he'll walk into this garden and he'll be your Abel again, fully restored. It'll happen, you'll see."

"I hope so, Tula, I really do. Because that will be a truly wonderful day."

After a pause, she asked, "Did you know these people, Enoch and Ruth?"

"No, not really. They were older than us. And we knew nothing about their plans to free Opal. Damien and Wincorn thought otherwise because they accused Geb, but my husband has always protested his innocence. And I believe him. But Geb could have done more to rescue her himself, instead of leaving it to chance and allowing two strangers to do it."

"The bridge is full of devils and sad memories, so why don't the townsfolk burn it down, or cut the ropes and sever the unfortunate connection to Unity forever?"

"The priests insist the bridge is a sacred part of our heritage. It was built by Herman, who led the citizens across it from Unity and laid the foundation stone of Topeth. Slender though it might be, the aspiration is that one day the devils will leave, allowing the angels to return. That's why we've not destroyed the bridge. There's always hope. Perhaps that's what you've brought."

"Me? What have I done?"

"In the old days, people used to come here, searching for the angels, seeking the enhancement they offered. Nowadays, no one believes in angels anymore. All this talk of devils has frightened them away. But not you."

"I believe they're still here and are hiding, or perhaps they are themselves lost."

"Lost? How can angels be lost?" Sarah scrunched up her eyes.

"I don't know. If we can lose our way, why can't angels?"

Sarah wiped her moist eyes and asked, "Why do you think the angels are still here?"

"I'll tell you. You shared your secret with me, so now I'll share mine," Tula said with a smile. She shifted on her seat, took a deep breath, and went on, "In the city when I grew up, my parents were poor and toiled day and night. I was often left on my own, so I found a place on the top of this hill overlooking the city. It gave me a superb view of the valley and the mountains in the distance. I had visions there, dream visions I suppose they were. One of them stuck and it came to me as a short verse."

32

"What was it?"

"Here, I wrote it down. I keep it with me all the time. It's why I trekked across valley and plain."

Tula took out a piece of paper and stared at it with a mix of awe and wonder, before reading:

"That you are the key.
With the angels of Unity."

"What's it mean?" Sarah asked.

"The home of the angels is the town of Unity. So, that's why I believe they're still here. And that's why I'm here. To find them. To join them. To be with them."

"And you are the key? The key to what?"

"I don't know. I've pondered these same questions for years. Eventually, I felt as if the angels of Unity called me and here I am."

The sound of a bell echoed across the rooftops. Abel left his trail of black ants and dashed back into the house.

"What's that?" Tula asked.

"The town bell; it's rung from the Bell Tower when there's an emergency or to call the townsfolk to gather together. Today is market day, so, maybe it's that."

As Sarah opened the back door, Abel was standing by the front door, waving goodbye to someone. Then he closed the front door and turned to greet them.

"Was that your father going out?" Sarah asked.

Abel nodded.

"Where's he gone? Who came to fetch him?" Sarah asked.

Abel glanced away and stared at the ground. The poor boy: it was as if he lived in his own invisible pod of fear.

"Kalim came. I like Kalim. They've gone… to the bridge," he whispered the last phrase as if repeating a forbidden spell.

"To the bridge? Why? What's happened?" Sarah asked.

Abel shrugged his shoulders.

"I'm going to see what it's all about," Tula said. "Coming?"

"No, I have to go to the market later. You go."

For the second time in as many days, Tula set off to the bridge.

CHAPTER 5

The Topeth Copper Company

In the thin mountain air, word flew around the alleys, weaved through the by-ways of the town and awoke the sleeping dogs. A swarm of mosquitoes buzzed with excitement, the flock of starlings swooped down over the derelict Acropolis while even the town's underground population of large, brown rats emerged out of their dark, forbidden hiding places to sniff the dawn vapours. Everyone wanted to find out what the matter was.

It was akin to one of those sudden, tumultuous summer storms infamous in the region. Scores of people moved shoulder to shoulder through the market square, now cleaned up and restored to its pristine state.

For an indescribable moment of relief and joy, Tula imagined they had found Jevros alive and well and the tragic events of the evening before had been a forgettable nightmare. But even she knew in her innermost self that that would be one miracle too far.

As she turned through Bridge Gate, there it was, the rope bridge swaying gently in the soft breeze.

The sun was rising directly behind Unity, dowsing the bridge in long, slanting shadows. The gorge was like a huge, gaping mouth separating the two towns. The ravine ran north to south, with Unity to the east and Topeth to the west of it. Because of this quirk of geography, the sun rose behind Unity and set behind Topeth, bestowing a subtle, ethereal quality on the light on the area's crags and canyons.

A crowd was heaving around by the entrance to the Devils' Bridge. With more townsfolk joining at every moment, the line of people backed up onto the snake path as far as Bridge Gate. Tula used her diminutive stature to squeeze her way to the front, only to find herself next to Zach. He tipped his straw hat to her, but his eyes were full of rue and sorrow.

"You, you…" he stammered. "You witnessed my son-in-law's demise last night."

"Jevros was your…?" Tula replied.

The lines on Zach's face furrowed into a deep frown and he nodded. She sensed that the old man had seen death in his life, but that this one was close to his heart.

"You poor man… you lost your granddaughter too… and what about your daughter? I'm so sorry," she replied, touching the old man's forearm with compassion. "So, you came here anyway?"

"I'm hoping and praying," Zach said, chewing his gums, "that what they've found on the bridge will shed light on the truth of what happened last evening."

"They found something on the bridge?" She stretched onto tiptoe.

"Yes, look over there. Commander Geb will find out what's going on. He stands for the town; unlike other folks I could mention," Zach said, and muttered various deprecations under his breath.

In the middle of the flagstone entrance to the bridge was a pair of huge pillars about eight feet tall set deep in the ground, to which the thick bridge ropes were securely attached. Now, in the light of day, they appeared like two massive digits protruding skywards.

The crowd was corralled behind makeshift wooden barriers. Guards prevented access to the flagstone area. Standing tall, Commander Geb was confronting Musa and Kalim.

"You two, come on. Tell me again," he was saying. "What did you see?"

Musa fingered a pair of eyeglasses in his huge hands. He spoke quietly, but quickly.

"A shadow, a box, or something. There, I thought it was in that bit where the bridge sags in the middle."

"Where? I don't see anything," Geb murmured. "The bridge is still in shadow, so it can't be a glint. The sun needs to rise above Unity. Then, we'll see what we can see."

"It's comin' soon," Musa said. "Then it'll be clear enough."

"Give me the eyeglasses," Geb said and peered into them.

The early morning rays of the sun breached the podium where they were standing. In a subtle dance of light and dark, the sun's shadow edged across the snake path. Like a huge supernatural being, it shifted slowly over their heads until, as the minutes ticked by, it slithered onto the flagstones. In a short while, she had to cover her eyes to shield them from the sun's rays. Soon, the sun would chase away the shadows and they would be able to glimpse this mysterious object on the bridge.

"The vulture didn't drop it there, did it? Someone got onto the bridge," Geb said.

"Someone or something," Kalim said.

Geb turned to see her standing in the crowd. "You, Tula. Do you know anything about this object?"

"No, Commander, not much," she said, approaching him. "When I arrived at the bridge last night, Jevros was bending down, examining something on the matting. It could have been this object, I don't know. It was dusk and I couldn't see much."

"You put it there, didn't you?" Geb peered straight through her.

"Why would I do that when I want to get across the bridge?" she asked.

"I want my town to be safe from the demons. You could have put it there as a protest, a diversion, or a subterfuge; I don't know, but I will find out."

"Listen," Tula said. "I was standing by the bridge gate. Yes, I wanted to cross, but my legs were trembling. I suffer from vertigo. Then you came along and used me for target practice and nearly blew my head off. Even now, I've got this ringing in my ears. So, no, it wasn't me."

Geb turned to Musa and asked, "Well, someone must have left it there. Maybe it was Jevros."

"We'll soon find out," Musa said.

"Why doesn't someone simply go and fetch it?" Tula asked.

"Nope, can't do that, Miss Tula. Not without permission," Musa said. "Sometimes we get on the bridge to replace all them ropes. Other times it's to get rid of any dead birds. Whenever we do, we got to have permission. Me, I'd never go on that there bridge without the right permission, no, not for all the copper in Suria."

"Permission? From whom?" Tula asked.

"From me," a voice boomed.

A man strode through the crowd with an air of bloated confidence. He was stocky, with a strong forehead and ice-blue, reptilian eyes that seemed to devour everything in their path. Some of the crowd averted their eyes, as if afraid to meet the man's stony gaze. His henchman brought up the rear.

The man headed for Geb.

"Well, if it isn't the head of the Topeth Copper Company, Master Damien himself," the Commander said.

"I hear you've been busy – for a change," Damien said. "A child's death, a riot and a demonic possession. Not content with that pretty trio, there's now an object on the bridge."

"And in every way, the first three were because of *your* copper mine," Geb said.

"I don't think so. The child's death was nothing to do with the mine," Damien protested, waving his arms in the air as if he was about to take off.

"I think you'll find the good folk of Topeth disagree with you," Geb replied. "Ask Jevros. Oh, no, you can't. So, ask his wife. Yes, ask Irit. She'll tell you about the copper dust and how it killed her daughter."

"Speculation." Damien spat the word out as if it was a foul taste. "Pure speculation. But Jevros went on the bridge with no protection. He was asking for trouble. The bridge devils got him. I wonder what you do in this town because you can neither care for the good people of Topeth nor can you control the bridge devils."

Geb gritted his teeth and shook his head. "Well, *have* you found their bodies?"

"Rufus set out with a search party along the river valley at first light. He'll report his findings as soon as he can," Damien said. "Now, what's this on the bridge?"

"It's a small object," Geb said.

"Let me see." Damien peered through a pair of eyeglasses. "How did it get there?"

"If I knew, I'd tell you," Geb replied.

"Don't be insolent, Commander."

"If I could act freely and without…"

"… recourse to me, yes, but I'm in charge of Topeth now and don't ever forget it."

Geb replied, "Well, what are *you* going to do about it?"

"I'm not going to talk to you all day. I want this object retrieved and quick. Who spotted it?"

"Me, sir," Musa said.

"Good. Then you can fetch it."

Musa grinned nervously. "Can't Kalim go instead?" he suggested.

"No, he can't," Damien said. "You will go. That's an order. And I don't want to see any more of this cowardice, understood?"

"Sir," Musa said. And he stood there, his feet growing roots into the ground.

"Well, what are you waiting for?" Damien asked.

"There are them devils on the bridge, sir," said Musa.

"Where? I can't see any," Damien replied.

"Like the wind, them devils are. Can't see 'em, you know that, sir." Musa's hands were shaking and his cheek twitching. Tula felt a pang of sorrow for the lad. He was trying his best.

"Oh, so you want protection. Why didn't you say?" Damien asked.

"Yes, sir, protection, that's it, sir," Musa muttered. "Them holy words and them coin things with those magic lightning things on it."

"You want a blessing and a sigil. Well, I can't give you those, but the old priest can. Where's Wincorn when you need him?" Damien asked, glancing at the crowd.

"Here, Damien." A small, squat, rotund man, with a charcoal black beard, stepped out from the back of the crowd. He wore a priest's crimson frock and a black and white chequered keffiyeh wrapped around his head. His narrow eyes flitted from side to side as if he was expecting a devil to devour him at any moment.

With him was his assistant, who was carrying a bag over his shoulder and holding the lead of a Canaan dog. Tula's neighbour in the city had one as a patrol dog. On her travels, she had seen them used to herd sheep. The animal had a distinctive wedge-shaped head, while its dense coat was creamy brown with small white markings. There it was, obedient against the assistant's side, with an alert, fierce look in its eye. The dog's protective presence seemed to lend Wincorn a supreme confidence as he hobbled over to talk to Damien and Geb.

Musa pointed at the dog. "Hah! Kebel can go. He can run on that bridge, fetch the object and be back in time for breakfast!"

"No, that's not his job," Wincorn said in a voice full of sand and grizzle.

Musa's shoulders slumped. Kebel growled at him and he shuffled back a step or two.

Damien turned to Wincorn and said, "Musa needs protection on the bridge. Would you mind doing the honours? And make it good, because I want no more of these irritating accidents or unfortunate hauntings."

"Of course, when have I ever let you down?" Wincorn said, with the air of a practised flatterer. He turned to his assistant and said, "Chimor, pass me my shoulder bag."

Wincorn opened the bag and pulled out a shiny lightning rod sigil, which was about the size of a large coin. The priest smiled in a wry, gruesome way and said to Musa, "First things first, keep this holy sigil on your person at all times."

Musa's bottom lip was quivering like a child's and his face had morphed into a petrified grimace. "The object," he said. "It's 'alf-way 'cross the bridge. That's where them devils gather. That's where Jevros lost it... Ain't it?"

"Have no fear, the sigil will protect you. COIL is all-powerful," Wincorn replied.

"What's COIL?" Tula asked.

"The Church Of Iridescent Light," Zach replied. "It's the name of our religion."

"Musa, kneel, here, in front of me. Good man, that's it. Now, lower your head," Wincorn said.

The crowd stopped shuffling around. A few high clouds scudded overhead, while the sun had risen high enough behind Unity to light the whole of the bridge. The air was thinner than a strand of hair. A solemn silence descended on the witnesses to the ceremony.

With his index finger, Wincorn wove a sacred circle above Musa's head, saying:

"Oh, Iridescent Spirit of Light that dwells amongst us,

Protect this man, Musa, from the terrors of the ravine.

Keep him from the devils of Unity,

And bring him home safe to Topeth."

Musa heaved himself up, but his anxiety remained etched hard on the lines of his face.

"That it? Nothin' else?" he asked.

Kebel let out a low growl. Wincorn, his master, added a growl of his own.

"I'll be here, watching you, guiding you every step of the way."

"Yeah, yeah, 'course you will." Musa rubbed the sigil for all he was worth.

"The prayer and the sigil form a sacred bond and will protect you from the wily devils," Wincorn said.

"Good. Now get going," Damien said.

CHAPTER 6

Pandora's Box

Geb unlocked the bridgehead gate and there in all its glory was the rope bridge, lit by the rays of the rising sun. Musa shuffled through the gate and clung to the hand rope stays with feverish intent. Tula guessed there was a way to walk on a rope bridge to prevent it bucking like a feral horse, but Musa was too frightened to follow that course of action. He edged along it with this curious sideways crab-like motion. It swayed to the left and right and gently sagged as he approached the dip in the middle.

The flock of starlings wheeled high in the sky and enjoyed the wispy clouds. With their pretty black and yellow markings, the little birds were a glorious natural spectacle blessing the morning skies.

Without warning, they flew off into the sunrise. The griffon vulture had arrived on the scene. These huge raptors were strange creatures. They were feared by mankind for obvious reasons. Yet, they were the cleaners and janitors who removed decaying organic matter, which, by any other name, was a noble function within the great scheme of things.

Musa crept along the bridge with the speed and determination of a tortoise. Finally, he reached the middle. He stopped and peered at the object, before bending down and grabbing it. He turned it over this way and that, and then waved it above his head with an air of cautious triumph.

"It's a box about as long as a child's forearm," Damien announced, peering through his eyeglasses.

"What's in it?" Tula asked.

"Who knows? Could be a devil or an angel?" Zach chipped in.

"Hope, reckon it's got hope in it." Vitus's curt, gruff way of talking seemed to match the spirit of the times.

"Isn't there a Greek myth about a box with hope in it? What's it called?"

"If you ask me, them Greeks had over-active imaginations," Vitus added.

40

"Pandora's Box, that's what it's called," Zach blurted out.

"Yeah, so, whatever's in this 'ere box, is a blessing or a curse," Vitus said.

With the box tucked under his arm, Musa clung to the rope stays and lumbered back to the bridgehead. The closer he got, the more it stirred the good citizens of Topeth. When he set foot on the flagstones, their cheers roused the heavens. After giving Damien the box and returning the sigil to Wincorn, Musa's knees gave way before he collapsed in a heap of nervous exhaustion.

Tula went to comfort him. "You were so brave," she murmured.

"Do you think so?" he asked.

She nodded and helped him back to his feet.

Everyone gasped at the box. A pall of silence descended as Damien examined it. After experimenting with the box and the lids, opening it every which way, instead of having a flat bottom and a top lid like a normal box, it was possible to open both the upper lid and the bottom lid, but not simultaneously. To add to the mystery, the lid of one side was a clear, white mirror, while the lid of the other was a black, dark mirror.

After Tula had described it to Vitus, he asked, "What's Damien doing now?"

"He's seeing if there's anything inside it," Zach said.

Damien held the box up to the light. Its white-mirrored lid reflected the light in the same way a normal mirror would. He turned it over and investigated the black mirror. Nothing. No reflection at all.

He opened one lid and said, "Here. These markings look familiar."

"Well, they should," Wincorn said. "They're sacred symbols. They're lightning rods. In the skies, a rod of lightning is a formidable display of the power of the Creator. It shows we live by His grace and that we can be destroyed by it at any moment. It reveals His ultimate authority over us."

"Are you saying this box was left... by higher powers?" Damien asked.

"Those markings are a unique sign of His presence," Wincorn added.

"Wait," Damien said, delving around inside it. "There's something wedged in the corner of the box. It's a piece of paper."

"Give it to me." Wincorn snatched the paper. He unfolded it, read it and with a smirk, held it aloft for all to see. It had one word written in large capital letters.

"What's it say?" Vitus wanted to know.

Without even reading the word, Tula's inner voice told her what it was. She spoke the word to herself at the same time as Damien said, "Help."

Geb must have noticed her because he shouted, "You mouthed the word 'help' at the same moment as Damien spoke it. How did you know that was the word he was going to say?"

"I just knew, that's all."

"Don't act so meek and pretentious," Geb said. "Yesterday, you arrived here unexpectedly, and I caught you about to wander onto the bridge. Then you claim you witnessed Jevros's sad demise. Your pleas of innocence are becoming tiresome."

"What exactly do you mean?" she asked.

"Let me spell it out," Geb said. "Last night, you almost trespassed on the bridge. Now, you knew what was written on the paper. I reckon the person who left the box was... you."

"I told you, it wasn't me." She raised her voice in frustration. "If I'd got onto the bridge, why would I go halfway, deposit the box, turn around and come back to Topeth? I've told you. I want to get to Unity, which was where I was going until you stopped me. If I never took a step onto the bridge, how could I have left the box in the middle of it?"

Tula was shaking, her eyes stinging with tears. Damn. They did not believe her. The ravine gaped in front of her, like a huge primordial mouth ready to devour the youthful innocence of the world. She swallowed a momentary pang of regret for leaving her home city.

"You must believe me." She was pleading with them. "It was Jevros. He must have written the note, put it in the box, and then left it there before he fell."

"It's true," Zach piped up. His grizzly voice seemed to betray the man's emotional torment. "The death of his little girl deeply troubled him. This was his cry for help. That's what the message says – help."

Geb frowned and shook his head. He said to Tula, "I'm not convinced. I don't know how or in what way, but you're involved. I can feel it in my bones."

Damien stepped between her and Geb. Now, it was his turn to point a finger at her. "I do too."

"Well, there's a rare sight, Geb and Damien agree on something," Zach chortled in her ear.

Damien carried on, "I'm watching you, young lady. I can smell a troublemaker a long way off. You're probably an anarchist from the city. I bet you threw stones at the guards in the market square to incite the riot. If I find any evidence against you, or that you've deceived me – and these good people here – I'll have you up on a charge quicker than you can fall to the bottom of the gorge. In the meantime, don't leave Topeth. I will need to talk to you again. Do I make myself clear?"

Tula nodded, albeit reluctantly. She had walked into a turmoil of innuendoes, accusations and uncertainties. This restriction meant she could neither cross the bridge nor get out of Topeth. Stuck in limbo, she had to think quickly.

"I-I remember something else," she stammered. "Last evening, coming down the snake path, it's possible I glimpsed another person on the flagstones. He or she was moving around in the shadows cast by that solitary lantern."

"More excuses. There was only Jevros. It had to have been him," Geb said.

"That's what I thought," Tula said. "But a few moments later, I arrived on the flagstones and saw Jevros on the bridge. He couldn't have been in both places at once."

"Are you sure about this?" Geb asked.

"Yes, I am," she said. "I remember now. I saw a shadow on the flagstones, only for a moment."

"If it wasn't you and it wasn't Jevros, then there must have been a third person. They didn't just fly off with the starlings, so where did they go?" Geb asked.

Tula shook her head. "I don't know. Whoever it was, they didn't go on the bridge and they didn't pass me on the snake path." All she wanted to do was get to Unity. And it was proving so difficult.

"Who was this mysterious third party?" Damien asked the question on everyone's lips.

"It's obvious, it's the devils," the High Priest said with worrying certainty. "They're devious, they really are. There's no question in my mind. They left the box there. This help message, it's for one thing and one thing alone, which is to lull us into a false sense of security."

"You could be right," Damien agreed.

"Of course I'm right," Wincorn said. "I'm always right. COIL is my benefactor. I am guided by the light of heaven. There can be no doubt."

"Then it's possible the devils threw Jevros and that third person off the bridge. Or this mysterious person has crossed the bridge and is hiding in Unity. Either way, we must find out if anyone else is missing," Damien said in a moment of revelation. "We need to account for every living soul in Topeth. Where's Samuel?"

"Here, sir," said a tall, stolid man. He walked stiffly over to Damien with minimal arm movement; it was as if they were glued to his sides. What a peculiar anomaly of a man. His neatly pressed robe was as shiny with age as his sunburnt face.

"I want you to carry out a census," Damien said to him.

"Yes, sir," Samuel said, scribbling in his notebook with feverish intent. He reminded her of one of her schoolteachers back in the city. "But sir…"

"Yes, what is it?" Damien asked, whirling round at him.

"I-I, well, Topeth has a large population of vagrants, bootleggers and interlopers, folks who come and go willy-nilly, all feeding off the last copper workings. It'll take time to account for them all."

"Well, now's the perfect opportunity to bring your records up to date," Damien said.

"Will you want the usual restrictions put in place during the census period?"

A shadow of doubt flitted across Damien's craggy features before he realised to what Samuel referred. "Why? Yes. Of course, we must be vigilant. No one must leave or enter the town without first being checked against the census. Lock Copper Gate. Guard Bridge Gate. Everyone comes and goes through South Gate. Vitus, you got that?"

"Yes, Damien," Vitus said.

"Anything else, Samuel? No, so you've got a lot of souls to count. What are you waiting for – a chariot? Get on your way."

"Sir," Samuel said and scuttled off, followed by his assistants.

"Now what are we going to do? Sit and wait for the census results?" Geb said.

Damien shook his head. "Oh dear. Commander, what am I to do with you?" he asked, raising his arms in mock despair. "I'm the leader of the town and you are, well, what are you? Listen, Wincorn's right, the devils are nasty, malicious foes. To combat them, we must break our own rules. We've no alternative but to do the unthinkable."

"What are you suggesting?" Geb shuffled on his feet as if he was uneasy with the direction in which the conversation was heading.

"We must grasp the initiative. We're going to send a search party…" Damien said and paused as if making sure everyone was listening to his next words, "… into Unity."

Everyone gasped. It was as if he had said the sun was green.

Damien pressed his palms into his temples as if gripping his head in a vice.

"Hang on a mo," Musa said. "That could be dangerous. It could be just what them there devils want us to do. They're canny creatures. You seen what they done to our Jevros. And I can tell you, it's scary out there on that bridge."

"Is that what you think?" Damien scowled.

44

"Sir, what I mean is – what if the message is a trick?" Musa replied, in a grovelling way. "They could be gatherin' at the far end of the bridge right now. That there search party could be all tossed into the gorge to their deaths. Worse still, they might come back, but all loopy in the head and mad, just like poor Abel."

"Don't bring my son into this." Geb seemed to bristle at the mention of his son's name.

"Sorry, sir, didn't mean to be rude, like," Musa went on. "Yeah, we've been on the bridge, but we've never set foot in Unity for ages, not in my lifetime anyways. Them devils are out there, they are, and we ain't got a clue how many of them there are. Could be tens or 'undreds, we just don't know. See what I'm saying?"

"Musa's right," Geb said, opening his arms as an appeal to the crowd. "I say, let's be cautious. Let's wait until we've heard from Rufus about Jevros and from Samuel about the census. If no one's missing, we can be certain the devils planted the message. In the meantime, we double the bridge guard and make sure the gate's locked."

"I agree," Zach added a decisive nod of the head. "We've enough trouble dealing with the rioters and now this tragic event with my poor Jevros. We can hardly spare men to send across the bridge and—"

Damien interrupted, "No, no, no! The box is as real as my hand." He held up the offending article as though it was a precious icon wrenched from the dread clutches of a devil. "Someone left this box on the bridge and wrote the note. It needs a response – and more than a 'wait and see'."

There was a pause until Damien added, "I'm the man who's made for this moment. My bravery will save the day, you'll see. Now's the time for action, not prevarication. I will lead the search party myself. And that's my final word on the matter."

People in the crowd turned and muttered to each other. Zach shook his head and mouthed a silent prayer. Vitus made a forked lightning religious sign with his hand, like the letter 'z'. A pall of silence descended on the crowd who seemed to have fallen into a hypnotic slumber at Damien's decision.

"Silus and Kalim will come with me," Damien said.

"Fine by me, sir," Silus said. He was a lanky fellow with a chin almost as broad as his forehead. His vapid, brown eyes wore the expression of a bedraggled youth, thrust into a dangerous world and drowning in its toxic vapours.

"This is too hasty. Don't follow this reckless course of action," Geb said.

"No, we hit back now, before anything else happens to us." Damien's eyes were bulging out of their sockets. "We strike first – before the devils possess us all and we're throwing ourselves off the bridge like lemmings in a grotesque act of mass suicide. I don't want to follow Jevros to the bottom of the gorge. Do you? Do any of you? Is that what you want? Good, then support my course of action."

No one spoke. She was not sure if that was because they were compliant or dumb, or both. Those in the crowd exchanged anxious glances. Zach and Vitus shared a muted conversation. Damien waited and looked around until the old priest shuffled over to him. Wincorn had this odd way of walking where he would push his right leg, pause as if wondering what to do next and then, as if suddenly remembering, move the left leg, or rather drag it forward. It made for a merry, if unconventional, dance. After a while, he reached where Damien stood. Kebel, his dog, was loyal by his side.

"Listen to me, all of you," Wincorn said. "These are anything but normal times. The forces of evil align themselves against us. We must face them, challenge them and defeat them, once and for all. We must retake our town and its sacred heritage."

"Thank you, Wincorn, I'll take that as a sound endorsement of my proposal," Damien cried, lifting his arms as if appealing to the crowd for acclaim. When none came, he said to Wincorn, "I hope you've brought your religious box of tricks with you because we three need to get going. We're placing our lives in your hands. Give us your spells and your sigils. Let's get on with it."

Silus stood there, arms crossed and legs slightly apart, peering down from his great height on all and sundry. Whereas Kalim, with his expression of fearsome apprehension, looked as if he was about to meet his maker and was woefully under-prepared for the final interview.

A middle-aged woman with high cheekbones and a gaunt, narrow face and strong, squarish chin pushed through the crowd. She wore a black mourning headscarf. The woman approached Kalim, clasped him by the hand and said in a soft, warm voice, "My family has a motto: go out with courage and come back with pride. I know you will."

"Amina, sweetheart, thank you. I will do that," Kalim said, puffing out his chest.

Kalim leaned forward to kiss her on the lips, but, as he did, Amina turned away from him and he made do with a peck on her cheek. The woman affectionately squeezed his hand. Before she merged back into the crowd, Amina turned and threw a glance of daggers, first at Wincorn and then at Damien.

With an air of blithe indifference to the gravity of the task, Wincorn blessed the three men in the prescribed manner and presented them each with a protective lightning rod sigil.

Damien turned to Geb and said, "Listen to me, Commander. If we're not back before sunset, you are to cross the bridge and come and find us."

"Are you sure? It'll be getting dark."

"I know. I don't want to spend the night over there. You're to form a rescue party. This mission is too important. I am too important. It's an order. Disobey it and you, and your family, will pay the price."

"Are you threatening my family?"

"I will do whatever is necessary. Follow my orders. Understood?"

Geb swallowed hard on his pride because he murmured, "Yes, Damien."

"Again? I didn't quite hear you."

"Yes, Damien," Geb said, louder this time.

"That's better. And don't even think about leaving me to rot over there," Damien said.

"Would I do that?" Geb shrugged.

"What did you say?" Damien snapped.

"Nothing, Damien. Nothing at all," Geb said.

Damien stomped off, Kalim and Silus trailing behind. The three of them moved in a bizarre, slow-motion, synchronised dance to keep the bridge sway to a minimum. They paused on reaching the midpoint. Everyone expected them to be jettisoned over the edge by some gigantic invisible hand – but that failed to happen, so perhaps Wincorn's peculiar magic spells were working, or there were no devils anyway. The low clouds drifting around the bridge swallowed up the three of them. Soon, they were out of sight and entering the dangerous, forbidden town of Unity.

"Get on with you all," Musa said to the crowd. "There's nothing more to see here. Get yourselves home or go pray in the chapel. Better still, go visit the market. Yeah, it's market day today. And you'll know when they're comin' back just as soon as we do. 'Cos that there town bell will echo down the ravine. You'll hear that all right."

"I never thought I'd see the day when folks from Topeth voluntarily entered Unity." Zach seemed to choke on his emotions as they joined the crowd heading up the snake path. "Anything could happen to those three brave men. Who knows what devils are lurking, unseen, there?"

"The bridge is not haunted, and neither is Unity," Tula said.

"Don't be naïve, lass," Zach replied, adjusting his straw hat. "I wouldn't cross the bridge for all the copper in Topeth. Nor even set foot on it. You may believe you've escaped the curse of the Devils' Bridge but watch out.

It'll catch you when you're unaware, like Bethany when she's upset. That old girl's got a kick on her. You want to see my bruises?"

Tula shook her head. That was one of her easier decisions of the day so far. Because she was in two minds; while desperate to fulfil her dream of entering Unity and mixing with the angels, she had witnessed a tragedy, a man plummeting from the bridge. Despite what the townsfolk believed and what Wincorn said, it bore all the hallmarks of a heart-rending suicide. Geb, Damien and Wincorn were an unholy trio spouting rubbish about a supernatural explanation, one that chimed with the citizens. Everyone seemed to have forgotten that Jevros's daughter was suffocated by toxic air.

The tragic incident was not only a suicide; it was also a burial. And it was a severe test of the strength of her belief in the angels.

CHAPTER 7

Hidden Paths

Tula headed for the market and trudged up the snake path into the main square. The stalls were arranged in neat lines like soldiers on parade. All signs of the riot from the day before were long gone. People swarmed up from the bridge to meet old friends and feast on the rich sights and aromas of a traditional Topeth market. The square was bustling with shoppers young and old, men and women, miners and guards.

Amidst the melee of people and cattle, Tula enjoyed the hustle and bustle of the colourful stallholders. She breathed in the animated and sometimes heated bartering between them and the townsfolk, as though it was a draught of fresh mountain air.

She was excited to find the stall of a man selling all the paraphernalia of domestic lighting, including candles, wicks, lanterns, clay lamps and olive oil. He even had a famous seven-lamp, a brass menorah with its six tributary branches emerging from the main stem.

As she passed by, she glanced into a corner and noticed her new friend, Musa, standing with his back to her. He was next to a flower stall and was either talking or listening to another trader, she could not tell which it was. Tula wandered over to him, only to discover that he was there with the Commander who was conducting some serious business with a cattle trader.

Musa greeted her with a broad smile. Then, just as the flower stallholder was dealing with a customer, Musa reached over and snapped off the stem of a yellow rose. He presented it to her and blew her a kiss at the same time. To hide the blush, she turned away.

The Commander was saying, "How much, Saul? That's too much. Far too much. It's nearly twice what I paid last year."

Saul the cattle trader was dressed in little more than a large brown hessian sack. The rough style of his attire seemed well-matched to his mode

49

of expression because he replied, "Dah! Not my fault." He added a solemn and convincing shake of his head. "Life's tougher than an old bull's hide. It's not too much, I can tell you. I mean, what with the taxes and all that. They want shekels for atonement, shekels for the temple, shekels for—"

"Yes, Saul, I know all about the shekels," Geb interrupted. "But there's a war on in the plains and everyone has to pay the levy, including me. Please allow me to take a closer look at what you're offering me." He bent down on his haunches to examine a large, gentle heifer with a smooth brownish-red coat. The beast could have been mistaken for a statue if it had not been for its tail, which was swishing this way and that to keep away a swarm of irritating flies.

"Well, she looks in good shape," Geb said, walking around the heifer.

"And so she should do. I tended to her myself, like, I was knowing you'd be wanting her for... the proper ritual."

"And she's fit?" Geb was asking. "If the priest refuses her, they will ridicule me. I'd have nowhere to hide my shame. I can't afford that to happen. My situation here's bad enough as it is."

"Oh, she's fit and ready. Never pregnant, never milked and never yoked. Them's the three rules. That's gotta keep the priests happy enough. That's what you gotta pay all them shekels for. You takin' her or what?"

"Yes, I'll take her," Geb said, handing over a pouch of coins.

"I'll leave her at the temple and 'cos it's you, there'll be no extra charge for that. Always a pleasure to do business with the likes of you. Until next year," Saul said, counting the shekels with the practised manner of a banker.

Geb set off through the market, Musa and Tula a little distance behind him.

"What's all this about, Musa?" Tula asked him in a whisper. "What's he buying a heifer for? And what's the ritual?"

"You'll find out soon enough, Miss," Musa said. "The Commander, he don't like to talk about it much. In two days, on Midsummer's Day, there'll be a special festival. The heifer's for that. You'll see it then. But now, I'm on duty. Gotta keep up with the Commander."

"Thanks for the rose," she murmured, as he smiled and headed off in pursuit of Geb.

As she watched Musa disappear into the crowds, she felt something warm and moist nuzzle into her palm.

"Oh, Bethany, it's you. I should have known," she cried.

"You can have my job," Zach said with a chuckle. "You seem to have a way with the donkeys, especially our Bethany. Anyone would think she knew you."

"I don't know about that, Zach," she murmured.

"I'm taking these two to the underground cistern. It's their turn at the water wheel. Want to come along?"

"Yes, why not?" she said.

Zach led her and his donkeys out of the busy market and along a narrow defile until they encountered an open arena. In the middle of it was a huge metal bust, human from the midriff to the neck and with the head of a bull, white horns and a snout as black as the night.

"What on earth is that?"

"Moloch," Zach grunted. "The bronze Temple of Moloch."

"What's it for, this bronze Moloch?" she said, screwing up her eyes. The statue sat on a large plinth. Access was by several steps which led to a large domed opening in the beast's belly. Above that, in the midriff, were four open rectangular cabinets, one above the other, with the uppermost just below the neck.

"Devilish and malevolent forces are unleashed when we sin. They play havoc, attack our people and our town. Moloch is great, for he keeps them at bay."

"How does he do that?"

"We make a sacrifice to the god," Zach said. "According to the severity of our sin, the priests announce a sacrificial offering, which is placed in one of those four cabinets."

Tula's head started pounding and her chest felt heavy. She gave a dry, hoarse cough. "So… This temple… No, I can't stay here. This place is suffocating me. I have to leave."

"I'm sorry, this is the only way to get to the cistern," Zach said. "Come along this way, lass." As he led them away from the statue, they passed through a cluster of red poppies next to the altar before the temple.

When they had left its gruesome presence, she mused, "The poppies… How do such things of beauty grow in the presence of that ugly demon?"

She was not expecting an answer, but Zach had one ready. "What you are seeing are the great and unseen powers of Nature at work."

"What do you mean?"

"Don't you know that poppies like to grow where blood's been spilt?"

"No, I didn't."

"And yew trees are drawn to where bodies are buried in the ground. They're another one of Nature's cleaners. We have some in our own cemetery. Poppies and yew trees; they're Nature's way of healing wounds in the land."

"Makes sense. So, what about the carpet of blue thorns just outside the town?"

"Like you, I suspect they're a healing of something or other, but I don't know what," Zach said. He led them through an alley between Acropolis Hill and the Amphitheatre. There, the street was heaving with men and women carrying rounds of cheese, loaves of bread, and barrels of water into the Amphitheatre. Amidst the banter and the singing, another group was porting theatre props.

"Ah, it's nice to see folk enjoying their work," she said. "The women in the city used to sing songs when they got together at the well to do the washing."

"Tomorrow's the Grand Fete. It's an annual event on Midsummer's Day Eve and features a re-enactment of our history. You'd enjoy it. You might learn a thing or two about Topeth."

They emerged into a narrow area, with Acropolis Hill trailing away to ground level and, in front of them beyond a safety wall, the great ravine itself. Full of subtle winds, sumptuous rainbows, and a susurration of starlings, the cavernous gorge occupied a different realm. Above her, a few high, fluffy white clouds tainted the immaculate purity of the aquamarine blue skies. They resembled wisps of air sealed with teardrops. Perhaps they housed thrones woven by ethereal threads of magic on which the angels sat, peering down with curiosity at the world of men.

In the searing heat, Zach took his two jennies to the water trough, who slurped with enormous satisfaction. Tula found a round, flat stone nearby in a slither of shade and sat down to relieve the weight on her ankle. With the tip of her walking stick, she drew lightning rods on the bare earth, trying to unravel the mystery of the strange z-shaped glyphs.

Bethany came and stood next to her and she stroked her, saying, "There, you are a sweetie, aren't you?"

Zach tugged on the donkeys' harnesses and they set off again, passing alongside Acropolis Hill. Looming ahead of them was a steep vertical wall of earth.

"Where is this mysterious cistern?" Tula asked.

"Over there." Zach pointed his walking stick at a small door cut into the side of the hill. Its wooden support struts resembled the entrance to a mine shaft. He ducked his head beneath the lintel and led her and the donkeys onto a path along a narrow downward-sloping tunnel. On either side of the pathway was a gulley half-full of pebbles and stones, which she assumed was to carry water run-off into the cistern.

The further down the slope they went, the cooler it got. She loved the fresh, chilled air on her skin and the abiding silence. Their footsteps echoed in the cavern. The underground confinement was new, exciting and full of promise. The nearer they got to the base of the slope, the more she could hear the whispering waters.

The cistern lay inside a huge cavern, with clean water lapping against the artificial shoreline. The domed cave was lit by wicker lanterns, which sent tiny sparks into the air. Enjoying a moment's freedom, the flames leapt out of their cradles, before dying as golden-red embers on the ground, as ephemeral as humanity's existence.

A round platform surrounded the water wheel. She followed Zach and his donkeys along a walkway into the central platform where a waterman was trudging along with two other weary donkeys around the circular plinth.

Zach was animated, apparently in his element. "The wheel raises the water from pools, reservoirs and aquifers lower down the mountain. These collect water by a lot of trenches, gullies and streams cut into the side of the mountain to haul fresh water up to the thirsty men and women of Topeth. Since it doesn't rain often, we have to keep every drop when it does."

The other waterman changed over the donkeys, hitching Betty and Bethany's harnesses to the shaft to begin their shift.

To one side were four grottoes carved out of the cistern walls. Each one contained a life-size statue.

"Who are these?" she asked.

"Let me introduce you to our founder and his wife, Herman and Kendra. They're the two in the middle. They're flanked by their sons, Joel and Victor. Herman knew his children would argue over their legacy, so he decreed that Joel and his descendants were to govern the town, while Victor and his family were to run any commercial enterprise. Geb is Joel's descendant, and Damien is Victor's."

"So, Geb and Damien, they're what… distant cousins?"

"You wouldn't think so the way they fight each other," Zach said. "But yes, you're right."

"My family in the city wasn't much different," she confessed. "My mother was always at odds with her sister over the way to run the orphanage."

"For Topeth to survive, Herman knew they had to have water. That was Victor's one and only task and he constructed the network that serves our water supply. After excavating this cistern beneath Acropolis Hill, it was Victor who discovered copper and zinc-bearing ores to the west of the town."

"So, that's how the mining began."

"And ultimately what Damien inherited. Listen, we need to take the two other donkeys back to the stable. Before that, I have to clean the water filters. Please, wait for me here. I won't take long."

As Zach shuffled off, she stood in the half-light watching Betty and Bethany pull the rotary arm around and around. They seemed extremely content in the repetitive nature of their daily tasking. If only she could be satisfied with such mundanity. After everything that had happened since her arrival, the gentle sound of water dribbling into the main pool cooled her blood and calmed her fraught nerves.

"What do you think of our cistern?" Zach asked on his return.

"Aside from its importance to the town, it's a nice, quiet place of retreat," she mused. "In its reflective presence, you can sit and hear and watch your own thoughts wing their way across your mind, like those starlings wheeling around in the sky on a clear, cloudless day."

"You've got a pleasant way with words, lass, you do," Zach said. "I've one more task to perform. I need to check the overflow pipe for blockages."

"There's an *overflow* pipe?"

"I know, it sounds odd," he chortled. "But on rare occasions, there are flash floods."

He led her to the back of the cavern. In one corner, a large cylindrical pipe protruded out of the ground at eye level.

"This is it," he said, with pride oozing from his voice.

The pipe sloped steeply downwards and was wide enough for her to sit inside. Even on tiptoe, she couldn't see the end of it. Zach found her a stool which gave her an unobstructed view of the area outside the walls by South Gate and towards the Welcome Boulder. Beyond that was the carpet of blue thorns and the little cemetery.

"This is an amazing feat of engineering," she said.

Zach gave the nod of a man who had seen and heard it all before.

From outside the cistern sounded the chimes of a bell. "Is that what I think it is?" she asked.

"Yes, it is. Time to go."

"I wonder what Damien found in Unity."

*

Tula and Zach arrived back at the market square, pushing and shoving alongside everyone else. A passer-by accidentally elbowed one donkey on the head, making it stand still and refuse to move an inch. The other one joined in the slow-down. Zach pulled on their leashes. Tula tried cajoling them. The two jennies only budged when Zach offered them each a conciliatory carrot.

"Come on," Zach said. "We have to get to the Devils' Bridge."

"The bridge?" a voice said.

"Musa," she chimed. "It's nice to see you again."

"And you too, Miss." Musa gave her a cheeky wink.

"The bridge, yes," Zach said. "We're expecting Damien to come back with the search party."

"Nah," Musa said. "This time it's South Gate."

"What's happened there?" Tula asked.

"Dunno. I got told to ring the bell. So, I rung it good," Musa said.

By the time they arrived, about thirty people had gathered by South Gate, shouting and yelling. Blind Vitus had his back to them and was facing the closed gates, shaking his fist at an imaginary foe. There was a loud banging on the other side of the gates.

"Get on with you!" Vitus cried at the top of his voice.

"With who?" Tula asked.

"With the devils," said Taurus. "They're outside the gates. We gotta keep 'em out."

Taurus was with the other bully. They were like a couple of baboons... fierce and provocative. Tula had hoped she would never have to meet either of them. But there they were again and now they were in cahoots with Vitus.

"Oh. It's you," she said. "What are you doing here?"

"Helping my pa."

"Your father, who's that?"

"Vitus, who d'you think?" Taurus replied.

"I didn't know," she murmured.

"Well, now you do. My pa might be blind, but he ain't stupid and neither am I. You're a stranger 'ere. You know nothin' 'bout our battles with the devils. Now they're just beyond these 'ere gates."

"Yeah, keep out of what don't concern you, got it?" the other lad said.

"Luca, you tell her." Taurus slapped his friend on the back. This Luca was as thin as a strand of grass and just as wispy. One puff of wind and he would blow over.

"Well, it does concern me," she said. "If there are truly devils outside the gates, I want to know about it."

Taurus puffed out his cheeks.

"How do you know they are devils?" she asked.

He folded his arms. "Little cub, they're banging on the outer gates."

Tula was not sure there were any devils, either outside the gates, or anywhere else for that matter, but Taurus, Vitus and the rest of the crowd seemed convinced. Panic spread amongst them like a firestorm through a dry, grassy plain, filling the air with alarmed and anxious voices.

"They're coming for us," one shouted.

"We've nowhere to run," cried another.

Confusion reigned as a man pushed his way through the crowd from the town.

It was Commander Geb; at last, the presence of authority.

"Everyone, shut up!" he railed. "Good, now can someone tell me what the hell's going on here?"

After Musa had explained, Geb said, "Right, we hold on here for dear life."

"That's what I'm doing, isn't it?" Vitus added.

"I got an idea, sir," Musa butted in. "These devils are as airy as them clouds. Let's see what they're really made of." With that, he picked up a stone and with one almighty throw, lobbed it over the gates. Geb nodded his approval, picked up another stone and chucked it over the top of the gate.

The response was immediate.

"Oi! Stop throwing the bloody stones!" a voice cried out from the other side of the gates.

"There," Musa said. "That's clear enough. That don't sound like no devil to me."

"Who's there?" Geb yelled.

Everyone bent their ears.

"It's me, Rufus. Open the damn gates, will you?"

"You sure it's Rufus who's out there?" a woman in the crowd cried. "Could be a devil, imitating him and fooling us to open the gates. How do we tell the difference?"

"It's Rufus. Remove the barrier," Geb said. For once, Taurus, Luca and Vitus did as they were told.

Fearful about who or what lay outside the gates, the crowd retreated. Some ran off chasing the shadows of their own fear, others covered their eyes with their keffiyehs.

The gates swung open. A short man with a long chin stood there, arms folded, with a square mouth, from which two front teeth protruded like a couple of unwelcome guests. Behind him was a small entourage – a temple servant, a half-dozen men and a donkey cart.

Relief spread across the crowd like the rays of the sun after a rain shower.

"Pa, it's Rufus. It's really him," Taurus said.

"Well, I'm damn pleased to hear that," Vitus added.

Weary and covered in mountain dust, the small party had travelled up the winding mountain road from Seliga. As it trudged through the gates, folks removed their head scarfs and bowed their heads. Tula soon realised why.

At the back of the donkey cart were two wooden coffins. One was adult size. The other one was only slightly bigger than the blue thorn wreath that lay on top of it. The sight of the tiny coffin drew a gasp of sorrow from the crowd. A woman hummed quietly to herself. Soon after, others joined in, a song of lost love and love lost; a lament of bitter tears.

"I-I was following orders not to open the gates," Vitus said. "Sorry."

"Bah. I might have known it was all the Commander's fault," Rufus muttered under his breath.

"Actually, Damien gave the order, not me," Geb said in his own defence.

"No matter," Rufus said.

The crowd parted to let a woman through, a small child trailing behind her alongside another woman, who Tula recognised as Amina. The woman dragged her feet along the ground as if she carried the weight of the world on her shoulders. She was small with puffy eyes and wore a black dress and keffiyeh, despite the heat of the day. She headed to the back of the cart and frantically threw her arms over the coffins, wailing and moaning.

"Who's that?" Tula asked.

"My poor Irit," Zach murmured, going over to comfort her and Amina.

As Vitus and Taurus closed the gates, the crowd fell into line behind the entourage. Their bare heads hung low, they traipsed solemnly together, carrying their grief.

Tula found herself near the front, within earshot of Rufus and the Commander.

Rufus asked him, "Where's Damien? Why isn't he here? Wot you done to him? Finally got your revenge on him?"

"I've done nothing to him," Geb protested his innocence. "He's across in Unity, hunting for whoever, or whatever, left the box on the bridge. Ask anyone. Now, can we stick to the business in hand?"

"I suppose so," Rufus said.

"Then tell me, where did you find Jevros and his daughter?" Geb asked.

"A little way downriver."

"Anything else to report?"

"No, nothing I should tell you," Rufus said, his voice heavy with scorn.

"Please, this is important. The dead man's wife and daughter are right behind us," Geb pointed out. "And we're all fighting for the same cause."

"Are we?" Rufus asked.

"Listen, just tell me, will you? What did you find?"

Rufus said in a low voice, "Jevros's body was... deformed."

"Deformed? How?"

"His neck was twisted around the other way."

Geb seemed visibly shaken and said, "So, it's happened again."

"It's a terrible coincidence," Rufus said.

"It's more than that," Geb said. "It's an omen."

"Yeah, bloody right," Rufus snarled.

Tula's skin was crawling. Geb was right. This did not bode well; this did not bode well at all.

Heads bowed and in full regalia, the priests waited for them at the chapel entrance. As a mark of solemnity, Wincorn made the sign of the lightning sigil and sprinkled the coffins with holy water. Chimor arranged for the pallbearers to take the coffins inside to lie in rest. Irit, her daughter, together with Zach and Amina, staggered in after them, their lives hollowed out by this tragic event.

As Wincorn finished a prayer, the town bell resounded over the rooftops.

Now, surely, that was Damien returning from Unity.

CHAPTER 8

Dancing Butterflies

"Hello, Miss Tula," a voice said from amidst the crowd.

"Hello, Abel. You going to the bridge?"

"I am. I love the bridge."

What an unusual thing for him to say, since it was home to a horde of devils – at least according to prevailing wisdom. It occurred to her that she and Abel shared some things in common; they both liked the bridge and the angels, they were about the same age, and the paths of their lives had crossed in the alley.

"On that day, twelve years ago, were you with your sister on the bridge?" she asked.

He lowered his head and stared at the ground, so she probed again, "Please tell me about it."

"I-I," he stammered, tilting his head.

"I'm a friend of the family, aren't I? You can trust me." She smiled.

"Don't know."

"I helped you with that bully Taurus."

"Suppose so," he said, returning her gaze with soft brown eyes.

"What was it like on that day?"

"I was with my big sister."

"Do we know where she is now?"

"No, but I wish I did. I miss her. I miss her a lot and I feel that her going missing was, you know, all my fault." Tears welled up in his eyes.

"Why? What did you do?"

"That's the thing, Miss Tula… I don't remember," he mumbled. "And when people see me in the town, they hide their mouths behind their hands, like they don't want me to hear what they are saying to each other, but I know they are talking about me and my sister and that… horrible day."

"Horrible day?"

"Yes, Miss Tula. Because before that day, there was me and my sister. My family was happy, and we were all together. And after that day, there was just me. And my family was unhappy. That's horrible. Do you... do you believe she's still alive?"

"Yes, I do," Tula said with a conviction that surprised even her.

"I do too," he said. "I remember the sunshine was nice and warm on my skin on that day." Abel rubbed his forearm as if recalling the feeling. "Big Sis was dancing with the butterflies. She liked dancing with the butterflies, white ones and especially blue ones. Me, I've always liked the bridge. It's a special place, it joins two big bits of land together; otherwise, they'd be lonely, wouldn't they, Miss Tula?"

She chuckled. "Yes, without the bridge, the bits of land would be lonely. Go on."

"I don't know if I should."

"Why?"

He crumpled his face in a shy gesture.

"Abel," she whispered. "Did *you* go on the bridge that day?"

He looked sheepish and nodded. "I could get into trouble, you know, just like Opal did. I don't want to get into trouble, Miss Tula."

"I know, Abel," she replied. "I won't tell anyone, promise."

"I'd never been on the bridge before. It was so high up; it was like riding in the clouds. When I peeped down, the river below was sparkling like a long ray of sunshine. Then I saw what was on the other side of the bridge."

"You mean Unity? I want to go there. You were so brave to go across the bridge. Can I tell you a secret too? I dreamt of you last night and how you met the angels."

"That must have been nice for you. I like angels."

"Did you speak to them?"

"Yes, I did, at least I think I did. See, they're not the same as us. When I reached the other side of the bridge, there was this moving shape – a white cloud with bright golden lights inside – that came and said hello to me. It was friendly. It made me feel happy. But the height of the bridge made my head spin and I-I fainted. When I woke up again, I was back on the other side. Mmm, I think my big sister helped me back across the bridge."

"What do people say about the angels?"

"Father says they've all gone. He says there are only devils now."

"Why does he say that?"

"Because the devils frightened me. Daddy says they gave me a trauma,"

Abel said, furrowing his brow. "I don't rightly know what a trauma is, but since then, I'm not afraid of tall heights."

"That's good for you."

"It is. But the boys still make fun of me. I don't like it, Miss Tula. When they do that to me, it makes my insides all squishy and squeamish."

"I know, I'm sorry they do that," she said, patting his hand.

"Me too." He twirled the tassel on his coat.

"Do you know anything about the box and the message?"

"Box? Message?" Abel's face was a picture of innocence. His eyes glazed over as if he was contemplating the galaxies of the Milky Way.

They dawdled on the snake path and by the time they reached the bridgehead, the sun had nearly set, bathing the bridge in evening shadows. There she caught up with Geb and Musa and the rest of the burgeoning crowd.

"I never thought I'd be pleased to see Damien," Geb said. "But there's a first time for everything. And look, even Tabitha's graced us with her presence."

"Tabitha?" she asked.

"The bridge cat," he said, bending down to pick her up and cuddle her. "Isn't she adorable? One of the copper miners abandoned her. You know what cats are like; she wandered in one day and took up residence. Now, she acts like she owns the place."

Wincorn arrived from the chapel to give thanks at Damien's safe return.

Tula narrowed her eyes as she counted the men coming across the bridge. Three of them had crossed it this morning, but now only two were returning.

Musa must have spotted it, too, because he asked, "What's happened to Kalim?"

Like a sword of Damocles, the question hung in the air as only Damien and Silus stumbled onto the flagstones.

Silus leaned on one of the bridge pillars, his face drained of colour and his head hung low. "I don't feel too good," he said.

"Get over it," Damien said to him, his lips turned into a snarl.

"Tell us all about Unity," Musa said.

"Yeah," Damien grumbled. "Let me get my breath back. That bridge. We survived the bridge. That's something."

"It's thanks to COIL," Wincorn said, full of religious piety.

"Unity," Damien said, sticking his chest out like a rooster. "So you want to know about Unity? Well, I'll tell you. It's not what you'd expect. It has an Acropolis, an Amphitheatre and a Cathedral with two graceful

spires. The streets are arranged in a similar layout to Topeth. The houses…
the buildings… the stonework… and the plaster mouldings are pristine, as
if they have just been built. Even the alleys and by-ways are swept clean."

"Err, how's that possible?" Musa scratched his chin.

"The devils make things look normal," Wincorn said. "They deceive
us into believing their intentions are good and noble. But it's all a trick, a
delusion. They make us imagine that it's clean, but it's just a mirage."

"Please sir, we all wanna know. Tell us, what happened over there?"
Musa asked.

"When we arrived," Damien said, "the three of us searched the
buildings, careful to keep each other in view. We looked in the cellars, the
houses, even in the Bell Tower, but there was nothing, no one… only hot
air and everywhere… this eerie, shining cleanliness."

"You mean, you didn't find no one there, not even them devils?" Musa
asked.

"Not as far as we could tell," Damien replied.

"The devils were in hiding," Wincorn said, adjusting his gold chain of
office. "You may underestimate the power of my protective sigil, but they
do not."

"That would be it," Musa agreed.

Tula frowned. She was not so sure.

"Around midday, the heat was stifling," Damien went on. "We sat
in the shade of the twin turrets of the Cathedral. We drew water from
the well; it tasted so fresh. After that, my limbs felt heavy and my eyes
drooped. The next thing I knew, it was late afternoon, and I was waking
from a deep sleep. I suspected it was something in the water. I was anxious
and confused – so was Silus. Everything had this aura of quiet calm. Yet
something was wrong."

Amina pushed her way through the crowd to the front. "Damn right!
I'm comforting my grieving sister in the chapel and I have to come down
here. I just heard the awful news. My Kalim's missing! Where the hell is
he?"

"Calm down. Truth is, I don't know," Damien said. "When we woke
up, he'd gone."

"Did you even search for him?" Amina's voice was shrill.

"I wanted to, I would have liked to, but look, we had no time, dusk
was falling," Damien said. "We had a choice; stay in Unity during the night
and risk both of us falling foul of the devils or return to Topeth before
dark."

"You did the right thing," Wincorn said. "To stay overnight would have risked life and limb. Those devils would've nibbled away at your spirit. You're fortunate they didn't corrupt you while you slept on the steps. My sigil and blessing protected you."

"Of course they did!" Amina yelled. "But they didn't protect my Kalim."

Wincorn gave this vacuous smile and hunched his shoulders.

"I'm never going to see him again, am I?" Amina went on in the same shrill tone. Her knuckles white with fury, she turned her scorn on Damien. "Because you abandoned him to the devils."

"No, that's not it. Don't worry about him," Damien said.

"Worry about him? I'm petrified for him!" Amina said. "You don't leave a man behind, not for anything or anyone. I smell a rat here. You and Wincorn have been out to get at me for years, ever since… you know what. You couldn't succeed, so you went after the one man who truly cares for me. You know that he's asked for my hand in marriage?"

"Of course, we all do," Damien said. "Just as everyone knows that you've yet to give him an answer."

"And you know why that is, too." Amina drew her face into a scowl. These undercurrents of fury and mistrust were new to Tula. Up to now, she had not witnessed a challenge to Damien or Wincorn. So, good for Amina.

"And you had better thank our High Priest," Damien replied, "for your even being here to speak to us today. It could have been very different."

"Oh, I'm ever so grateful." Amina rolled her eyes.

"Don't you dare talk to me like that," Damien said. "You're upset, I understand that. But listen, I'll make sure we find him and bring him back to Topeth."

"You will? And how will he be? Mad? Possessed by the devils?" Amina went on, her voice shot with anxiety, her eyes blazing with fire. "He could have been thrown from the bridge when you were asleep and none of you would be any the wiser."

Wincorn interrupted, "As long as he keeps hold of his sigil, he'll be safe."

"Safe? What? From the likes of you?" Amina asked.

Some distance away, Silus clutched his stomach and vomited its contents onto the ground. The smell was putrid.

"Someone look after the poor man," Geb said, entering the fray.

Tula liked that. Despite the duress, Geb still showed care and compassion to the man. Perhaps he was not so bad after all.

Geb's forehead was drawn into a deep frown. "So, you've lost one of my guards."

"Only temporarily." Damien lowered his head.

"And the devils, are they missing as well? Now, that would be an achievement," Geb said.

Wincorn's grimace was a truly gruesome sight of bushy eyebrows, wrinkled mouth, nose and forehead.

Geb turned his anger on Damien. "It's too late to cross now. But tomorrow, I'll come with you. I'll find him. Kalim's one of mine. I'll see him brought back safely to Topeth."

"No, you won't," Damien said. "Tomorrow, you will officiate at the Grand Fete."

"This is hardly the time for celebrations," Geb reminded him with a shake of the head.

"You will do as I say," Damien said.

"Why?" Geb countered. "Have you any idea what's going on?"

"I do, but do you? Tomorrow is a special anniversary, particularly for you," Damien replied.

"Yes, and you won't let me forget it, will you?"

Damien smirked and folded his arms.

Behind him, Silus was dry retching.

"Poor lad," Geb said. "It's the exertion of crossing the bridge and the fear of those devils."

As Geb and Musa and some others gathered around the stricken man, Damien pulled away and waved Rufus to his side. The two turned their backs on everyone else. Tula edged closer to keep them in earshot.

"I've brought back an item of interest from Unity," Damien was saying.

"Yes, sir," Rufus replied.

"Don't let anyone know about this. Understood?" Damien handed Rufus a piece of cloth wrapped around an object about the size of a man's fist.

Rufus clutched the weighted bundle in his palm. "What is it?"

"That's exactly what I want to know," Damien said. "Get it assayed at the mining laboratory. When the report's ready, let no one else see it and bring it directly to me."

"Understood," Rufus said as he tucked the object in his knapsack.

Geb noticed their secretive conversation. "Hey!" he said. "What's going on here?"

"Trust me, it's nothing to concern yourself about," Damien said.

"Trust you? After what you did to my family, that's impossible."

Leaving the two men arguing, Rufus set off up the snake path, followed by a portion of the crowd and a posse of guards holding wicker torches to light the way. In the evening gloom, the gorge possessed an ominous presence that pressed down on them, as if glowering at the puny humans who dared live in its perpetual shadow.

Tula walked next to Amina.

"They'll find Kalim in the morning, I'm sure they will," she said.

"I doubt it," Amina replied.

"Why do you say that?"

Amina glanced over her shoulder and said, "You're a stranger here. You haven't lived through all the nooks and crannies of our history."

"True enough, but I'm getting to grips with it," Tula replied. "Tell me, what did Damien mean when he said you had the High Priest to thank for being here?"

"It upsets me to talk about it," Amina said, lowering her eyes.

"I understand."

"Well, actually, you don't. It's a terrible story and I'll tell you if you want to know. Come back with me to our house. We can talk freely there."

Amina's house was in the suburbs, amongst wooden shacks and stone cottages, some with the paint bleached by the incessant glare of the sun, peeling like sunburnt skin. Others had their front doors hanging off their hinges, broken windows and strands of grass growing out of the mortar. While candlelight flickered in some, many were vacant and in darkness.

Tula tapped her walking stick on the threshold as she and Amina entered the stone house.

The kitchen had a delightful aroma of herbs. Next to a larder, a stove and a sink, sprigs of mint and rosemary hung from the low ceiling. Jars of almonds, flour and olives stood obediently on the shelves. Tula sat down at a kitchen table; its legs wobbled on the uneven stone floor. Amina brewed some mint tea, to which she added a heaped spoonful of honey. Tula took a sip; the sweetness of the honey and the aromatic freshness of the mint swirled around her mouth, a delight to the senses.

"What do you want to know?" Amina asked.

"What's Damien got against Kalim?" she asked.

"Before Damien went on the bridge, do you remember Kalim advised him not to act hastily? Well, Damien ignored him, which was no surprise. He's never got on with Kalim. And never will. Kalim's one of Geb's men. Damien and Geb hark from two strands of the same family. They're like two tribes and their continual feuding paralyses the town."

"I'd heard as much. Talking of families, what about yours and Kalim's? He's asked for your hand? You must be so excited."

"Yes, I am, but I'm keeping him waiting for an answer." Amina bit her bottom lip. "He's a sweet man and I love him desperately. But, well, it's… complicated."

Her hands shaking, Amina poured another cup of mint tea. "It's a long story. It always is, isn't it?"

Amina's face was etched with tension, so Tula waited while she composed herself.

"After the exodus from Unity," Amina went on, "things were fine until the mining of the copper ore. The town grew rich but at a cost. Out of greed came debauchery, followed by thuggery. Then Godal, a distant relative of Wincorn, tried to repair the damage. He replaced the wooden bridge pillars with those made from copper and zinc. And because people had abandoned the true way, he founded the COIL religion. He gathered all the bits of unused and discarded metal from the mines and out of it built the Temple of Moloch. The people were to make offerings to Moloch, who would intercede for us and bring us back into the iridescent light."

"What kind of offerings?"

"At first, it was plant seed and fruit. It worked for a while, but people soon returned to their greedy ways. So, Godal decreed animal sacrifices; small rodents like mice and rats. Then about two hundred years ago, the High Priest of the time demanded offerings of larger mammals like sheep, heifers or bulls."

"So, that's where you are now?"

"Well, no, it's not," Amina said, fighting back some tears.

"I'm sorry, this is distressing for you."

"Yes, please give me a moment."

Amina wiped her eyes and carried on, "This next incident took place thirty years ago when I was seven years old. Marcus, Damien's father, ran the Topeth Copper Company. A young Wincorn had just risen to the exalted position of High Priest. The bridge was in disrepair. Wincorn wanted it fixed. Marcus and his men risked their lives for over a year, replacing every thread and loop. As a reward, Marcus wanted permission to cross the bridge. Wincorn refused."

"Why was that?"

"Because Wincorn suspected – with the deposits in Topeth running out – that Marcus wanted to look for copper in Unity and Suria, that's the area nearby."

"No wonder Wincorn stopped him."

"But he didn't. At dawn the next day, Marcus crept onto the bridge and entered Unity. Later that day, he was on his way back when the bridge swayed uncontrollably – even though there was not a breath of wind.

Marcus was thrown from the bridge, arms flailing, into the abyss below. His body was found washed up on the shoreline of the River Naddee. It was awful."

"Why?"

Amina looked straight at her and said, "His head was twisted round the other way."

"But that was exactly how they found Jevros. Now I know what Geb meant when he said it was an omen."

"According to Wincorn, the angels were harmless, and it could not have been them who threw Marcus off the bridge. So, he claimed that the angels had been chased out of Unity by some devils, who now occupied the bridge. We had brought this peril on ourselves, through greed and debauchery. After that, no one was allowed on the bridge, or into Unity. That was when they changed the name of the bridge."

"What happened then?"

"Wincorn demanded a sacrifice."

Tula felt sweat break out on her brow. "Another one? A heifer wasn't good enough?"

There was a long pause. Amina's face was a sea of turbulence. Tula waited. The silence was heavy and oppressive.

"No, not this time. Wincorn insisted it had to be something both innocent and precious to the town."

"Wait, what are you... you don't mean... a human sacrifice?"

Amina nodded; every muscle in her face tightened into a strong frown. "Worse."

"What could be worse...?"

"Yes, a child. Tula, a child was to be sacrificed to Moloch... and passed through the fire."

"That's inhuman."

"They put the child in the Galling Chamber and lit the oven in the hearth beneath it. The bronze was heated, the drums were beaten, the child screamed, but... there was a last-minute reprieve."

"The child was saved?"

"Yes, she was. Wincorn substituted a goat at the last minute. Since then, she suffered not from the flames of the ceremony, but from the mental and emotional trauma of its memory."

"Who was... she?

Tula's inner voice told her who it was before Amina replied, "Me."

At that moment, Amina was as innocent and vulnerable as a lamb, so much so that Tula could hear the cry of her soul, rebelling against the cruelty.

Amina said, "That's what Damien meant when he said I had the High Priest to thank for being here."

Amina paused, her chin quivering with the sheer emotional impact of the memories.

There was one last confession. "And that's why I can't say yes to Kalim's proposal. I have a delicate balancing act to perform because, if I refuse, it will break his heart. Now, do you understand, little one? I'm so afraid that if I marry him, I will bear him children, and they will end up... being passed through the fire... but this time with no reprieve."

CHAPTER 9

The Grand Fete

During the night, the little room at Sarah and Geb's house was like a theatre of nightmares. Tula felt awful for Amina and the children and townsfolk of Topeth. She wondered what the angels thought about a god-like Moloch and his lackey, Wincorn, performing human sacrifice – on children. Perhaps they glanced the other way, fearful of what they witnessed. Perhaps they looked on in mute disbelief. Blinded by hatred and fear, the people of Topeth ignored the angels.

With her nightdress stuck to her body with sweat, Tula's meagre night's sleep was made worse by screeching noises coming from somewhere outside the house.

The next day, the eve of Midsummer's Day, was the Grand Fete, held in the Amphitheatre. On a scorching hot, sunny day, the mosquitoes buzzed around the town as though they were its masters. The cats and dogs slept in whatever shade they could find, and the market stalls were closed for the day. The locale was crowded with the good citizens of Topeth, no doubt seeking a way to escape from the scorching heat and the continuing stream of dreadful news.

Tula sought shade wherever she could as she strolled around the compact, imposing arena, guided by her trusty new friend – her walking stick. The stonework on the walls and quaint arches showed fraying and signs of heavy weathering. The area had a tangy, musty smell like decaying herbs. Alongside the Acropolis, the Amphitheatre was one of the oldest buildings in the town. The arena resembled a sleeping giant of marble, stone and brick, with Romanesque colonnades and sturdy columns. Outside was a sign. In Topeth, there was always a sign:

The Great Amphitheatre.
Built by the Topeth Copper Company.

A guard stopped her at the outer entrance. Samuel stood a few steps behind him.

"Name?" the guard asked.

"Tula."

"Not on the list, Miss."

"I'm a visitor."

"How do you spell your name?"

"T-U-L-A."

"Ah, I've got you now. It's here on the bottom of the list," the guard said.

Samuel waddled up to them with his pad of papers. He walked like a penguin, stiff and with a quaint shuffle. It brought a snigger to her lips.

In the city, she had never taken part in a census. Edging closer to Samuel, she asked, "Is everyone present and correct?"

"That's what we're trying to find out, Miss," he said. "And remember, during the festivities, the gates remain locked and bolted. Anyone who leaves before the official end contravenes the Law of Census, which is a grave offence."

"It's a strict arrangement," she said.

"Damien's orders, Miss," Samuel explained.

"I'll bear that in mind," she said, trying to sound compliant for once.

Tula refused to stay cooped up in the place all day. So, she loitered in the entrance area and discreetly checked the padlocks and chains on the exit gates. But to find the right exit gate was a different matter altogether. And she had to avoid arousing the guards' suspicions.

The Amphitheatre was shaped like a huge horseshoe with a keeper bar connecting the two open ends, where a stage was situated. Behind the wooden stage area, two flags billowed in the wind, one showing the red spade and silver sickle flag of the mining company and the other, the white, blue and yellow lightning rod flag of the municipality of Topeth.

As the citizens occupied the rows of wooden benches, the place hummed with anticipation. Everyone from Topeth was there. Well, they had to be – for the census. Upwards of a thousand people, she estimated. Friends, old and new, chatted amiably at the anniversary event. Overlooking either side of the stage were two balcony boxes with chairs sumptuously decorated in bright purple, adorned as for an emperor and his entourage. They soon filled with local dignitaries.

She found a place next to Amina. Deposited on every seat was a pair of eyeglasses. Tula tucked hers into her pocket.

"How are you today?" Tula asked.

"Still worried sick," Amina said. "Of all days to be stuck in here. I want to be at the bridgehead to greet my hero, my amour, my Kalim."

Amina wiped away a tear from her eyes, puffy and red raw. "Please meet my sister, Irit, and her little daughter, Esther." Next to Amina was a tiny woman in her early forties, still wearing a black dress and keffiyeh.

"My condolences," Tula said and then added:

"Woe for his leaving,

Woe for our grieving."

"That's kind of you to say so," Irit said. "Amina's coming for a family supper tonight. We won't be the most entertaining company, but you'd be most welcome to join us."

"I'd love to," she replied.

A blast of trumpets announced the Commander's arrival. Alongside Sarah and Abel, he entered the main balcony. Abel had the bag for Miriam's heat stone, no doubt to amuse himself during the day with her antics.

The Commander announced, "Welcome, citizens of Topeth. Enjoy the festivities of today's Grand Fete. Let the celebrations begin."

Everyone cheered and waved their bunting.

At the far end of the Amphitheatre was a portcullis gate. Accompanied by another blare of trumpets, it was raised by two men pulling on its lifting chain. It revealed an ornate two-horse chariot, which charged around the oval auditorium. The crowd's acclaim was deafening.

Behind it came a colourful procession of locals dressed in red and white quartered tunics. The crowd was ecstatic when they saw two burly men in a sword fight, jousting with flair and energy. Acrobats turned wild somersaults and performed elaborate feats of balance and agility while a dozen jugglers and a handful of jocular clowns amused the heaving crowd. Then came a man dressed as the mellow moon and another as the bright sun wearing a pointed hat. The 'sun' was leading a brown bear which was almost twice as tall as its minder. A third man waved a couple of long, thin, metal rods, prodding the bear to keep the beast at a safe distance.

Last, but not least, came a proud eagle perched on its handler's forearm. It squawked so loudly that Esther hid her face under Irit's armpit. The crowd clapped as the procession wound its way around the stage, before exiting to applause and shouts of glee.

Stagehands cleared the arena of debris, before hauling a model church from the wings and plonking it in the middle of the stage.

"What are they doing?" Tula asked.

"It's a passion play with actors showing the events of the exodus,"

71

Amina said. "I'll explain to you. You'll follow it. Look, there's a model of the Cathedral in Unity. See what happens next."

Two actors emerged onto the stage dressed in white robes and with graceful, swan-like wings.

"They represent the angels of Unity," Amina said.

Then two actors, a man and a woman, strode in a dignified manner onto the stage, heads held high and dressed in imperial robes.

"And that's Herman and Kendra."

The actor playing Herman held up his palms to the two angel figures, saying, "There's no unity here anymore."

One of the angels replied:

"Emissaries of the Creator are we,
And Unity is our home and embassy.
Cared for you we have, so,
Watched over you, seen you grow.
Guided you every day,
Now you're privileged, in every way."

"That may be," Herman yelled in defiance. "Without free will, humans were innocent of life, like the birds and animals. We could only carry on within narrow, prescribed confines. It was a perfect state of grace, a brilliant communion. But it was sterile because we made no mistakes and so learnt nothing. There was no progression, no development, no evolution.

"Now, all that's changed. The Creator wants us to emerge from your protection. That's why He's granted us free will. We'll learn right from wrong. We'll use the power of reason to survive, prosper and understand. We'll court the future."

The other angel replied:

"We angels have no free will.
But love the Lord our God.
We have no doubts to hold us back,
And lay us on the awful rack.
Like and dislike, we cannot entertain,
Nor keep to any preferences in the main.
But one thing, we seek to find,
The refinement of humankind.
Waiting every day to be,
Agents of your future are we."

Herman puffed out his chest and replied, "We don't need you. With free will, we'll forge our own future!"

Then the first angel said:

"The Creator too must sow seeds,
Like humans too, by many deeds,
Must grow and change in a line,
Make more of kind and refine.
Of love, we angels cannot know,
Yet you humans may teach us high and low.
The Creator has writ the angels' symphony.
Yet humanity's song will be His epiphany."

"We will not change our minds if that's what you think. We're still going to leave Unity," Herman said. "We can do what we like. And you can't stop us."

This time, both angels spoke in unison:

"You are as children before the Maker,
Be not rash as a decision-taker.
Stay, and with us, abide,
For we will always provide,
To you, feelings fine and clear.
Keepers are we. To us, be near."

"No, we're going," Herman replied.

"No, we're going," the audience repeated. The call echoed around the theatre and spurred Herman to action.

"We're humans. We have free will. Angels don't," Herman scoffed. "In the eyes of the Creator, that makes us higher than you, at least in possibility. We don't need you angels anymore."

The angels replied, their voices as sweet as seraphs on high:

"Let's both grow in service higher,
Together in our glorious desire.
Leave us not in Unity alone,
Facing tomorrow in the unknown."

"No, we can't," Herman cried. "Wait and I'll show you what human beings can do."

Two stagehands rushed into the arena. They laid two long pieces of rope flat on the ground and parallel to each other, both leading away from the house representing Unity.

Herman walked between the two guide ropes, edging his way to the other side and fixing his eyes on it. Despite a few wobbles along the way, drawing gasps from the crowd, he made it. Stepping off the other side, he said:

"Now we're free of the old, angelic shackles. We'll find our own way. Build our own town! Shape our own future."

The crowd loved it and shouted, "Herman! Herman!"

He took off his hat and gave a long, low bow.

The stagehands brought on a second model house and laid it at Herman's feet. He pointed to it and said, "I name this town Topeth because it's 'The Top' town in the world. And free of angels."

"Top-eth! Top-eth!" everyone roared.

Against the angels' sensible and cautious advice, Herman had led the exodus because he had disagreed about the best place for humans to exercise the gift of free will.

Geb stood up. "Now, everyone. This is our time, your time. I am your Commander and I want you all to enjoy the rest of the Grand Fete."

The charioteer returned to the stage, gripping the reins of the two dappled horses. Driving them faster and faster around the arena, he courted danger and death with each turn of the wheels until his theatrics were abruptly interrupted when a half-dozen men and women spilled from the front seats onto the stage.

"Every breath, nearer to death! Every breath, nearer to death!" the intruders shouted.

The wily Taurus was their leader. Luca and the rest of Taurus's band of baboons were not far behind him. The guards rushed onto the stage and chased them around the theatre. The crowd shouted and jeered. After a comical pursuit, they arrested Taurus's co-conspirators. Only Taurus escaped their clutches. Occupying centre stage, he danced and jigged this way and that. He let them catch up with him, then used his youth and agility to escape their flailing grasp.

Amina's snorting laugh was contagious. Tula joined her in a moment of light relief. With the guards and the audience distracted, Tula sniffed an opportunity and stood up.

"Where are you going?" Amina asked.

"I won't take long."

As Tula headed to the exit, cohorts of guards rushed past her to deal with the havoc Taurus was causing centre stage. One shouted at her, "Go back to your seat. You're going nowhere. All the gates are locked and bolted!"

She pretended to go back inside, but as soon as the guards were out of sight, she spun round and darted for the exit she had identified earlier. The protestors' shouts and chants reverberated around the old arena.

Then, a flash of white. A guard's kaftan. Move. Fast. She ducked into a broom cupboard. Footsteps. Coming her way. Had he seen her? Moist palms. Quickened breathing. Trouble now. She had left her seat. Think of an excuse. Back pressed against the wall. She peered through the slit in the cupboard door, watching, her breathing shallow, as beads of sweat broke out on her forehead. She prayed. He had to walk by. He had to.

More footsteps. Another guard. Coming the other way.

The guards met outside her broom cupboard. She could see them through the thin crack in the doors where they joined. She wished herself small. Invisible would be better. She waited for an eternity for one of them to spot her. They were talking.

"Hot one today, eh?" one of them said.

"Damn those mosquitoes," the other replied.

"And the protestors. Making us run around like idiots."

"I know. Where you posted?"

"I've just been with Samuel to deliver the results of the census."

"It's finished then?"

"Yup. As soon as Damien returns from Unity, Samuel will report to him."

The sound of claxons blaring, and angry shouts drowned the other guard's reply. Tula wanted to melt into the wall. With closed eyes, and her heart thumping in her chest, she waited, expecting to be arrested. She blinked and when she looked again the guards had gone.

What a relief.

She poked her nose out of the broom cupboard. The principal thoroughfare was clear. She headed for the exit gate. It was chained. She shook the gate and the chain fell off onto the ground. Earlier, she had noticed that the padlock was not properly secured on that exit gate. Was that providence or serendipity? Or was it watchful preparation on her part? She did not mind what it was, because she cried, "Eureka!" as she shoved the metal gate open, replaced the chain and padlock as she had found it, and strolled into the sun-kissed street. For a few brief moments, she tasted the clean waters of freedom and the release from bondage, seen and unseen.

There was shade in the narrow alley between the Amphitheatre and Acropolis Hill. Stray cats fought over scraps. Two black-hooded crows watched with marked disinterest from the safety of a rooftop and then flew off in tandem. She nearly stepped on a Greek tortoise which was doing an extremely good impersonation of a rock.

But she was free. Other than the dogs, cats and birds, and the ever-present mosquitoes, the streets were deserted. This would have been a great opportunity to cross into Unity, but Damien was over there. So, she decided to explore the town and unearth some of its secrets. The people seemed so wrapped up in COIL and its metal monster, Moloch.

She threaded her way through narrow alleys, past houses with open doors and with window shutters flung open. Following the promptings of her inner voice, she moved across the deserted market square, by the Bell Tower and out towards Bridge Gate.

Turning the corner through the gate, there it was, the rope bridge, soaked in the sun's golden rays. The flock of starlings eased through the air, gliding serenely above and below the bridge. She loved their glossy, lustrous black plumage, flushed with an orange streak on the outer wing.

Today was different. So was the ravine.

A man was shuffling around on the flagstones near the copper pillars. Wearing a white robe and black and white keffiyeh, it was Rufus, Damien's lackey. Tula retrieved her pair of eyeglasses from her pocket. He was adjusting the harness of a horse, tethered to a covered wagon. To keep out of sight, Tula ducked behind a stone wall at the top of the snake path.

The bridge was still, the air quiescent.

Damien was at the Unity end of the bridge. Waving his arms about as if he was about to alight with the starlings, he was instructing Silus. They set off across the bridge, Silus leading with Damien five paces behind him. Theirs was the pace of a tortoise, moving in the synchronised way demanded by the bridge.

She trained her eyeglasses on them. Damien and Silus were wearing thick gloves, which seemed out of place, considering they were not carrying anything. Perhaps they had already found Kalim, because after the pair reached the flagstones, Rufus locked the bridge gate behind them.

The three of them peered into the back of the wagon which faced away from her line of sight. She wondered if Kalim was in there. The three were laughing. To cap it all, Rufus took out his pistol and fired it into the still air. Damien slapped him on the back as the sound rebounded off the ravine walls. Her eardrums were already sensitive, and this made it worse.

When they finished shooting off their pistols and their mouths, Rufus strode to the front of the wagon and climbed on board. Silus jumped up and sat next to him. Grasping the horse's reins, Rufus guided the wagon up the snake path.

They were heading directly towards her. She had to get back to the Amphitheatre before they missed her. She crawled along the ground, keeping out of sight behind the stone wall. The wagon was trundling up the snake path and slowed to a crawl as it reached the top of the hill near where Tula was hiding. Silus and Rufus were chuckling to themselves.

Knees and palms scraping in the dust, she reached the end of the wall. To avoid being seen, she would have to wait until the wagon had passed by before going on any further.

She glanced at the ground ahead. There it was, curled in a perfect circle under a rock; a black whipsnake.

Everything in her wanted to scream, or flee, or grab a rock and pummel it.

But she couldn't. Either way, she would give away her hiding place.

The snake had seen her and lifted its pointed head.

Still on all fours, she froze. Fear gripped every sinew. The blood drained from her face. Everything stopped: the day, the clouds, her breathing, even her command of her body. Everything was motionless, except for the snake's forked tongue and the wagon trundling ever closer.

With its scaled skin glinting in the sunlight, the snake danced in front of her, staring at her with its ringed eyes, paralysing her emotions, her mind, her being.

The whipsnake raised its head to strike.

A pistol shot rang out, the bullet whistling by just above her head. She nearly jumped out of her skin.

"Got it!" Rufus crowed.

The shot separated the snake's head from its body.

And… shredded Tula's nerves. Gasping for breath, she slumped onto the ground behind the wall and waited until the wagon had passed through Bridge Gate.

Slowly, life returned to her sinews and normal thoughts filled her mind.

She got up and stared at the snake, then stamped her heel on its bloody head. That felt better.

Taking care to keep out of sight, she retraced her steps. Fortunately, the same gate from which she had left was still unlocked, so she re-entered the Amphitheatre and carefully rechained it. She returned to her seat in time for the closing ceremony.

"Where've you been?" Amina asked. "With that look in your eye, I can tell you haven't been for the call of nature. Come on, young lady, what've you been up to?"

"Don't tell anybody. I-I went outside," she whispered.

"I thought so… And?"

"I saw Damien coming back from Unity."

"That's wonderful news," Amina said. "Did you see my Kalim? Is he safe? Oh, tell me he's safe, please. Is he there?"

"I don't know. He might be with them. I just couldn't tell."

"When they let us out of this place, I'm going to see for myself," Amina said.

"I'm coming too," Tula said.

CHAPTER 10

The Curse of Topeth

As the wings of dusk were falling, Tula and Amina pushed through the crowds departing the Amphitheatre and headed straight for Bridge Gate. When they breached the bridge flagstones, the place was deserted and there was not a trace to show the men had even been there. They were about to leave when Tabitha meowed. They turned to see the door to the guards' hut swing open and Damien stroll out.

Before he could say a word, Amina was in his face. "Where is he? Where's my Kalim?"

"We didn't find him," Damien said.

"I don't believe you," Amina replied. "You've probably disposed of him, as you did the others. He told me about your financial sidelines and how all the shekels you collect for the war effort never quite reach the coffers in the city."

"Innuendoes, all innuendoes."

"Did you even look for him?"

Damien backed off, but not by much. "We did search for him. Ask Silus. Ask Rufus."

"I will," Amina replied. "But you didn't try too hard. If you had, he'd be here with me now. You've left him there amongst the devils. He's probably at the bottom of the River Naddee. Oh, no. With his head twisted round." Amina's body was shuddering.

"Listen." Damien softened his tone. "We're going back tomorrow."

Amina pulled herself together. "You had better find him and deliver him back to me or there'll be hell to pay. Zach will see to that."

"What's your father going to do? Set his donkeys on me?"

Before Amina could defend her father, Geb and Samuel strode onto the flagstones. Despite the clouds of dust billowing around the ravine,

Samuel had kept his long, white robe pressed to perfection. He stood before Damien.

"Well?" Damien asked.

Samuel said, "Sir, I've finished the census."

"About time too."

"I want you to know that I paid meticulous attention to detail, as these papers attest," Samuel said, shoving his wad of papers in Damien's general direction.

"I don't doubt it," Damien said, shooing away the papers. "But I need some good news. Give me the results."

Samuel cleared his throat and spoke as if he was addressing the town elders. "The count was one thousand and forty-two souls."

"That's a sizable number. After all the departures, I thought it would be less. I'm interested in any notable deaths, absentees, exiles or additions."

"Let me find that sheet. It's here somewhere," Samuel went on, licking his thumb and forefinger and leafing through the papers. "Ah, here it is. Would you like it, sir?"

"No, I've got ears and you've got a tongue. Read it to me."

"Sir. Recent deaths: Jevros and his daughter. Recent addition: Miss Tula. Recently missing: Kalim. Other than that, there are six absentees."

"And they are?"

Samuel cleared his throat and said, "Ezra, Mina and Didi are the most recent. They are all unaccounted for."

"How? What happened to them?" Damien asked.

"I encouraged them to go," Amina said.

"You did what?" Damien narrowed his eyes.

"Their daughter's young," Amina said. "Didi's eight and about the same age as me when I suffered the Moloch ordeal. Her parents were terrified you would pass her through the fires. So, they left. And can you blame them?"

"Wincorn should have passed you through the fires when he had the chance!"

"It's too late now," Amina said.

"Sir," Samuel interrupted.

"What is it?" Damien snapped at the record keeper.

"Shall I carry on?"

Damien took a deep breath and asked, "Who were the other three?"

"Enoch, Ruth and Opal, sir," Samuel said.

"Well, well, well, Enoch and Ruth," Damien chirped. "Along with your missing daughter, Commander, they're all wanted criminals."

"I don't need reminding," Geb said, lowering his head.

"One day, I will apprehend Enoch and Ruth," Damien replied. "Then they'll lead us to Opal and reveal how you helped them escape the Law of Topeth."

"You have no proof I did anything wrong," Geb said.

"White as winter snow is our Commander."

"I pay my penalty to Moloch every Midsummer's Day."

"Which is tomorrow. And as you well know, I look forward to it every year." Damien added a menacing grin.

Geb spat on the ground, missing Damien's sandal by the width of a shoelace. Damien thrust his face in front of Geb's and they stared at each other until Samuel fumbled and dropped his precious tranche of papers.

The record keeper scrambled to pick them up and then asked, "Damien, sir. I have a query. The Law of Topeth states that, until the person is found, or a corpse identified, the person is treated as being alive. Enoch, Ruth and Opal have been on the absentee list for many years, so what shall I do about them?"

Damien rubbed his chin. "Let's ask our esteemed Commander."

"What do you want to know now?"

"Why is it that all the search parties you've sent out over the years have never found them? Not one trace of them; it's almost as if you knew exactly where *not* to look for them!"

Geb frowned and glared at Damien.

"I thought so," Damien went on. "Admit it, you don't want them found."

"That's not true. I'd love to see my daughter again."

"I can imagine. I'd love to see her too. As would Wincorn and Moloch. But since you've failed so miserably to find her, I'll arrange the next search party myself. And they *will* find her."

"Good luck with that. After twelve years, the trail has gone cold. While you're chasing your tail," Geb replied, "I'm going to look for Kalim. I owe it to him and Amina."

"No," Damien said. "You'll attend Jevros's funeral tomorrow morning and offer your condolences to his family. I myself will go to Unity and bring back Kalim."

"Will you now?" Amina said. "You didn't find him today. What makes you so sure you'll find him tomorrow? Ah, it's another ruse. Your promises are empty. Mine have substance; don't forget, you'll die exactly as I predicted."

"Still banging on that drum?" Damien shook his head. "I thought you'd have grown up since those days. When was it now, all of thirty years ago? But no, your brush with death still terrifies you. I don't know, Madam. Have a good look around you. We're in a town on top of an arid mountain. How can I die of *drowning* here? That's a stupid prediction and you're a pathetic charlatan."

"You're going to drown in a pool of your own wrongdoing." Amina spat the words out.

Damien clenched his fists, so Tula pulled Amina away, saying, "Come on, he's not worth it."

"My prophecy will come true, one day, you'll see," Amina claimed.

Tula led her up the snake path and they headed to Irit's for supper.

By the time they reached Irit's house, Amina had calmed down. Outside there were two flickering candles in a window arranged in traditional mourning fashion; there was a framed pencil portrait of a man dressed as a doctor, a tiny item of baby clothing and a porcelain vase of white lilies, their delicate flower heads drooping in grief.

They trudged up to the front door and Amina lifted the bronze knocker. No one answered although noises were coming from inside the house.

Footsteps were approaching the door.

"Who's there?" It was Irit, her voice shot with alarm.

"It's me, Amina. I'm with Tula."

"I'm so glad you've come," Irit said, opening the door. Her face was wrinkled and her cheeks sallow and puffy.

Tula stepped inside.

"Welcome to my house," Irit said. Her voice sounded dismembered, as if her soul had temporarily departed.

One of the candles in the window spluttered, gasped and went out.

"Here, let me," Amina intervened and lit it again with an iron and a flint. Light splashed onto the lawn. A row of blood-red narcissi bobbed their heads in the gentle evening breeze.

Irit wore a pinafore over her mourning robe. Cooking smells emanated from a stove in the kitchen. Irit lifted her head, revealing a pair of pleading, doleful eyes. Her voice was a gentle whisper, like a breeze through the leaves on the trees. "I've prepared a stew and, well, I've cooked a lot. I hope you both have a healthy appetite."

Inside, the house was as tidy as the front garden. But everything wore a sheen of empty abandonment and sad loss as if the guts had been ripped out of it. Another bouquet of white lilies decorated the dining table.

Esther sat cross-legged on the floor, playing with a doll dressed in a staid pinny, cap and cloth shoes.

"Esther, sweetie, come and sit at the table. And behave yourself, we have a guest," Irit said.

Without a word, the little girl climbed into her chair at the table and, realising she'd left the doll on the floor, slid off to retrieve it. Hugging it to her chest, she retook her place.

Five places were laid: one for Esther, one for Irit and one for Amina. There was a fourth place set next to Esther and a fifth at the head of the table. It dawned on Tula that one was for Irit's dead baby daughter while the other was for Jevros. Irit had laid the table as she had done only a few days previously – before her tragic losses. On the night before the burial, their errant spirits seem to roam the house, searching for, yet unable to find, the last resting place.

"Where shall I sit?" Tula asked.

"I'm so sorry," Irit said. "I've forgotten to lay a place for you."

There was a touching silence, akin to the solemn gap between the peals of a church bell, waiting to hear if another was coming. Irit said these words as if they were the most poignant thing she had ever had to say. "He won't be coming home anymore, will he?"

Her hostess stifled a tear and said in a shaky, quivering voice, "Please, take his place. It's the seat of honour, Miss Tula."

Irit went to serve the stew but realised she had forgotten to lay the serving spoons. When she went to fetch them in the kitchen, she broke down in tears and sobbed into a kerchief. Amina went to comfort her sister.

Left alone with Esther, Tula was sitting in Jevros's seat. It was cold and empty – a place prematurely abandoned by its rightful occupant. Her limbs were heavy, a great weight pressed down on her chest. The skin on her face thickened, her eyes narrowed, her chin jutted out, her body was taut and wiry. Lord, what was happening to her?

Her inner voice said: "*Don't worry.*"

What do you mean, don't worry?

She was more than worried. Terror gripped her by the throat. Because something, someone, was taking over her mind and her body and there was nothing she could do to prevent it. She licked her lips at the smell of the stew, yet she had never enjoyed the dish. Grabbing some cutlery, she closed her right hand around the knife and her left around the fork. She never handled cutlery like that and, besides… She was left-handed.

She knew not how, but she was thinking Jevros's thoughts, feeling his feelings. She was Jevros. He enjoyed lamb stew. He was right-handed. He adored his wife and children.

Her chest ached and her heart beat like a drum.

Images presented themselves in her mind's eye – pictures of Jevros weeping by the corpse of his little daughter. Despite his skills as a doctor of medicine, he had been powerless to save his child. What good were all those years of dedication and all that training? Witnessing his little girl struggle to breathe, his heart had been savaged. She had fought valiantly, but it was a battle the little girl had been destined to lose.

An awful sense of desolation weighed on Tula's chest. Her breathing was shallow. The room was spinning and the walls pulsating. Clouds of pale-yellow dust billowed before her eyes. When they cleared, Jevros was there again, this time at the moment when she had seen him at the front of the riot in the market square.

In the depths of her soul, Tula heard him cry out, "Every breath, nearer to death!"

That was the moment Jevros went to the Devils' Bridge. Rightly or wrongly, he believed that he would encounter the devils there.

Grasping his dead child in his arms, tears rolled down his cheeks, just as they rolled down hers. Fractured doubts and black thoughts of his failure to save her swooped on him like a murder of crows, preying on his spirit, invading his mind, perverting them towards their nefarious intentions and turning him against his family.

Tula could not condone the act, but she understood why he had chosen suicide. Such was the shame at his failure to save his precious little girl, that he had feared that, in the madness of his grief, he would lash out at the very things he loved so much, his wife and older daughter. To kill the very things he cherished, that was something he could never, ever, do.

Then, he had seen his suicide as a mercy killing, as a way to salvage life from death, to save his wife and other daughter.

She realised that the devils were an illusion; they were the thick, dark reflections of his own fears and anxieties. Walking in their shadow, they had persuaded him to take his own life – long before he had even set foot on the bridge.

As her mind hovered on the edge, on the subtle boundary between her consciousness and Jevros's, a final thought winged into her mind from his. It was so shocking, Tula immediately recoiled from it. It was an instinctive act of self-preservation on her part. Something in her had decided that she should know this thought, but not think it, and that she would consider it when she was good and ready and that this was not the moment.

"Are you all right? You're crying," someone spoke to her.

"Urrghh," Tula murmured. Twinkling stars pulsed before her eyes.

"Are you unwell?" The voice spoke again. It sounded muffled and far away.

"The room's going round and round," Tula said.

A woman was standing over her, a hand resting lightly on her shoulder. "There, that's better. You blacked out. You're exhausted. It's been too much for you. Here, take a kerchief. Do you know where you are?"

Tula mumbled something; she was not quite sure what. She wiped the tears from her eyes.

"I'm Amina. We're at my sister's house. This is her daughter."

"Now, I remember," Tula said. "Jevros. His child."

The moment she spoke his name, the veil lifted from Tula's eyes. His errant spirit left her body and moved on to the next stage of its journey, back to the world of ephemera from whence it had come. It was a world which had always seemed as far away as a distant constellation but now she was painfully aware that it was much closer than she could have possibly imagined.

"Esther, run and get Tula a drink of water. Quick now, there's a good girl."

Tula was coming round. The weight had lifted from her chest. She could breathe again. The spinning room came to a shuddering halt. The stars vanished. In their place were two concerned women, a dining table, a child with a beaker of water and the pungent smell of a rosemary-flavoured lamb stew.

"Here, drink this," Irit said, lifting the beaker to Tula's lips.

"Thank you," Tula said. The water was cool and refreshing.

"What happened?" Irit asked. "Was it a dizzy spell?"

She imagined that mentioning Jevros and their dead little girl would only upset Irit, so she complied. Sometimes, a white lie was justified when it spared the recipient further suffering. "Yes, it was a dizzy spell."

"Feeling better?" Irit asked.

"Yes, thank you, and I'm sorry. It's never happened to me before."

"It's the thin air. Topeth's built on a mountain top. We've lived here all our lives and you're a plains-dweller, aren't you?" Amina piped up, rubbing Tula's hand with affection.

"Well, are you ready to eat?" Irit asked.

Tula nodded.

"Esther, sweetie," Irit said. "You can stop cuddling your doll now. It's time to eat. Put Annie down, there's a good girl."

She gave Annie a big hug. Gently, carefully, she held the doll's right hand and bent down. Only when the cotton plaything nestled safely on the floor did she let it go.

"Try and eat something, sweetie," Irit said.

"I'm not hungry, Mummy."

"Come, dear, your daddy would want you to."

"I suppose so. I miss my daddy. He's gone to heaven and won't be coming back. And I'm so sad. I had a little sister, you know. Now that she's gone to heaven too, I'll never get to know her. I would have liked to introduce her to Annie, but now I won't be able to do that, will I?"

"No, I'm afraid you won't," Tula said, trying hard to hold back her tears in front of the child.

The start of the meal stalled because no one was hungry. Esther tried to serve Annie a spoonful of stew, but the doll maintained an expression of glum defiance. Tula had hardly eaten since the meal on her arrival two days ago, but her appetite had disappeared, consumed by the presence of Jevros's ghost.

Amina and Irit were united in sorrow and in sisterhood. Both had suffered recent abandonment; Irit, by her husband's tragic demise, and Amina, by Kalim's recent disappearance. If Kalim was never found, there would be not one, but two sisters grieving for their men. It was too awful to contemplate.

Irit sent Esther and Annie to bed. Amina tucked them both into bed and read them a goodnight story.

Tula sat with Irit, quietly listening to the mantelpiece clock tick away its seconds, which seemed like hours. The silence wore a heavy cloak – a ponderous weight from the other world was pressing in on them. It had an ominous sense as though it was about to break through into their world and create havoc. As she stood up, Irit let out a strangled cry, like that of a crow, a squawk, from deep in the throat, which seemed to break whatever spell had settled on them.

"I don't like what's happening in Topeth," Irit blurted out and turned as Amina came downstairs and re-entered the room.

"I know what you mean," Amina said.

"Listen," Irit said. "Herman led our people out of that hell-hole called Unity. What a name, Unity. There's more unity in the bones of my little finger. And now they've taken my precious child. Six months old, she was. *How could they?* I've milk in my breasts for her. I can still feel her in my body, growing and kicking. And they've taken Jevros too. My Jevros. I'll never understand why he did it. I'll never be the same again. Never. Curse on the devils. Curse on the witches of Unity."

"Why has it come to this?" Tula asked.

"Wincorn claims it's because of Opal," Amina said. "Because of her, he reckons there's a dark, forbidding cloud of ill fortune resting over Topeth.

The town remains an accursed place, at least until Opal's punishment is fulfilled."

"What? You mean until she's passed through the fire?" Tula asked.

Amina nodded.

"What kind of place is this?" Tula cried. "I don't know how you stand it."

CHAPTER 11

The Lights of the Future

It was late when Tula got back to Geb and Sarah's and she went straight to her room. She found it hard to sleep and lay there tossing and turning, plagued by the unnerving way the evening had unfolded and then by more squealing noises coming from outside the window.

Witches of Unity was how Irit had described the angels. Now, they were witches from whom the curse on Topeth derived. Her words were another dent in Tula's faith in the seraphic beings.

The other day, Damien had returned from Unity with a strange object wrapped in a cloth to avoid identification. He had secretly despatched Rufus to the mining lab, so it must have been a piece of ore. Damien's family had a history of wanting to explore Unity. That greed had cost his father, Marcus, his life, thirty years before. The town of Unity was sacred, as was the land of Suria, so surely that intrusion could not happen again.

Her understanding of the history of the town made little or no sense because some essential pieces of the puzzle were missing. She had no idea where to find them, what they looked like, or was even sure, if she saw them, whether she would recognise them for what they truly were.

The good folk of Topeth laboured under an illusion, that what she believed were angels were in fact devils, terrible entities who protected their domain, their town, their Unity, by throwing people off the bridge or rendering them insane.

The waxing moon was nearly round, a lamp in the sky, shining through the thin attic room curtains. She had to be certain that her vision of the angels was real and was going to bear fruit. If, and when, she found these mysterious entities, these seraphs, what would happen then? Perhaps they would lower their angelic wings, bow their heads and prostrate themselves before her. No, she did not expect adulation, but she

87

imagined an ambience of mutual respect, high discourse and profound learning.

A screeching noise interrupted her musings. And there it was again. Then a high-pitched shrieking. It was not human. It was more like the cry of an animal. She got up to investigate. It sounded as though it was coming from outside her room. On the previous night, a similar noise had been less intrusive, and she had ignored it, and gone back to sleep. This time, it was accompanied by a shrill squeal. She went to the window to listen.

The other evening at dusk, she had noticed them flitting over the roofs of the houses.

Bats.

The fear of the little beasts momentarily crushed her, and she could barely breathe. They were coming for her, trying to burrow through the wall, invade her space, pollute her life. She would be deluged in bat goo.

Her inner voice had something to say about it:

"If you never face your demons, you'll never advance.

If you never advance, you'll stay the same.

And your tomorrows will be the same as your yesterdays."

She would not let that happen. She would advance. She would change. Gritting her teeth, she wrapped herself in her robe.

On her first night in the room, she had noticed a ceiling hatch. She grabbed the small ladder and placed it beneath the hatch. One step at a time, she climbed the ladder, opened the hatch and found herself on the flat roof. She closed the hatch softly behind her, so as not to wake her hosts.

Thankfully, there were no bats. They must have flown off somewhere else, guided by some great planetary hand.

Above her, the moon hung amidst the canopy of stars – thrown like glittering jewels into the great sea of the Milky Way. The panorama was as eternal as it was ephemeral.

Her heart stopped racing and she took in the night-time view. Below lay the town of Topeth and beyond it to the west, the copper workings, full of dark scars across the landscape. To the south, the gate at the Topeth end of the bridge was lit by a flaming torch in a cradle on the flagstones.

Unity appeared quite different at night. The silhouettes of its buildings were hazy in the subtle light of the moon. They seemed to shimmer as if they were lit from within, just as the human is lit from within by the charisma of the spirit.

Her eyes rested on the Cathedral's twin spires. It had an energy field that stood out from it by a foot or so, vibrant colours with pastel shades – light blues and pinks, yellows and pale greens – like sequins flashing from one side of the building to the other, quivering with lithe astral power. As abruptly as the vision had come, the astral colours disappeared and she was back to seeing the physical colours, flat and bland.

The place tugged at her soul like a lost love. Unity was where she could and would grow and refine. It was akin to her home. Unity was where she belonged and where she would stay forever. She felt a yearning to get there.

Once again, she felt close to the city of angels, yet so far away.

Over by one end of the roof was a stone shed with a wooden latch door. It was slightly ajar, inviting her to look inside. The shed was lit by the dim light of the waxing moon, but it was enough for her to make out a wooden chest engraved with lightning rods.

She was about to shut the door when her inner voice whispered:

"Open the chest."

But it's not mine. I don't like to pry.

"What's in it will help you realise your dream."

There might be some disgruntled jinn inside.

"Trust me, there isn't!"

She relented, lifted the lid and moved her hand around the inside of the chest. There was a short, curved dagger, a slingshot with a broken elastic strap and an old pistol with the handle missing. Amongst other debris, she found a collection of discarded children's toys. It was both poignant and unusual, in that all the toys wore the sheen of newness, none were broken, and, without scratches or blemishes, appeared as though they had never been handled or even enjoyed.

She was about to head back to her room when her inner voice whispered:

"Look again."

She delved inside the chest. There, shoved to one side in a cotton cloth, was a box. She ripped off the cloth. It was *the* box. The one from the bridge. The note was still tucked inside.

HELP.

Handling the box drew her nearer to the angelic presences of Unity. She rubbed the note between her fingers, certain there was a hidden message in it, waiting for someone to unlock. She stepped outside the shed and into the moonlit night.

Recalling what Vitus had done with her travel pass, she pressed the note to her cheek. Then she touched it to her other cheek. At first, nothing happened.

Her inner voice whispered:

"As usual, you're trying too hard."

She breathed deeply and relaxed.

Her mind was filled with natural sounds – the gentle lapping of the waves on the seashore, the awesome power of lightning, the music of the spheres – and images – the gatherings of people living in harmony, the talk of great enterprises and universal plans. This was Unity. This was a glimpse of the town before the exodus.

She put the note back and was about to shut the black lid when, out of the corner of her eye, there came a glimmer of light. That could not have come from a wooden box, so she stared at the lid again. Nothing.

Again, she turned her head to one side and out of the corner of her eye, caught sight of a flash of colour – a peerless incandescent orange, a livid red – a cone of living fire.

That time, she had seen it. She had to peer into the black mirror out *of the corner of her eyes*. That was the secret. That was the way to *see* the reflection in the black mirror.

This time, keeping her gaze steady, she looked again until the full image resolved itself in the mirror.

What it revealed took her breath away.

There, hovering above Unity, was a glory of angels. Towering entities of light suffused the dark, tenebrous night with a milky glow. Shaped like a large cockle shell, they were taller than the tallest tree and glided above the gentle township of Unity. Some still had their thinner lower part in the earth and their upper heart-shaped part above the ground. Like lithe, ethereal beings, they arose out of the mountain. One by one, they lifted themselves out of the crags and rocks of the hill and floated effortlessly up into the chill night air.

Her mouth dropped open as she gazed at this ethereal procession until the last one emerged from the hill, shifted itself above the twin Cathedral peaks and slowly drifted off into the heavens above.

When no more came and the air was silent and the night thick with possibility, she put the box back and returned to her room filled with wonder. Where was 'home' for an angel? Perhaps they didn't have a home or need a sanctuary in the same way that humans did. Their birthplace was probably in the depths of the Milky Way, or close to the primaeval origins of the universe, or perhaps in the outer reaches of the most distant galaxies as they expanded into the void. For the moment, they, or at least some of them, lived in Unity. If they were born, could they 'die'? Was 'death' for an angel caused by abuse or misuse or neglect? She imagined that the angels were always unified and always would be, and it was humanity that was perpetually short-sighted and bloody-minded. Such was their beauty, the glory of the angels' natural form, the reflections on the black lid and its mysterious mirror had entranced her.

The note made sense now. The box was a gift from the angels, to enable humans to witness them. It was a facilitation, a HELP.

How a gift was received told a story about the receiver, revealing their attitude and state of mind. Topeth folk shoved that help, that divine assistance, into a gloomy place hidden from the light, from where it could no longer be seen or found.

Such were the lights of the future.

CHAPTER 12

Passing Through the Fire

A clamour of bells rang through Tula's head, dowsing the last embers of her slumber. The town bell was ringing. Something urgent had happened. She sat up and shook her head, trying to throw off the doleful events of the night and her lack of sleep. Once the bats had roosted, it was time for the cuckoos and the cocks to remind her, and everyone else, of the dawn.

By the time she got downstairs, Sarah was letting someone out of the front door. Tula assumed it was Geb. Abel had gone. Sarah turned and stared at Tula, static, like that statue of her missing daughter in the grotto.

"The bell pealed. What's it for now?" Tula asked.

Sarah's bottom lip was quivering, and she said, "F-follow the crowd."

"Why? You not coming?"

"No, I can't face that dreadful place. It brings back fearful memories of what might have been."

"Where?"

"I think you know where."

Sarah was upset and Tula had an inkling as to the reason. As Tula left the house, the sun was rising over Unity, casting a bloom of shadows over Topeth. The eastern sky was shot with shafts of rose pink and crimson red. The morning was fresh, the winds strong and the air as clean as a whistle. Puffy, white clouds scudded across the sky like a shoal of mysterious, incipient fish. The shadows cast by the mountain on which Unity sat, silent as a ghost on the opposite side of the ravine, were like long fingers of fate reaching into every aspect of people's lives.

Amidst a clutch of folks heading into town, someone asked, "You still 'ere, little cub?"

The voice was familiar, as was the aggressive tone.

"Yes, Taurus, I am. Leave me be, will you?" Tula said.

"Why's that then?"

"Because you're a bully. I saw you with Abel."

"Bah. He's an idiot. He ain't worth nothin'." His voice was bitter like lemon.

"He's doing the best he can, just like the rest of us. So, leave him alone. And me!"

"I'll do what I like!"

Turning a corner, she found herself on the edge of a large crowd in the open arena in front of the Temple of Moloch. It confirmed her suspicions as to why Sarah had refused to come.

Today, the bull-headed temple seemed to glow with a hideous light that emanated from within its cold bronze heart. In front of it was the white marble altar.

"Is there... a sacrifice today?" Tula asked. Her knees were trembling.

"Wait an' see, little cub," Taurus said with chilling malice. Thankfully, he spotted Luca and darted off to meet his mate.

Up above them, a timeless dance was taking place: a flock of starlings wheeled above them as if to bear witness to the high endeavours of mankind, only to vacate the skies in fear of a predator – the griffon vulture.

The early morning crowd was shouting amusing and derogatory remarks and causing waves of laughter.

Clad in his long crimson robe, Wincorn was in deep discussion with Damien. The Commander stood next to them. From his slouched shoulders and bowed head, she guessed this was the ceremony for which Geb needed the heifer.

All three stood before the altar on which Chimor was arranging various religious items. At either end of the altar was a large, white, curved bull's horn. In the middle of it was an incense censer and a cup, both of bronze.

Tula was too short to see over the heads of the crowd. Searching for a stool to stand on to get a clear view, she eventually found a small, abandoned cart with a missing wheel. She hauled the cart a short distance against the wall at the back of the temple arena and balanced herself precariously on it.

A cry arose over the hubbub of the crowd.

"Mo-loch!" It was Taurus. He was up the front near the altar next to Luca and the rest of his group of baboons.

"Mo-loch! Mo-loch!" the crowd repeated with hypnotic fury. Their voices rose out of the temple yard, through the wispy morning clouds and to the Creator on high. Tula did not think He was listening.

Everyone quietened when Wincorn stepped in front of the altar and raised his arms above his head. "Today, we gather to mark a special anniversary. On this day, Midsummer's Day, a dozen years ago, there was a great calamity."

"Moloch! Moloch!" the crowd bellowed.

"Moloch was cheated," he went on. "His sacrifice was ripped from him. Opal is a fugitive from the fire. We will find her and bring her in chains to Moloch. She will have her limbs wrapped in flame. She will feel the scorching wrath of Moloch on her skin. I promise you, and him, that the fugitive will pass through the fire."

The crowd roared in approval. Tula could barely believe that these people were desperate to witness a child burn. She had only come to see for herself how far Topeth had fallen. The wings of mercy had either failed to open or had fallen off completely. It seemed the angels' vision for the future of humanity had been abandoned. For better or worse, Herman and the exodus had delivered them to this place and this moment in time. A chill ran up her spine. She mouthed a silent prayer that Moloch would never see the unfortunate girl or any other human being for that matter.

"To mark the anniversary and in homage to Moloch," the High Priest said, "we humbly offer a substitute for the sacrifice. As his penance, and as he has done every year, Commander Geb will provide that sacrifice – and will continue to do so until his daughter is brought before Moloch."

Geb shuffled out to face the crowd.

Encouraged by an animated Taurus, the crowd erupted with wild cheers and obscene gestures.

"Mo-loch!" Taurus's voice carried over the temple, past the Acropolis and plunged deep into the ravine, before being echoed back to them all, "Mo-loch!"

When even the sound of a voice could not escape from Topeth, there was surely no escape from the accursed place.

With each shout, Geb winced and shifted uncomfortably on his feet. This was a ritual shaming, a stripping, strand by strand, of his integrity and reputation. This public ordeal bore all the hallmarks of Damien's handiwork – calculated, conniving and cruel. Damien was trying to rip away Geb's power for good, leaving him in total control.

The High Priest was in full cry. "Great Moloch! We implore you. Accept this animal as a surrogate."

Chimor sprinkled incense onto the burning coals in the censer and wafted it along the length of the altar. It had that woody, lemony aroma of frankincense.

Leading Geb's red heifer, a temple assistant emerged from the nearby stable. The animal lumbered forward. This bovine killing was a metaphor,

Tula thought, symbolising the awful compliance of the masses. Wincorn had won; Topeth was reduced to a place of death and mutilation, yet he seemed to cleave all the more to the sanctity of his mission.

Gradually, as the sun rose higher in the sky, its shadow moved serenely and silently over the crowd, guided by the hand of the Creator.

With the consecrated dagger, Chimor slit the heifer's shoulder and placed a bronze cup beneath the wound. The great beast of burden bayed in pain. Blood streamed into the cup. When it had filled, with his index finger, Chimor sprinkled the blood on the bull's horns at either end of the altar. With slow, ponderous movements, he repeated the ceremony three times, murmuring prayers and incantations.

Wincorn peered up to the skies and cried, "Great Moloch, hear our prayer! What we do here today is to atone for the sins of the people of Topeth."

A temple assistant led the heifer up the steps, into the large central opening and then up the ramps inside the temple. After a brief delay, both heifer and assistant appeared in the fourth, and uppermost, cabinet.

The assistant tethered the animal by the neck and by each of its legs to the bronze hooks on the cabinet walls. The heifer peered at the crowd below with innocent, bovine eyes. If she believed it would have made any difference, Tula would have cried out and beseeched the sacred heavens above for mercy, but those in the secular realms below would probably have had her arrested. From fighting phantoms down a dead end, she had learnt to choose her battles with care.

From the stable emerged a dozen temple servants dressed in fiery red robes carrying kindling. They laid it down, branches and twigs inside the central opening, which housed the hearth. Rushing back and forth like devils, they lumped larger and bigger logs and pieces of wood, until a good-sized bonfire was built in the hearth, directly beneath the upper cabinets.

The temple servants lined up, six on either side of the altar, each with a drum hung around their neck.

Chimor lit a wicker torch and handed it to Wincorn. The drums rolled, the heavens stared, and the people gaped. With precise dramatic timing, Wincorn waited and waved the flaming torch at the crowd, who voiced their approval with yells and shouts. He thrust the torch into the heart of the bonfire and moved around it, prodding the kindling, kissing flame to wood, until the whole of it was ablaze with the cleansing fires of COIL.

The flames spread across the dry tinder, devouring each branch and lighting each log, hungrily spreading across the entire woodpile. The heifer bellowed, pulling and yanking on the ropes that held it in their grip. The excess smoke gushed out over the top of the crowd.

The drums beat; primordial, elemental.

In time to the drums, Taurus took up the chant again, "Mo-loch! Mo-loch!"

The heifer roared, fearful. One tether snapped by dint of the brute's defiance, but the others were less merciful. Waves of heat, smoke and ash billowed out of the four cabinet openings. The bronze Moloch crackled and guffawed, holding the head in its belly, satiating its appetite on the heifer.

The lithe orange flames licked the upper cabinet. The smell of scalded flesh and scorched hair was excruciating.

Tula had seen enough. The disgust made her dry retch. They had not even bothered to stun the beast before lighting the fire.

Well before the terrible end, she got down from the rickety cart and edged along the back wall. When she was staggering out of the exit, a voice shouted from behind her, "Too much for you, little cub?" It was Taurus again.

"I've seen enough," she murmured, swallowing the acidic taste in her mouth.

"You and Abel, you're two of a kind. Cowards, both of you!" he snarled, following her out of the arena.

"Leave me alone!"

"Bah! Run away, then. Your fears'll catch you up. I seen it before, I have. A frightened animal runs for its home and that's what you'll do. Run for home, little cub," he said, before heading towards the crowd.

She stumbled out of the arena and turned her back on the clouds of smoke, the pathetic bellows of the heifer, the heavy, sonorous drum rolls and the crowd's raucous cries of malicious glee. Above all, she turned her back on his taunts.

Somewhere, anywhere, she sought solace away from 'The Top' town.

CHAPTER 13

The Acropolis

Tula staggered away from the Temple of Moloch to escape the toxic atmosphere. The air was thin. Her body was sweating, her stomach, knotted. Once in a while, she paused to gather her breath. Her head swirled with conflicting views about the townsfolk. At one turn they were kind and hospitable, but then they seemed to flip into a collective madness, in which they were possessed and intoxicated by a deluded sadistic pleasure.

There were no devils, other than those believed and invested in by people's hearts and minds. The devils had no power without the freely given will of the people. She did not think this was how the gift of free will was intended to be exercised.

Then there was the bridge, a bridge to the future, away from the past and into the bright lights of tomorrow. Was its true name Via Angelica or the Devils' Bridge? After Jevros's fall and the tragic death of his baby girl, she had entertained her doubts. And now Moloch – the terrifying monster.

She needed a quiet place to meditate. The sun was arcing in the sky and sending waves of heat onto the town. The sunlight glinted on the derelict temple columns on Acropolis Hill. On first arriving in Topeth, the old structure had intrigued her. It would be an ideal sanctuary, at least until the gruesome ceremony at the bronze temple had finished.

Occupying the highest point in the town, the old Acropolis had been abandoned to nature, a monumental relic to a past era. She found herself at the head of a causeway leading to the first of three tiered terraces or courts, each separated by a low boundary wall running around the hillside like a girdle. The Acropolis building itself, or what was left of it, stood bleak and proud on the uppermost peak.

On entering the outer court, she scrunched up her nose. The stench was coming from a mound of rubbish. Blotches of weed poked through the gaps in the pile of old rotting clothes, discarded sandals, broken bottles and more of those nearly new children's toys. The tip had attracted vermin, who, on her arrival, scampered for cover into the tall, thin spindles of dry grass. Schooled both by the adversity of the heat and the rarity of the atmosphere in Topeth, the rats seemed as big as beavers and mountain-ready.

Rats she did not like, neither the four-legged variety nor the two-legged. She had encountered a few of both in her short time on Earth and bore a particular disgust for the latter. Both smelled; the four-legged were putrid and the two-legged, well, they were even worse, since they had free will and therefore had volunteered to act like the four-legged variety.

Then there was the compliance, the serial inability to think for oneself and to follow others as a matter of course. She did not like that either. Yet it was as infuriatingly difficult to spot as to eradicate. Her pet hate was the giving of a name by its parents to a child. Her parents had named her Tula. She had not asked for it, condoned it, or even agreed to it, yet the name had stuck. One day, she would give herself a new name, to mark the beginning of her life-long quest, with a name chosen by her that chimed with her perceived destiny. Now that sounded like the proper exercise of free will.

She was Tula; Tula was she. The name had echoes of the tulip, the flower. Did her cheeks bloom with their fiery reds? Did she smell as nice? Could she smell her own body odour or her own clothes? They mostly smelled of sweat and fear, but on the odd occasion that she found that quiet, listening space in herself, she smelled as sweet as the turban-topped tulip.

The buildings in the outer court of the Acropolis were dedicated to public life. Here was a building where public records were once deposited; over there was a large open stadium surrounded by tiered seating for athletic events.

She wandered into a cave beneath one of the temples. Inside the entrance was a pile of debris – leaves, twigs and small branches blown in by the desert winds. She heard a soft scuffling. She paced up and down the cave trying to find its source. There were only shadows on the cave walls. There was no one. Not a soul. She was about to leave when she heard the sound again. It was a rustling like autumn leaves being blown along a rocky surface. Then she saw it on the ground. It was a bird, a starling. She bent down to examine it. It had gorgeous orange and black markings on its plumage. But it was trapped. One of its wings was ensnared in the twisted branches. The poor thing was struggling to fly away.

"Keep still, little one," she whispered.

She reached down and gently freed its trapped wing. As she picked up the bird, it gave her hand the tiniest little peck. Nestled in her cupped hands, the bird was soft and warm: a little piece of the planet's soul, so gentle and alive. Tula walked out of the cave and threw her hands into the air, releasing the starling back into the airy expanse that was its natural home.

This act of kind mercy strengthened Tula's resolve to find her own natural habitat, her spiritual home, the place where she could fly high and free.

Further exploring the Acropolis, she found the remains of the library, where all sorts of stone tablets, large and small, broken and intact, were strewn around the ground, covered in more of the red-brown dust. Yet because of the warm, dry climate, the writing on them remained legible. In this area, the strong and mildly nauseating smell was like a stagnant pool covered by rotting leaves.

Next to it was the site of the building that once housed the Topeth School of Art and Wisdom, or at least that was what it said on the engraved plaque. One end of the temple was intact, a row of five columns standing tall as trees, piercing the upper reaches of the sky. The other columns lay on their side, smashed into small pieces. Once the elaborately carved stone frescoes had stood proud and defiant; now they were decaying fragments. And the length of that column, flat on the ground and its tapered capital, reminded her of a beached whale – and it had a thick piece of copper wire attached to it. So, once it had served as a lightning rod; not anymore.

The smell in the school was pleasant and kind to the nose, reminiscent of the soft, peachy fragrance of a frangipani leaf. Her eyes wandered around the broken stonework until, absorbed in the mysteries of the place, she stubbed her toe on a tablet, sending a shock of pain through her toe and up her leg. Her body tensed as she hopped around on her bad ankle.

Damn.

She examined the writing on the stone tablet. It revealed that the building had been used for marriage guidance counselling, but not of the kind she had encountered before. This one advised on the suitability of a match; an assessment that was carried out by a priest who specialised in the subject. What a thought. The priest would assess the physical, soul and spiritual compatibility of the couple. He would decide if their union was beneficial not only to themselves, but to Topeth, and the Creator. Tula was filled with a sense of nostalgia for a time when a person possessed such skill and insight, and a society upheld such elevated values.

She read the inscription on the stone tablet:

Women are designed to manage the eternal in the now.
Men are designed to manage the now in the eternal.

This was a glimpse of how Herman and his people had conducted themselves in the time after the exodus. If only she could recapture that eternal truth in the now; perhaps the angels would help her do exactly that.

As she climbed the path, passing the boundary wall and entering the inner court on the upper terrace, the view across to Unity became clearer, as did the panorama of the hills and mountains surrounding Topeth. Before she had even explored the peak, she was seduced by the aromas; a subtle blend of soft rose plume, refreshing mint and sweet jasmine.

The inner court contained a solitary building, or rather its remains – the inner sanctum or Temple of the Creator, dedicated to Herman and Kendra, the twin founders of Topeth. Once, the old stone temple had boasted a roof and a proper frieze, as well as lintels and capitals. Today, these lay forlornly about the site like broken pearls from a once-beautiful necklace. The columns were laid out in meticulous order, marking the boundaries of its rectangular site. A few of them had resisted the ravages of time and retained their original stature. The rest of the columns were stubs of stone fallen on hard times, neglected and abandoned. Grass grew in solid tufts around the rubble. Bits of metal were strewn about the area; vestiges of how once, during the commercial heyday of the town, the site had housed the metal market.

The starlings nested in the few remaining capitals.

The only things intact were the stone etchings. The columns were grimy and covered by copper dust accumulated over the years. The heat was stifling and so was this place. A tall, defiant cypress tree offered a modicum of shade.

A waning sadness descended on her. The Acropolis was a relic to a forgotten era, less a celebration than an epitaph on the solemn tomb of a once great and formidable human race.

She scrubbed one of the entrance columns clean. Faced with a cloud of copper dust, she turned away and coughed heavily.

But what she uncovered amazed her. It was an etching of the profile of the town of Unity as viewed from Topeth. There were the bridge pillars. The name inscribed beneath it was Via Angelica. She wiped away the rest of the grime, revealing the whole etching. Floating above Unity were huge heart-shaped entities – the same cockle shell shape of the angels that she had witnessed with the aid of the black mirror.

Standing in the derelict Acropolis gave her an elevated view of Unity, partially visible through hanging clumps of mist. Just as Damien had described it, the houses, temples and courts of Unity were similar but different to those of Topeth in that from each building emanated a fine, subtle glow.

She was on top of the world. She tried to imagine what had happened in the original Acropolis, but her head was spinning, and her legs ached from the walk up the hill in the stifling heat of the day. Finding some shade, she sat down with her back against the central column.

Her eyelids felt heavy. An ethereal mist rose before her eyes. When it cleared, her imagination had taken her to the Acropolis – not in the present day, but when it was first built, with gleaming limestone columns and a full entablature. It was majestic, mysterious and pristine. People with shining eyes and youthful expressions wore white robes and laurel wreaths. They clamoured on the rows of seats, occupying every small space to witness the proceedings.

A figure dressed in lime-green priestly robes strolled onto the podium at one end of the Acropolis. A temple servant waved his censer, sending clouds of incense into the skies, a message to the Creator on high. Tapping his wand on the ground, the priest called for silence and announced, "Everyone, please, a warm hand for our leader, the First Man."

To great applause, a tall, thin man with tired, beady eyes, a balding head and a sprightly gait stepped onto the podium.

"Elders and citizens of Topeth," Herman began. "Welcome to the inaugural meeting of the Acropolis. When we lived in Unity, the angels nurtured us, gave us their virtue and lent us their light. In return for these gifts, we served them fully, with passion and vigour aplenty. Our compliance, though, was automatic and, in the absence of free will, not freely volunteered. Despite the angels' reluctance, I made the tough decision to leave Unity. We needed to find our own way – with me in charge.

"In Topeth, we'll plot our own course. We'll discover the way laid out for us by the Creator. To help us in this quest, we've designed a special place, a temple dedicated to reading the runes of the future; the Topeth Acropolis. It's aligned to the four quarters of the Earth so that, each dawn, the sun, as it passes overhead, will wash the temple in its enhancing rays. We need to conjure high spiritual entities to help us find our way, so the structure has these high columns to allow the entities to fit inside the temple. The gaps between the columns allow the excesses of the proceedings a way out. Using marble in the temple is to anchor the great atmospheres generated by our deliberations.

"From here, we have an uninterrupted view of the snow-capped mountains surrounding us. From this elevation, we can consider the far-reaching questions that face every nation during every age; how best can we serve the Creator? As a race of people, what is our purpose and how can we align ourselves to it? How do we fit into the great universal plan? What is the best way to apply free will in our lives, individually and collectively? The future is incoming, so how can we prepare for and respond to it?

"As history unfolds, every civilisation will need an Acropolis, a place where the tribal elders can parlay.

"I, Herman, will be the First Preceptor of the Acropolis, the seer who divines the future. I will interpret the runes of the times and explain them to you in simple terms. Now, as we begin our separate journey away from the protection and guidance of the angels, we need stability and surety. I will provide that too. With me at your head, you will never be lost. With me leading the way, I will mediate for you."

As the cool breeze whispered through the statuesque columns, everyone sat back and pondered the profound ramifications of Herman's words.

CHAPTER 14

The Funeral

Slumped against the column, Tula awoke. She had been in the presence of Herman and the originals of the exodus from Unity. To have borne witness to the first-ever proceedings in the Acropolis was a privilege. Back in the present day, her eyes dropped at the decayed state of the buildings. The past was richer than the present. Perhaps that was why so many people were nostalgic for a golden age. But she was looking ahead and at how mankind could navigate its way towards a brighter future.

The people of Topeth had set out with such great hopes but had gradually got lost and abdicated the responsibility they once prized, something for which Herman inexplicably had never made provision. While a profound sense of purpose guided Tula to an overriding belief in the angels and their existence, everything about her journey was turning into a nightmare, what with bridges and bullying, devils and death.

From Herman's speech in her dream, she had understood his vision for the three tiers of the Acropolis. It was such a shame that his persona, arrogance and self-love had blinded him to the truth of his situation. It could have been so different for Topeth and humanity.

She had a strong inkling that historians misunderstood history, because they failed to take into account one important fact; that history was alive. It lived, all of it, all the time. Some parts were dormant, but every past event, every past life, lived, breathed and could be, and often was, re-enacted in the present. Perhaps history was an enigma, a labyrinth of coded patterns that could, given the right motive, be unravelled and re-enlivened. It was not extraordinary that history repeated itself, it was inevitable that it did.

What must it have been like for the people of Topeth at the time of the exodus? They had departed the angels' protection and set out on their own to take up the mantle of their newly found independence offered by the gift of free will. Herman had seen to that. It was his initiative that drove them out of the maternal embrace of the angels and into the dangerous, uncharted waters of freedom and liberation.

Herman might have had regrets about their journey so far. If humanity, armed with its unique power of free will, had remained in Unity, it would have evolved differently. Since the exodus, it had regressed. From what she had done, learnt, and experienced in her short eighteen years, she thought that humanity had yet to grasp the mantle of free will and apply it humanely and with wisdom.

At least it banished her lingering doubts; there were angels in Unity. They had lived there in the past. She had seen them in the present. Herman had led mankind away from Unity. She would have understood if the angels had performed their own exodus, after growing tired of waiting for the human race to wake up and live. But they were still there, waiting and watching.

While she was proud of her belief in the angels, the good citizens of Topeth discounted them and were convinced they had neither seen them nor witnessed their works. Their original pledge to pursue the proper use of free will had been conveniently forgotten. More than that, they were now convinced that the angels were devils in disguise.

And the devils. Topeth folk had named the bridge after them. They existed in the nether realms as a figment of people's overwrought imaginations. Since arriving in Topeth, someone had delivered a box with a message, a man was lost in Unity, while another had lost his life over the bridge, leaving behind a distraught family and a fearful township. If a staunch family man like Jevros could succumb to the wiles of the devils and witches of Unity, no one was safe from them.

Yet, with the help of the box, she had 'seen' angels in Unity. It was possible that there were devils over there and that they now controlled the angels. These nagging doubts brought a painful discomfort as the dark wings of uncertainty cast a shadow over her soul.

By the time the sacrifice at the Temple of Moloch had ended, the sun had reached its zenith. She headed to South Gate to join the procession for Jevros's funeral. There was a shortcut through a deserted alley. Unexpectedly, a man stepped out of the shadows.

Her heart skipped a beat until she recognised him. "I should have known it was you."

"Why's that, little cub?"

"Because you're always hiding in the shadows."

"What you just say to me?" He bent his ugly face towards her.

"You heard me."

Taurus glanced up the alley as if to check if anyone was there. No one was. He folded his arms.

"What you doin' with my pa's whittlin'? You steal that walkin' stick from 'im?"

"No. He gave it to me. He's kind. Not like his errant son!"

"You don't belong 'ere."

"What are you saying?"

"I'm sayin', go back to the city where you come from."

"What? No. I can't. I won't." Grasping the walking stick gave her strength and courage.

"You ain't wanted 'ere. You tell people about them angels an' that. There ain't no angels. All your wise words confuses 'em. You're stirring up a hornet's nest of trouble."

"Look who's talking! You're the one who provokes riots and leads rebels."

"That ain't nothin' to do with you. You gotta leave Topeth. By tonight. Hear me?"

"Or else?"

"Or else, I'll make you!" Taurus jabbed a finger towards her face.

"No, you won't!" Gritting her teeth, she brandished the walking stick in the air and threatened to smash it on his head.

"So, you're 'uman after all. We all got a nasty streak, haven't we, little cub?"

"I'll protect myself! Now get lost!" She edged closer to him, still waving the walking stick above her head.

He turned to leave, then spun around, and in one swift movement, snatched the walking stick, broke it in two over his knee and flung the pieces to the ground. They clattered into a shop entrance.

There was the sound of footsteps approaching along the alley. Who was that? If it was Luca, she was in even deeper trouble than she was now.

"Oi! You!" a voice called out. "Stop that!"

It was Musa.

Musa, my saviour.

As he strode towards them, Taurus leaned over and whispered in her ear, "Get outta town. By dusk. Or you'll end up like that. Broken in two!"

With that, he stormed off down the alley.

"Taurus, come back 'ere. You're under arrest!" Musa shouted after him. Taurus ignored him and vanished round the corner. "I'll get him later," Musa murmured. Turning to her, he asked, "You all right?"

Tula's tongue was frozen. Her legs were shaking, and her heart was thumping. After a while, she dared to breathe again, live again. Her heart stopped beating so hard.

"I-I think so."

"Don't worry, he's gone," Musa said. "He ain't gonna bother you again."

"Oh, Musa. Thank you for coming to help me."

He picked up the broken pieces of the walking stick. "This 'ere was yours, wasn't it?"

She nodded. "It was a gift from Vitus. The old man was kind to me when I first arrived in Topeth." She bit her lip. Now those memories were snapped in two.

"And this is what the son's done," he said, shaking his head. "Him, Vitus and Damien, they're a strange family, they are that."

No one had ever intimidated her like this before, even in the city where there were gangs and groups of kids roaming the streets and by-ways. There, the play was rough and tumble, but ultimately good-natured, and never destructive.

"He threatened me. He wants me to leave Topeth – by tonight."

"Nah, they're empty threats. Don't believe anything he says. I'll look after you, I will. I'll not see you in any trouble."

"Thank you, Musa. You've been such a help."

"Here, you goin' to the funeral. You're nodding. Come along with me. I'm on duty. Gotta look after the Commander."

This was an unlooked-for boon. The young man had turned adversity into hope. She could stay in Topeth and be protected. This was all she could have asked for and he was handsome to boot. Those eyes, she could dive into those pools of warmth any day. Now, she knew she had an enemy who was out to get her, and she had better watch out for him, especially in moments when she was alone.

Arriving at South Gate, Musa went to the front of the procession to find the Commander, while she limped along at the back, accompanying the old and infirm. Ironically, Vitus was there, with his own white stick. He tripped on a stone and nearly fell. Without her lightning-quick reactions, he would have added a mouthful of earth to his breakfast. Helping the old man stand up and find his balance made her feel human again.

"Thanks," he murmured.

Tula insisted that he held on to the tassel of her belt and off they went, a small procession amidst a larger one. Vitus was munching on a tobacco wedge. He spat the accumulated contents in an orange-brown stream of liquid which narrowly missed the back of her sandals. Blind as a mole,

106

he was unaware of his misdemeanour. He reached into his pocket and pulled out a length of dried compressed leaf, from which he took another humongous bite.

"Where is it?" he asked her. "What you done with it?"

"With what?" Although she knew intuitively what he was talking about.

"The lightning rod stick, o' course. Whittled it for you, I did."

She paused for thought. She did not want to tell him the truth, but she was not going to lie either. Vitus's son was a bully and a thug. People said, 'Like father, like son,' but she genuinely thought Vitus was nothing like his son. And she would not be the one to tell the old man what a monster he had raised.

"It broke, I'm sorry. It was an accident."

"I'll whittle you another," he replied. "An unbreakable one. You'll see."

"That's kind of you."

Up ahead, Wincorn's shuffling limp kept the procession at a snail's pace. Chimor struggled to keep the hound, Kebel, in tow. Zach was with his two daughters, Amina and Irit, who walked hand in hand with Esther. The wooden gate at the entrance to the cemetery swung open and squeaked on its hinges. Cut to perfection, the individual stones of the low cemetery wall lay against each other, holding each other's weight and, together, formed a unified whole that had lasted for centuries. Pity the town was unable to emulate that.

In the middle of the cemetery was a prominent, stone mausoleum. It had two figures, a man and a woman, carved out of a single block of pale-yellow limestone. Below them was a plaque:

To the First Man, Herman,
And the First Woman, Kendra,
Who released us from a crushing past,
And led us into an enlightened future.

It was strange that the past – the time spent in harmony with the angels – was referred to as crushing. She read it again and she realised that Herman himself might have penned this epitaph.

The procession followed the eastern edge of the cemetery, which brought them near to the ravine. Draughts of hot desert air gusted across them, blowing off Wincorn's funeral hat. Obedient schoolboy that he was, Chimor gave chase and brought it back to his master. Kebel sat and guarded.

The drop was sheer. The searing wind howled through the vast gap as if the two sides of the ravine – like great jaws – were opening to take in a mammoth gulp of air. Tula's head was spinning. In her mind, she reached out and touched the town of Unity; it seemed so close, she could feel it, sense it, smell it. Yet after Taurus's threats, she feared she would never see it. At least Musa had shown some humanity.

The sound of two youngsters shouting at the tops of their voices interrupted her reverie. Lost in a game of hide and seek, Abel and an older lad had separated from the procession. They ran around the cemetery, skipped on top of the wall and hid from each other behind the gravestones.

Tula stood next to Amina, who tutted her obvious disapproval of the young men's antics.

By the graveside, the gravedigger and his mate waited as patiently as the dead. The beetles, ants and woodlice were less so and climbed willy-nilly over the heaped mounds of earth, blithely unaware of the awful gravity of their social transgression.

Digging graves was possibly older than the oldest profession. It required little or no training. Brute force, ignorance and previous experience of digging holes in the ground was useful. Dig a hole, lower a wooden box into it, then fill in the hole with earth. Then repeat. That was it. And do not, under any circumstances, spill the contents of the box.

Leaning on their spades, the gravediggers were nattering about the box found on the bridge and its poignant message – HELP. She was going to mention how she had found the box and the message but thought better of it.

She felt a tinge of melancholy, not only for Jevros but because this was her first funeral ever. In the city, she had gone to her aunt's wedding, at which she had made a pretty bridesmaid if she said so herself. But this, her first burial, was unremittingly sad.

Musa and the other guards stood behind the Commander as he recited a homily to Jevros, what a fine man he was; a father, a husband, a consummate doctor, good at all tasks, loved by many and revered by all. While Wincorn was saying a prayer for his soul, Tula wondered what had happened to the two hide-and-seekers. They had gone. The last time she had looked, they were loitering near a path that led away from the cemetery and which seemed to end *in* the ravine. That could not be right. They could not have fallen into it. Not on a day such as this.

Her heart thumped against her chest. Quietly, she moved away from the ceremony, walked through the cemetery gate, and strode down the path for a minute. It ran tantalisingly close to the edge of the ravine and seemed to come to a stop at a high stone wall. She peered around it.

Her mouth dropped open.

The two boys were perched on a narrow ledge cut out into the cliff face. With their backs to the ravine and facing the cliff, they were shuffling along the ledge.

Abel in the lead, the other lad behind, they appeared supremely confident in the execution of this frightening manoeuvre. Yet the drop below them was fatal. The ledge was so narrow they had to walk along it sideways, grabbing tufts of grass and cracks in the rock above their heads to keep their balance. The ledge was about fifty steps, of which they had traversed the first ten.

It reminded Tula of the high-wire circus act that had come to the city when she was eleven. It made her feel dizzy just watching. Even then, she was afraid of heights.

She felt as though someone had kicked her hard in the stomach.

"Boys, come back, please," she called.

"No, we're doing just fine," Abel yelled back, without even lifting his head.

Their level of concentration was astonishing and their courage even more so.

"Abel, what are you doing?"

"I've done it before." Abel's voice echoed once, twice, thrice.

She was scared, not only for them but also for their families. The boys were mad to attempt this escapade, especially at this time of raw emotional upheaval. Should anything untoward occur, they would blame the bridge devils.

At the top of her voice, she pleaded, "Abel! Come back!"

They carried on.

"Boys! Remember, we're here for a funeral."

They stopped. Abel glanced back at her.

"This is not the time to play games with your lives. Get back here. Now!"

They edged towards her.

Abel leapt across the gap between the ledge and the hill. He nearly fell and had to scramble up the slope, Tula hauling him up to save him. He fell into her arms and his legs capsized beneath him. He lay there flat on his face, arms akimbo, as if giving obeisance to the Earth goddess. Tula let out an enormous sigh of relief.

She noticed that the other end of the ledge ended at the flagstones by the bridgehead. Maybe Abel was one of the missing pieces of the puzzle. When he had got his breath back, she said to him, "What on earth were you thinking? You should know better. Your mother and your father have already suffered the heartbreak of a missing daughter. How do you think they would cope if you were to fall?"

"Y-yes. S-sorry, Miss Tula."

"Promise me you'll never do it again."

"Promise, Miss Tula."

"Good. Now tell me, when was the last time you were on this ledge?"

He smiled at her with that sheepish grin.

"Abel, be a good boy and answer me, please."

"I-I don't rightly remember, Miss."

"Oh, but I think you do, Master Abel. On the evening poor Jevros came to the bridge, I thought I saw someone else on the flagstones. That was you, wasn't it?"

He nodded, averting his eyes from her gaze.

"Was that a 'yes', Abel?"

He nodded.

"And what did you see?"

"I was on my own. I like the ledge. It makes me feel good. I got to the flagstones. I was near the guard's cabin. I saw a man on the bridge, so I hid in the shadows."

"Which man? Jevros?"

"No, Miss Tula. Jevros was coming down the snaking path."

"Then who was on the bridge?"

"I don't know. It was another man."

"What happened to him? Where did he go?"

He shrugged.

The maudlin sounds of solemn chanting swirled around the cemetery.

"Thank you, Abel. Listen, we need to pay our respects to Jevros and his little girl," she said, and led the boys back to the cemetery.

After that, she could wait no longer; she had to face her fears head-on.

CHAPTER 15

The Covenant

After the funeral, Tula offered her condolences to Irit and knelt down to give Esther and Annie a big hug. She lingered at the cemetery gate. She waved to Musa, who waved back to her, cheerily. He was accompanying the Commander and Wincorn at the head of the procession as it traced its way up the hill to South Gate.

Who had Abel seen? That was the question that consumed her. The more she thought about it, the more she grew convinced that the ledge was part of the puzzle. And she had so little time left to solve it.

With everyone departed, the gravedigger and his burly apprentice got to work with their spades and filled in the grave, the earth thudding onto the wooden coffins, father and daughter buried together.

Tula was alone. And she was ready. Well, with no head for heights, she was as ready as she could be, which was not ready at all. But she had to do this. The guards were ambling, and it would take them a good while before they returned to the bridge. If she hurried, she could get to the flagstones before they did and still have time to investigate. This was an opportunity she had to take.

She retraced her steps towards the high stone wall. She took a deep breath before looking at her nemesis, the ledge. It was fifty steps – only fifty steps, she repeated to herself, as if that would make it any shorter or easier to negotiate. In the valley's base ran the clear, crystal waters of the River Naddee, fed by a thousand and one sparkling mountain streams.

Low clouds descended, blowing in from the distant sea, shrouding Unity. For all she would have known, the town could have disappeared, swallowed by a thirty-mile-wide unseen vortex of force, one that caused typhoons, tornadoes and volcanic eruptions. Her inner voice had some sound but obvious advice:

"Remember, don't look down."

Before the first step, she glanced at her feet. Just one glance. But it was enough.

She looked down.

Oh Lord.

The ravine.

She froze. It was sublime and terrifying – at the same time.

The ledge was as narrow as her foot. And her foot was small. The drop was into the abyss, into Gehenna.

Tula pulled herself together.

The first step along the ledge was torture. Whoever built this path must have either been raving mad or a cat with nine lives. Her life was in her mouth, a knot was in her stomach and a vortex of fear spun in her head. She feared the drop.

"And don't look down."

She paused. If those fifty steps along the ledge were along a plank of wood that rested on the ground, she would hop, skip and jump over it in no time, without a worry or a second thought. Put that plank of wood on the edge of a mountain, with a sheer drop to one side and a vertical cliff face rising from the other, and on every single step, her nerves made a coward of her.

If she failed to conquer the mental beast inside her, she would never cross the bridge. She would never cross any bridge. She called for and demanded courage – to defy the bridge devils, whether they existed or not, and to defy her fears, which definitely did exist.

She gulped and lifted her right arm to grab the tuft of grass above her head. Her right foot searched for a place to settle, but a kind soul had previously carved out footholds. She planted her foot into one, reached up to grab the left handhold and thrust her left foot into the adjacent foothold. Even though she felt like a crab, edging sideways along the ledge, she felt exhilarated for having made it so far.

The unforeseen benefit to her venture was that she was physically incapable of looking down. The ledge was so narrow, and foot and handholds so precisely arranged, that her cheek was squashed against the rock. She took regular mouthfuls of rock dust and her eyes were watering.

A walk of fifty steps was not that far – if she was walking on a road, or on that plank of wood. But fifty steps on the ledge leading to the bridgehead – that was far, that was the longest fifty steps she had ever taken.

When she had taken about ten steps, she touched something odd in the rock above her head. Her hands seemed to clasp into the rock, but the indent differed from the shape of the handholds. She could not look up.

Equally, she could not look down. But as she shifted her weight to make another step, she inserted her fingers into the cliff face and felt more of the inscribed shape.

With each tentative step, her hands felt the crevices above her head, which appeared to trace out large curves and lines in the rock face. It might be a picture or an etching. A few more steps and she was sure. Her hands and fingers were clutching onto parts of letters.

It was writing – etched into the cliff.

She edged further along; her parched lips pressed heavily against the rock. Arms outstretched, her small body lay flat against the huge cliff face like a fly on a vertical wall. A burst of confidence surged through her aching limbs. Her fears plummeted into the ravine. A warm, soft wind blew across her face. She had grown to ten feet tall. Feeling the eternal in the now, the indomitable strength of youth surged through her aching limbs.

"You can do it. You can really do it."

A bird swooped by behind her. A rasping squawk made her whole body shudder. She crooked her neck and glanced to one side. Damn. The vulture. It was just passing, not stalking her. She pressed on another step. Halfway across now. She was getting there. Behind her, she sensed a second approach of the raptor. And this time, its wingtip brushed her back. Her body froze with the impact. Her limbs were like lead. She screamed, but no sound came out.

"Be careful. The bird's circling again. It's coming for you."

This was the end. Flung into the jaws of death – by a vulture. It was going to knock her off the ledge, watch her plummet into the ravine, then come and pick her bones on the valley floor. She was lunch.

Bracing herself for impact, she waited. It was getting closer.

Behind her came the sound of a hundred tiny squawks, a thousand little squeals and then a huge growling croak.

And: silence.

For a moment, she did not know what had happened. Her inner voice did:

"The raptor's gone."

She kissed the rock face. The dust particles were warm and dry. Her hands clung to the crevices as though they were her passage to heaven. A light breeze brushed her bare arms.

A small bird landed on her hand; it was so subtle, so fine. Its orange and black plumage stood out against the pale stone rock face. A starling. And not just any starling. It was the same bird she had released from the cave beneath the Acropolis. This was extraordinary. Before it departed, the little bird gave her hand the tiniest little peck and flew off to join the rest of its flock.

At that moment, she knew.

Somehow, the flock of starlings had fought off the vulture and saved her life.

With a relief as deep as the gorge, she stepped onto the bridgehead flagstones.

The bucketful of sweat from her glands had glued her clothes to her body. Exhausted mentally, emotionally and physically, she collapsed in a heap. If Musa or any other guards were coming, she could not care less. More than anything else, she was sure of two things: one, she would never walk across that ledge again and two, she would care for those pretty little starlings.

She lay on the ground, face-up, eyes closed, in the pose of a corpse. Not for any particular reason, except that it was the most comfortable. A piece of her soul had nearly suffocated during that momentous struggle with the ledge, the vulture and her own doubts and fears.

Out of death came life; out of the swamp grew the lily of the valley; out of ugliness came beauty.

Having got her breath back, she waited until her soul spiralled back into her body. It must have been as scared as she was and passed out of her body for a gentle sojourn around the locale. It left her with a bitter taste in her mouth. Now that it had fully returned to her and brought with it its superb mind-body coordination, she sat up. Conquering her fears only strengthened her purpose.

On this day, when she had nearly wet herself and used up several of her nine lives, she was sure the Creator was playing tricks on her. Perhaps he found it endearing to witness the timid endeavours of His charges.

She sighed and stood up. The bridge was there, looping across into the morning clouds. The ravine was there, plunging into the underworld beneath her feet. The bridgehead was there, flagstones and all, with its pillars and guards' hut. One of her local cuckoos – she was sure it had awoken her earlier that morning – was pecking at an outcrop of grass near the bridge pillars. The thick ropes of the bridge hung from the green copper poles as they had done for decades – solid, secure and safe, wrapped around them like lovers in an eternal embrace.

Tula was heading for the bridge gate when Tabitha emerged from the guards' hut, disturbing the cuckoo. The bird took flight and dropped its meal next to one of the oxidised pillars. Curious as ever, Tula, newly crowned queen of the flagstones, strolled over to see for herself. The pillars were filthy and probably had not been cleaned since they were first erected. Yes, the skin was uneven, thicker in some parts of the pillars, thinner in others. In one part, she could make out something beneath the green sheath.

She grabbed a handful of pebbles, wrapped them in a cloth she found in her bag and rubbed it against the surface of the pillar. It revealed a slit in the copper sheath. It was an engraving which read:

Via Angelica.

She scrubbed off some more debris, revealing a flap with a small handle. As she flipped it open, one of its hinges fell off, leaving the flap dangling from one hinge. Behind the flap was a rolled-up parchment tied with a gold-coloured ribbon.

With her hands shaking, she untied the ribbon, opened the parchment and read the title:

The Covenant of Angels.

Not only did the angels exist, but there was also a covenant with them. This was precisely what she had been searching for since she had arrived in Topeth, since she had left the city, perhaps from the moment she first drew breath. Instinctively, she knew this document existed. Here it was in all its glory. She read:

Angels of the Lord, are we.
A spirit life born away from home, are you.
Together we live in a place of mixing and marrying: Mother Earth.
Part of a huge, expanding Universe, is She.
This Universe – a gigantic machine governed by immutable laws.
The Creation – a sublime ordering of galaxies and suns, planets and moons.
But a machine is but a cold thing, an automaton.
For kindness and forbearance – it lacks.
Not freely given – these qualities, say, by a mother pigeon to her chicks.
Pre-planned in her, with no choice but to nurture her young.
And no freedom of election of these qualities.
Making the Universe an unfeeling, nay, a cruel, place.
Granted free will, mankind brings the warmth of human sentiment to a cold place.
This, then, the dignified purpose of Homo sapiens, man-the-wise.
We, the angels, are pods of spiritual advancement for man-the-wise.
Ethereal and dedicated are we.
The great sentiments of kindness and wisdom, consideration and

forbearance, Sagacity and humanity are yours alone – one day, to share with us.
A glimpse of the rare and beautiful things we cannot experience ourselves – your gift to us.
Trainee angels at distance – our gift to you.

She reflected on what she had read so far.

There were, or at least had been, angels in Unity. Now she was certain of their existence. Inside, she leapt for joy.

There were scuffling noises on the snake path. The guards were coming back from the funeral. She tucked the parchment in her pocket. She had to be quick if she wanted to cross the bridge and realise her dreams. Get into Unity and forget about all the troubles in Topeth. Standing by the copper pillar, she was in a perfect position to see all along the contour of the bridge. She got ready to make a dash for it before the guards could stop her. Glancing along the length of the bridge, she expected to see it empty of devils, angels or any other living soul.

She was wrong.

At the Unity end of the bridge was the stocky, overbearing figure of Damien. Behind him were others. They were too far away to see how many.

Between the guards on the Topeth side and Damien on the Unity side, she was trapped.

She had one means of escape.

The ledge.

Never again, she had promised herself. And how could she be certain the vulture would not repeat its attack on her or that the little starlings would come to her rescue? Once was karma. A second miracle would be impossible. She was going to be caught. The guards would know she was trying to cross the bridge. It would be the end of her. As she berated herself, the door to the guards' hut swung ajar and out walked the bridge cat.

"Tabitha, you beautiful creature." She stroked the feline as it rubbed against her ankles. "As a reward for showing me where to hide, I'll bring you a morsel of fish."

Singing the praises of providence – and Tabitha – Tula dived into the guards' hut and quietly shut the door. As she hid behind a desk, something niggled her. It was the searing memory that the flap hinge on the pillar had snapped and hung there, limp like a broken dream.

While Musa and the other guards arrived on the flagstones, the bell rang out across the rooftops with its customary urgency. Now, everyone knew Damien was returning.

CHAPTER 16

An Unexpected Arrival

Damien and his party were edging their way across the rope bridge as people surged down the snake path to welcome them. A few starlings circled the bridge and headed off to roost in the early afternoon, no doubt to boast to their friends of their victory over the predatory vulture.

People cheered Damien's return as if it was a victory over the bridge devils. Perhaps it was. Tula peered out of the hut and waited until the volatile crowd had grown large enough to distract the guards. She slipped unnoticed out of the guards' hut, closed the door behind her and even attempted some elementary running repairs to the flap on the copper pillar.

Musa and the guards were holding back the crowd as she shuffled up behind them. As soon as he saw her, he gave her a welcoming wink. She sneaked in next to Vitus, Zach and Amina at the front.

"Is Kalim with them this time?" Amina was asking.

Tula craned her neck to see how many were returning.

"Three went, I reckon two are coming back," said Zach. "I bet Damien lost another one. He's careless, like his father."

"Nah, there's three, the same that went," predicted Vitus. "And they didn't find Kalim."

Approaching the flagstones, Damien and the search party came into full view.

"Damn, Vitus, you're correct on one count. Kalim's not with them," Amina said.

"But you're wrong on the number returning," Tula said.

"Why's that?" Vitus asked.

"Because Damien's leading *three* other men," she said.

"Then who's the fourth?" Vitus scratched his chin.

"Silus and Rufus are with Damien," Tula said. "Whoever he is, the fourth man's in trouble."

"How do you know?" Vitus asked.

"Oh, I see him too. His hands are tied like a common criminal," Zach said.

"Who's this mystery man? Is he young or old? What's he look like?" Vitus asked.

"He's a tall, distinguished fellow," Zach said. "Balding, with a white goatee beard and blue, watchful eyes. Fellow must be a little shy of sixty. I know that man from somewhere, but for the life of me, I can't think where."

Despite his handcuffs, the mystery man walked with a dignified air, as if he was unconcerned by his predicament and the clamour surrounding his arrival. There was a light in his eyes and his presence cast a benevolent glance on them all.

Damien stepped off the bridge and onto the flagstones.

"Who's this other fellow with you, sir?" Musa asked.

"He looks familiar to you all, doesn't he?" Damien replied. "He should do because this is the man who twelve years ago ran away from Topeth. This is Enoch."

"Enoch. Yes, I thought I recognised him," Zach said.

"He's a criminal," Damien went on. "I'm the one who hunted him down. Another mystery solved by me. Well, what do you think of me now?"

It was as if Damien expected a roar of adulation for his success. He was met by a wall of silence. The crowd seemed more interested in the man he had apprehended. They stared at Enoch as if he had just stepped out of the clouds.

Vitus broke the spell. "You old yella' belly. What you been doing for all these years? Where you been hiding?"

"And where's my Kalim?" Amina demanded.

"And where's Opal? She over there with you in Unity?" Zach asked.

Damien raised his hands and shouted, "Enough. People, be quiet. Enoch, you heard the questions. Now, come on, you owe us some answers."

"I am Enoch," he said with a curt nod. His voice carried a richness and depth Tula found intriguing. "Twelve years ago, Opal was a child, innocent and filled with the urge to discover life. She wandered onto the bridge to play with butterflies and tend to her little brother. Then, you, Master Damien, and Wincorn, sentenced her to be passed through the fire for what was no more than an innocent transgression. That decision was cruel and inhumane, so we rescued her. We wanted nothing more to do with the town. So, we left.

"Since then, we've lived in a croft in Suria, a short distance from Unity. We attend to the angels in Unity on a daily basis, while making sure that we are never visible from anywhere in Topeth. We did not want to alert you to our presence there."

This news was like manna from heaven to Tula. With the Covenant and now Enoch, the shadows of doubt cleared from her mind and a burst of energy coursed through her veins. The angels existed and here was a man who dealt with them regularly. Inside, she leapt for joy and mouthed a simple prayer of thanksgiving.

"So, it was you who left the box on the bridge," Damien said.

"Yes," Enoch said. "It was."

"There, I've solved another mystery," Damien chirped.

Tula realised it must have been Enoch that Abel had seen on the bridge that evening.

"Once we found the box," Damien went on, "you must have known we'd come and search you out. So, after all these years, why take the risk of being discovered?"

"The angels are desperate and these ending times call for drastic action," Enoch replied, his voice like polished sapphire.

The High Priest limped forward; his lips curled into a rapacious snarl. "This is heretical nonsense. In Unity, there are devils and only devils. They forced the angels to leave. You, Enoch, are a purveyor of evil and a warlock."

"War-lock, war-lock," the people chanted.

Tula shook her head; the townsfolk could at least have given this newcomer the benefit of the doubt.

Despite the provocation, Enoch's expression was like stone mullion, craggy and unchanging, which further enraged the crowd.

Damien shot an angry glance at Enoch and asked him, "Tell us then, oh wise one, what have you done with Kalim?"

"Kalim's helping us to serve the angels," Enoch said. "He chose to stay in Unity of his own free will."

"I don't believe that," Amina said. "He'd never abandon me."

"He has not abandoned you," Enoch said. "He just can't stand Damien and Topeth anymore. When Damien and Silus fell asleep, Kalim stayed awake. That was when he wandered into the Cathedral where he found Ruth and me. He was as surprised as we were when we met. Then he begged us to let him stay."

"In that case, Kalim's a deserter," Damien said. "And also a criminal."

"Ruth and I are not as young and healthy as we once were and, with only the two of us, it's hard work keeping everything pristine. So, we were delighted to have another genuine servant," Enoch added. "He's free to leave Unity whenever he likes."

"Sweet-sounding words," Amina butted in. "I reckon you've captured him. You've befuddled him. You've sent him mad, like Jevros."

"No, nothing could be further from the truth. And Jevros is a different matter," Enoch said. Turning to Wincorn, he added, "Jevros died by your hand because of your rotten dogma. You frightened the poor man until he fell on the sword of his own fears. May his eternal soul rest in peace."

"They're the biggest bunch of lies I've ever heard," Wincorn said.

"Jevros was a good man," Enoch said. "During his final days, he was more afraid of his own shadow than anything else. After I left the box on the bridge, I went back to Unity. Then I saw him come onto the bridge. I knew straight away he was consumed by grief and what he intended to do about it. I tried to save him, but it was too late. But it could not have been the devils that pushed him off the bridge for the simple reason that they do not exist. He *fell off* the bridge. His death was a terrible, and avoidable, tragedy."

"Is that what'll happen to my Kalim?" Amina asked, wringing her hands.

"It's quite normal for you to feel anxious, but that will not happen to your man," Enoch replied.

"Now I remember you," Amina said. "You were a prison guard; now you turn up after twelve years with a fantastic story about helping angels. Why should I believe anything you say? I mean, is he actually alive? Has he been driven mad by the devils? Is he still sane?"

"Of course he is."

"Prove it!"

"I can. Here, he gave me something for you."

"Show me," Amina said.

As Enoch delved into his pocket, Damien asked him, "And how did you know about Jevros?"

"I know what goes on in Topeth," Enoch replied.

"So, you've been spying on us. Oh, and do tell the angels that the box you left for us was a great *help*," Damien said.

"How do you mean?" Enoch asked.

"Well, it flushed *you* out of the clouds, didn't it?"

Hemmed in by the growing crowd, Tula could hardly move, such was the interest in Enoch's sudden and surprising appearance. Urged on by an animated Amina, the mob was unruly, their frustrations reaching fever pitch. The guards drew batons and pushed them back. The crowd resorted to hurling barbed insults at Enoch.

"You're to blame for our situation!" one shouted.

"You've brought the devils onto us!" yelled another.

During the verbal fireworks, a cry rang out. It was Geb.

"Stop! Everyone! Hold your peace!"

His face was drawn into a scowl. "News travels fast. I heard you had come back and I had to see for myself. And it's true. Where's my daughter? In Unity? Take me to her."

"I can't," Enoch said.

"Can't or won't?" Geb asked.

"I can't because I don't know where she is," Enoch replied.

"You know, you must do," Geb said. All those years of pain spoke through his voice. "You snatched her from prison twelve years ago and I've waited that long to ask you what happened on that Midsummer's Day. You owe me and my family the truth."

"I admit that I rescued her," Enoch said. "But I don't know where she is now."

Geb pressed his palms into his temples. "Please, Enoch. With you coming here today, I thought we'd finally discover her whereabouts."

"If I knew, Commander, I would tell you. I tell no lies," Enoch said.

To Tula, Enoch appeared as a genuine, upright man. She believed him and, so it seemed, did Geb. Of course, Damien did not.

"Utter rubbish. Sling him in jail," Damien ordered. "He'll soon tell us everything he knows."

"I've done no wrong," Enoch said. "I saved an innocent girl from a terrible death. You and Wincorn are the ones who need to account for your actions."

"Hah! That's nonsense. You're the wanted criminal. You can't abduct a young girl from prison and expect to get away with it. And you've admitted it," Damien replied. "You're guilty of a very serious offence."

"No more serious than what you did in Unity yesterday," Enoch said.

"Yesterday, the day of the Grand Fete. What did he do?" Geb asked. His interest was no doubt piqued by Enoch's ambiguous reply.

"He's my prisoner. You're forbidden from questioning him," Damien said, physically inserting himself between Geb and Enoch.

"Enoch, tell me, what did he do?" Geb asked again.

"It's nothing, he's whipping up trouble," Damien said. "Guards! Take the prisoner away. Now!"

Silus had grabbed Enoch's arm when Geb stepped in front of them both and said, "Enoch, tell me, tell us all, what did Damien do in Unity?"

Enoch shrugged off the guard's hold. "He stripped the roof of the main temple."

"The roof? What are you talking about? Why did he do that?" Geb cast a suspicious glare at Damien.

"You don't need to know. It's mining company business," Damien said.

"Every damn thing is mining company business. You're just like your father," Geb said.

"How dare you stain his memory," Damien said.

"Your father's greed led him across the bridge in search of more copper to rape from the earth. And we all know what happened to him."

"Do not insult my family. You'll pay for this."

Turning to Enoch, Geb asked, "What exactly did he strip from the temple roof?"

"The temple roof," Enoch said, "is – or rather was – made of cylindrical rods laid one next to the other. Damien and his lackeys ripped them from their housings. One by one, they carried them across the bridge into Topeth."

"I don't understand. Why did he do that?" Geb wore a heavy frown.

Tula had a feeling that whatever Enoch said next was going to change her life.

"The rods are coated in metal," Enoch said.

"I knew it. So, he found copper over there," Geb said.

"Copper? No. It was far more precious than that," Enoch said.

"I forbid you to say anything more. Guards, take him," Damien cried.

"Ignore him," Geb said.

Enoch did. "It was gold."

CHAPTER 17

The Gold Rods

Geb puffed out his cheeks and turned to Damien. "Gold? You found *gold*?"

"There wasn't much," Damien said and paused. He was biding his time or fabricating a plausible excuse – Tula thought it was more likely the latter. He went on, "The rods on the temple roof weren't even solid gold. Only the part exposed to the air was coated in gold."

"And that made it acceptable to steal? Anyway, how did it get there?" Geb asked.

"Don't ask me. Ask him." Damien pointed to Enoch.

"You probably won't believe me," Enoch replied. "But in the presence of the angels, the gold rained out of the air in tiny droplets. Over time, it condensed on the roof in the same way that lichen gets deposited on stone."

"That's inventive," Geb hissed. "But I'm more interested in this thief," he added, shoving his finger at Damien.

"I only took two rods," Damien said.

"That's not true," Enoch said. "He took all of them."

"You're a criminal. Your word has no credibility here. Stay out of this," Damien said.

Silus pulled Enoch away.

"Let me see the ones you've brought back," Geb said. "I'll make up my own mind what they're worth."

"That's not possible."

"Why not? Have you sold them already? I wouldn't put it past you."

"They're safely stored away from prying eyes," Damien replied.

"That means one thing." Geb was onto it like a falcon to a hare. "If you're still here, they must be too. They're still in Topeth. And you haven't told us about the purity of the gold."

123

"That's confidential mining business," Damien replied.

"No, it's not; it's town business," Geb replied. "That's the fault line between you and me. You want wealth for yourself and your blasted Company and I want it for the town. You've always acted as if the two were separate. But, in truth, they're bound together as tight as the rope cables on the bridge. If the gold on these rods is pure and there are many of them, this is precisely the windfall the town needs to repair the derelict buildings, starting with the Acropolis. Now, what will you give the town that granted you your substantial wealth?"

"I'll answer your question later," Damien said. "Now I need to get this criminal behind bars."

"No, you can't dismiss me as easily as that," Geb said, gnashing his teeth. "A child has died. The copper workings are a blight on the land. The dust is a killer. We need to get back to how things were. The town is bleeding people. Its heart and soul, the Acropolis, is a relic. The gold will pay for that and more."

"I'll think about it," Damien snarled.

Tula knew Geb was right. The land was in a parlous state. The people were broken. The town was derelict. Repair was out of the question. Salvage was the only viable course of action.

Staring at Geb, Damien poked his tongue out of the middle of his mouth and just as quickly retracted it.

"I bet you're looking at this gold as a timely find," Geb went on.

"What are you talking about?"

"Well, you've been trying to sell the mine for months. Ah, you thought I didn't know anything about that, but nothing gets past me, not even your devious plans," Geb said. "But you've had no buyers, have you? It's not surprising, who's going to buy a copper mine with no copper deposits? Now you've come across this gold, you're seeing it as a rich cache for you and your minions to start a new life in the city."

"Pure speculation. Where's your proof?" Damien snarled.

Next to Damien was his lackey, Silus, whose hand was hovering over a curved dagger sheathed in the belt of his robe.

"Silus," Geb said, "you've crossed the bridge on each of the last three days. You must know the truth about the gold rods and what happened to Kalim."

Silus shuffled his feet on the flagstones and stared at the ground. He shrugged.

"I can't wait to hear what he has to say for himself," Tula said.

"That's not going to happen," Zach said to her. "Silus is a young man.

You know what the young are like: they make a big play of independence, but then they turn and follow the herd. He's never had an original thought in his life and probably never will. He'll certainly never say a word against Damien."

Before Silus could reply, Wincorn shuffled up to Damien. "I blessed your journey into Unity for you to discover who placed the box on the bridge and find Kalim. Instead, you pillaged whatever of value you found there. You've deceived me and you've betrayed COIL. Neither you nor the Commander will keep the gold rods. They are precious; they came from the temple in Unity. They belong to COIL."

"I won't let that happen. You're not going to steal them from me, they're mine," Damien said. "You have no right to them. I found them, I brought them back to Topeth. They are what my father is owed. They're compensation for his death. They belong to the Company now."

Kebel growled through bared teeth, his back arched for attack.

Wincorn touched the gold chain of office that hung ostentatiously around his neck.

"Abuse my trust and face the full wrath of COIL. No more will I bless your crossing of the bridge."

"You wouldn't dare withdraw your support!" Damien stared at the priest.

"Try me. Now you will tell me where they are," Wincorn said.

There was a heavy pause. Everyone waited. Their fate, the fate of the town and the townsfolk seemed to hang in the balance as these three men pondered their next move. Damien folded his arms and let out a long, slow hiss. Wincorn stroked Kebel, who sat obediently by his side. Geb paced up and down, muttering to himself.

Damien blinked first. "They're stored in our company offices," he said to the old priest.

"Good, you've made the right choice in telling me," Wincorn said. "It begins the process of forgiveness, but despite that, I won't bless any more of your visits to Unity."

Damien grunted.

"Move the gold rods into our custody," Wincorn said to Chimor. "Place them in the stables next to the Temple of Moloch."

Chimor scuttled off with his assistant to do his duty.

Geb asked Damien, "And when exactly did you find these rods?"

Damien folded his arms. "What's it matter?"

"It matters a lot." Although Geb's body was shaking, his powers of reasoning seemed lucid. "I'll work it out for myself. Today was your third visit to Unity in as many days. The first was to search for whoever left the box. That must have been when you spotted the gold rods, the same day Kalim went missing. The next day, yesterday, was the Grand Fete. Ah! That's why you insisted I officiate it. The census was a smokescreen to cram everyone into the Amphitheatre – you wanted us out of the way so you could get on with your theft. You're good, but I'm better. Because I know what a greedy, conniving snake you are!"

Geb raised his fist, as if to smash Damien to a pulp, but lifted his other hand and punched that instead.

In a moment of pressure, Damien opened his mouth and poked his tongue out so quickly it was hardly noticeable. But Tula had seen him do that before. It was as lightning fast as a rattlesnake. If Damien possessed the snake's lethal strike power, Wincorn was the boa constrictor, suffocating the life out of his prey, swallowing them whole before slowly digesting them. Both were dangerous predators.

"That's not true," Damien said.

Tula had seen Damien, Rufus and Silus celebrating whatever was in the back of that covered wagon as if they had stolen the crown jewels. So, perhaps Enoch was telling the truth and Damien had stolen more than two of the gold rods.

She had to grasp the moment by the horns.

"But it is. The Commander's right," Tula said.

"What did you just say?" Damien asked. "*You're* accusing *me?*"

"Two days ago," Tula said, "the first evening you got back from Unity, you sent Rufus to get some ore assayed. That was a sample of the gold, wasn't it?"

"What? How did you know about that?" Damien asked. "Did Rufus tell you? I'll kill him, I will. Bring him to me."

Tula had to tell the truth. "No, stop. It was me. I overheard you speaking to Rufus."

"Don't push me," Damien said. "You're incapable of minding your own business. I'm fast running out of patience. You're a little meddler and you should slide back into the hole from which you came."

Another one wanting to get rid of me! He will not speak to me like that. I'll show him I'm no fool.

"And I saw you," she said.

"You *still* talking about me, little one?" Damien turned on her again.

"Yesterday, I saw you on the bridge." She spoke loud enough for everyone to hear.

"Of course, I was on the bridge. Everyone knows that," Damien said. "I'd been searching all day for Kalim."

126

"No, wait. Tula, tell us exactly what you saw," Geb said.

"He was with Silus and Rufus. On the flagstones. They loaded something inside a horse-drawn wagon. It was covered, so I don't know what was in it. But it was heavily loaded. I'm sure there were more than a couple of those gold rods in it."

"I suspected as much," Geb said, as a satisfied smile spread across his face. "And that confirms Enoch's story. What have you to say for yourself now?"

"I'll tell you!" Damien snarled. "To see me on the bridge yesterday, you, little Tula, must have left the Amphitheatre. That is strictly forbidden. You broke the Law of Census."

"Ah. I forgot about… the Law of Census," she muttered.

"I warned you," Damien said. He was so smug now. She hated him when he was smug. "One more indiscretion, one more unlawful act and there'd be a penalty to pay. Silus, take her and Enoch. Cuff them both."

You're not going to do that to me.

She shoved her hands in her pockets.

"This is no time to be petulant," Damien said to her.

Silus grabbed her forearms.

"Get off me!" Tula yelled.

As Silus wrenched her arms out of her pockets, a metal object looped out of one and into the air and landed in a jangle on the flagstones.

"What's this?" Damien said, stooping to pick up the object.

Her heart was in her mouth.

With triumphant delight, Damien held it up. "I think this belongs to you, Commander."

"Yes, it does. I've been searching for this for days. It's the missing key to the bridge gate," Geb said.

Damn! Just as the Commander was showing me signs of sympathy, now this.

"Eavesdropper, law-breaker and now thief; get her out of my sight," Damien ordered.

CHAPTER 18

A Glory of Angels

Through long afternoon shadows, Rufus, Silus and the other guards led Tula and Enoch up the snake path. Below her, tentacles of white mist swirled around the lower reaches of the ravine, shrouding the River Naddee from view. Above her, a deep azure blue sky protected the world in its canopy.

Despite the glory of the panorama, Tula hung her head in shame. She had never been arrested before, let alone incarcerated. Once, in the city when she was thirteen, she had joined a protest against the deprivation caused by the incessant war. There had been trouble with the guards, but nothing like this. She might not agree with all the laws but, like the customs and traditions, they were part of the covenant between her and the land on which she lived. The laws were a part of the human heritage and so she tried to abide by them when and wherever she could. The laws she sought to discover were the natural laws that governed the Universe and everything in it.

Whipped up by Damien, an angry mob followed her and Enoch into the market square. They shouted and screamed at them as though they were animals. Then they passed along the narrow confines of an alley, forcing people to press in on them. The unruly mob pushed and shoved her from one side to the other and the guards did nothing to prevent them. Amidst the hubbub, a stone whizzed out of the melee and struck Enoch on the side of the head. His knees buckled and he fell, blood oozing from between his fingers.

"Help him, can't you?" Tula pleaded with him.

But Silus was about as sensitive as a lump of granite. The guard bent over Enoch and shouted at him, point blank, "Come on, stop loitering."

The poor man came to his senses and, clutching his forehead, stumbled on.

They emerged into the open area outside the Amphitheatre which lay swathed in shadows.

Whipped up by Damien, the townsfolk hurled insults at Enoch.

"Runaway!" one shouted.

"Absconder!" cried another.

"Warlock!" yelled a third.

While still dazed, Enoch was unusually accepting of his predicament. He seemed a kind, gentle soul, pressed into a madness not of his own making.

Tula ducked a shower of rotten vegetables but failed to avoid a large, overripe tomato, which splashed onto her shoulder. The pips and juice dribbled down her upper arm until the skin finally dropped to the ground. She struggled to control her emotions and tears welled in her eyes, but she refused to give the mob the satisfaction of seeing her weep. A piece of delinquent carrot hung from the front of her keffiyeh, shrouding her vision. With her hands cuffed, she motioned to the guard as best she could to remove it for her. She might as well have not bothered. She felt as unloved as a neglected wall plant.

She tripped, lost her balance and tumbled onto the hard, parched ground. Silus ignored her difficulty and yanked her along, her feet dragging behind. Her bad ankle snagged in a tree root and twisted. She squealed. Her ankle was hot like fire, sending pulses of pain up her leg, numbing her mind. Silus let go of his grip and she thudded to the ground. Stooping over her, he stared at her, wide-eyed, prodding a finger at her, yelling, "You. Get up. Now."

Her ankle burning, flat on her face, smeared in vegetable matter, surrounded by scores of angry people, the world was accelerating out of control and her purpose was draining out of her. She struggled to turn herself over and face upwards. Inside, she felt empty. The taste of disgrace was bitter in her mouth.

"Don't be so nasty to her," Zach was saying. At least someone was complaining about Silus's treatment of her.

During the melee, a cuffed pair of hands reached down to her. Instinctively, she took hold of them. They were warm and firm. It was Enoch.

He helped her to stand and asked, "Can you walk?"

"I-I can try," she stammered.

"Here," Enoch said, extracting the piece of stray carrot from her hair and moving her fringe out of her eyes. "That feels better, now, doesn't it?"

She felt warmed by the help he had given her and the simple care he had taken over her appearance. She returned his kindness with a warm smile.

Rufus waved his pistol at the building in the corner of the square. From the height of the walls and the noxious smell of guilt, fear and self-loathing emanating from it, it had to be Topeth Prison.

Rufus knocked on the prison gates, shouting, "Open up! And look lively about it!"

While they waited, Tula took the weight off her ankle and leaned against Enoch. The relief from the pain was immense and the world seemed to come back into focus.

As the crowd swarmed around them, she recognised a familiar face and then lost sight of him. The crowd moved away again, and, like an ebbing tide, he reappeared, white walking stick in hand. His clothes were grubby, and his old face was pitted with battle-weary defiance.

"Vitus, what are you doing here?" She patted the back of his hand.

Empty eye sockets stared into nothing, seeing everything.

"I might ask you the same thing," he said. The question hung in the still air, begging an answer.

What am I doing here? I'm going to be locked up in a prison cell. Why? For following my inner voice? For pursuing my dream? For seeking my destiny? Because I put a key in my pocket and forgot it was there. Because I left the Grand Fete. That's not right. What are they going to do to me?

The world was crumbling around her and she was falling through the thin veneer of her life into the dark, meshed bindings of the world.

Vitus shoved a small packet in her direction and murmured, "If you get the chance, give this to him, will you?"

"Oh, Vitus, I can't take it from you because my hands are tied. Here, shove it in my pocket, that's it, just there," she said, and Vitus felt around her midriff until he eventually found her pocket.

Before she could ask him who she should give it to, the gates swung open and Rufus pushed her into the prison yard, Enoch close behind. Two prison wardens awaited them.

"Ah. Cyrus, there you are. Two more customers for you," Rufus said. This Cyrus had a dishevelled salt and pepper beard topped by a bald, shiny pate.

"Oh, thanks for that," Cyrus replied. "I just had two more come in, moments ago. It ain't as if I got an empty jail, now, is it?"

"Well, do what you can, old man," Rufus replied.

"I'll still care for them as if they were my own," Cyrus replied, wiping his nose with his sleeve.

"I know you will." Rufus chuckled and turned to leave.

Cyrus's assistant bolted and closed the prison gates, metal clanking on metal.

"You two," Cyrus said. "Come with me. And no dawdlin', y' hear. This ain't no country walk." He led Tula and Enoch across a walled enclosure lit by a single torch. The flames sent ribbons of shadows scudding across the courtyard.

Tula, hobbling, and Enoch, nursing his bleeding head, followed him into the main prison building, down uneven steps and into a gloomy corridor. On either side were barred cells, packed with about twenty men each. Some cowered in the corner of the cell while others stared at her with a look of anger glaring from their eyes. When she spotted Luca amongst them, she assumed they were mostly protestors arrested during the riot and the Grand Fete. The place hummed of urine mixed with fear and loathing.

As soon as the inmates spied her, they rattled the bars. They probably did not see many women in the cells, let alone young women. She pulled her robe up to her neck and walked with her head hung low. She tried her best to shut out the whistling and the catcalls. Egged on by Luca, the inmates' choir sprang up, as they serenaded her with a song laced with lascivious overtones. She wanted to disappear down a large, cavernous hole.

To lengthen her humiliation, Cyrus dragged his heels. He seemed to possess the sensitivity of an old iguana. She had encountered the cold-blooded reptiles on her travels and here was another one.

Her one crumb of comfort was Enoch, who helped her along.

Cyrus got out the cell door keys and brandished them above his head, like some magnificent trophy. For his vanity, he received the tumultuous applause of the inmates. With more than a trace of sexual innuendo, he licked the key with lustful intent, plunged it into the lock, then released the key and plunged it in again, repeating the manoeuvre several times to howls of delight from the prisoners, before finally unlocking the cell door.

The other guard unexpectedly shoved her in the back, and she stumbled forward and fell flat on the ground. Spread-eagled on the mangy cell floor, she lifted her head and stuck her nose in the air only to find it lodged in the crotch of someone sitting there, knees up and legs wide open and with his back to the far wall of the cell.

"Well, well, well, if it ain't little cub," a voice greeted her out of the murky darkness. It reeked of arrogance.

At that moment, she was as low as she had ever been in her life. Waves of darkness were drowning her. Her throat was dry, and her stomach was pulled into a tight knot of shame. Scrambling up from the floor, she straightened herself and brushed down her soiled robe to ride out the embarrassment.

"Oh, we got company already. Just got here myself," Taurus said.

"Wh-what are you doing here?" she asked.

"Wouldn't you like to know?"

"He was on the run and got nabbed by them guards," Luca called out from a nearby cell.

"Yeah, it's true," Taurus said, scratching his pointed chin. "They didn't like my singin' in the riot. Nor in the Grand Fete. Nor in the temple."

"And yet you still found time to threaten me?"

"So what if I did?"

"Well, I'm glad they caught you. I don't like your singing either," Tula murmured.

"When I left you in that alley, I hid up in the derelict school," Taurus said. "Soon after, the guards busted down the door and found me there. No one goes to that old place, so I knows someone must've shopped me. And guess who told the guards?" Taurus jutted his chin out toward a huddled shape in the corner of the cell. It emitted a little whimper.

"*Abel*? Is that you?" she asked.

The young man sat with his back to the cell wall, his knees drawn in against his chest, his eyes looking down, his head resting on his knees. She had seen that posture before. Hearing her dulcet tones, he glanced up with a look of pity.

"I'm here now," she said. "I'll protect you."

"The guards," Abel said. "They arrested me as well, Miss Tula." He did sound pathetic.

She placed a hand on his shoulder. "What for? What did you do?"

"It wasn't me. I didn't do it, honest, Miss Tula."

"I believe you, Abel," she said.

Taurus butted in, "No one shops the Taurus and gets away with it."

Abel peered up at her with that hangdog expression. "He was punching me."

"Yeah, too right I was, and I'll do the same again when I get the chance," he said with a scowl.

"You're safe with us now," Tula said to Abel.

"So, now you know," Taurus said.

"I do," Tula said. "Oh, and I saw your father outside the prison gates."

"What's he doin' there?"

"He gave me something for you."

"What's that?"

"It's in my pocket," Tula said.

"I'll get it then," Taurus said.

"No! I don't want you to touch me. Abel, help me, please. Untie me. Please, you can do it."

When Abel had untied her, she retrieved the package and gave it to him.

Taurus unwrapped it. It was a chunk of bread and cheese. He took a bite and munched away, satisfied. Through salivated lips, he replied, "Thanks. I'm starving."

As she sat down, her ankle buckled under her weight and she groaned as she thumped to the cold floor.

"Untie me and I can help with your ankle," Enoch said.

Something about him made her trust him so she nodded, and Abel untied him. She stretched out her leg towards him. Enoch laid hands on her ankle and the pain eased almost immediately. After some prolonged massage, the swelling subsided and it stopped throbbing. A wave of well-being washed over her, rejuvenating her soul.

"I don't know what you've done, but it's feeling stronger. Thank you so much," she said, and her hand brushed against the parchment in her pocket.

"Ah. I've got something here I think you'll be interested in," she said, pulling it out.

"Yes, what's that?" Enoch replied.

"It's called the Covenant of Angels."

"I'd like to read it, but my eyes are not so good these days and the light is rather poor."

"Anyone got a flint?" she asked.

Of all people, Taurus came to the rescue. He delved into his inner pocket and produced a candle stub. What else did he have in there – the keys to the kingdom of heaven? Not quite, because from another pocket, he produced a flint and an iron, with which he lit the wick, spreading a welcome tranche of light across the cell.

"Thank you, Taurus," Tula said.

"That's for bringing me the food from my da," Taurus replied.

"So, you can be kind, if you want to be," Tula murmured.

Taurus grunted.

The light was enough for Enoch to read the parchment. He read it slowly, with long pauses and concerted deliberation. Now and again, he nodded his head. At one time, he closed his eyes and mouthed a phrase, presumably echoing something that had touched him.

"I've only read the first half myself, which I found fascinating," Tula said. "Could you read the second half out loud?"

He nodded and began:

"Humans are trainee angels at distance.
Homo sapiens by nature — are you.
Sapiens means wise, yet unwise and unkind — are you.
He who gives consideration is man-the-wise.
Yet, like ignorant brutes do you act.
Mature you should now be — as a race.
The planet — so loyal to you — you have turned into a circus,
Full of activities to distract you from your purpose.
Life for you is an agreed-to communal deception theatre.
We are the way to return to the light of the greatness of correctness of service.
For that is your true purpose.
Service is not servitude. Service never degrades.
Slavery is degrading. That is servitude.
Higher in function than humans, but lower in possibility — are angels.
Service to the Higher, help to the angels — the proper exercise of free will.
True service uplifts, inspires and enhances.
You have built a tower of confusion in a city of deception.
Your time and culture are a labyrinth of delusion.
Everything, everywhere, is invented to cause this delusion to deepen.
The highest kindness, a supreme wisdom — was our hope for you.
When that failed, you believed it was because we, the angels, had abandoned you.
We always knew that it was because you had abandoned us.
Because from your purpose, you have abdicated."

Enoch lowered the parchment. "This is a fair, true and profound statement of the angels' sentiments. Where did you find it?"

"In one of the copper pillars, inside a hidden flap," Tula replied.

"It's a sacred document and part of our human heritage. I'm so pleased you showed it to me."

"I'm curious about the angels of Unity. I've travelled here from the city to be near them. Finding this document, and being able to speak to you about them, is a dream come true."

"What do you want to know?"

"I've heard of Michael, Gabriel and Raphael. They're the famous ones. Are they amongst the cohort of angels in Unity?"

"Those are names given to them by humans. Their true names are different."

"What are their true names?"

"One day, you could introduce yourself to them and they might tell you themselves."

"Oh, I hope so, I really do," Tula said. "Tell me, what are they like to deal with?"

"Well, they are not like us. They aren't constrained, as we are, by the fleshly way of plenty. We're physical. They're metaphysical. We're natural. They're supernatural. They're subtler than starlight, brighter than sunlight and as mysterious as moonlight. Their speeds are incredible. They are faster than lightning and can move from one side of the planet to the other in the blink of an eye."

"It must be so strange to you. They're invisible, so you can't see them and yet you know they are nearby. You feel their presence. How do you know when they are close by?"

"They're like the wind," Enoch said, "in that you can see how they affect matters as they pass by. In our time, they can't fulfil their purpose because they're unable to bring their influence to bear on us. They're mostly unused by humans and that makes them desperate and alone."

"That's exactly how I feel," Tula replied. "There's an absence in my life, an ache in my soul. That missing piece exists; that's why I know that I will not be stopped if I try again tomorrow. It can be found, and I've found it. It's the angels. They're the missing piece."

"What makes you think it's any different for the angels?"

"I don't know. I've never thought they would be like us," she murmured.

This was not what she had expected to hear. She had conceived of the angels as seraphic, winged beings, with supreme capabilities, undaunted, if not amused, by humanity's bungling, error-prone ways.

"When they were able to influence us," Tula asked, "how have the angels appeared in people's lives and what effect did they have?"

"I'll give you an example. Once there was a composer whose early, prodigious talent drew the attention of the angels of music, who provide cadence and harmony. They tried to pass to him their high spiritual vitamins with which to infuse his compositions. But because his life was a raging tempest, the vitamins were too potent for him."

"What happened?"

"Because of his imbalance, he went as deaf as a doorpost, but he composed some of the most inspiring music ever heard."

"So, angels have been the hidden source of many discoveries and inventions?"

"Angels are midwives to human progression. They give permission, just as at one time they gave permission for mankind to perceive the wheel or gravity or the rainbow spectrum."

"Did the angels give free will to mankind?"

"No, they did not," Enoch said. "Angels don't have any choice in what they do. They're dedicated to their purpose, which is to provide humanity with the spiritual vitamins they need, but only when they call for them. They would not cast their pearls before swine, would they?"

"In the passion play during the Grand Fete, the angels said they don't have things like doubt, indecision, or likes and dislikes."

"Exactly. They're fixed entities. So the gift of free will must have come from higher up the Ray of Creation, from something that made both the angels and mankind. In other words, it was a gift from the Creator."

"Do they speak to you?"

"Yes. I often hear their cry."

"Their *cry*? What do they say?"

"Help us, O Lord."

Tula winced. "That's incredible. Because that's our cry, the cry of humans, to our Lord."

"It is, yes," Enoch whispered, as if they were exchanging the secrets of the world. Perhaps they were.

Tula was quiet for a moment, before Enoch continued, "Remember, Herman and Kendra led the people out of Unity. The angels did not eject them. The angels did not punish them. Herman and Kendra departed voluntarily. Then, with their fine ideas about life and living with free will, such as the Acropolis, they grew the subtle connections with the angels and everyone prospered, at least for a while. But over the decades and the centuries, people grew familiar. The Acropolis fell into disuse, along with the possibility of spiritual guidance it offered. The people preferred to pursue commercial gain rather than correctly exercise their free will. COIL, Moloch and child sacrifice were the final, terrible acts of self-resignation from the Covenant."

"People can self-resign? How does that happen?"

"It's a common occurrence. Look, every person is born with a human nature, but within that, they are granted an individual nature. If a person departs from both natures – human and individual – the angels cannot recognise them as human. I'm talking here about evil people who have committed heinous acts of cruelty."

"Then these people don't receive any enhancements?"

"Because they have gone below the standards required of a human, they have self-resigned from that great realm. That's the abdication. Also, most people are lazy and do not consider it their duty, or within their remit, to develop, advance or refine. They have reduced life and living to the pursuit of happiness. Nothing could be further from the truth."

"But tell me, how can I see the angels for myself?"

"The best time is at night."

"I thought so. I saw them the other night with the aid of the box and the black mirror. I want to serve them, as you do."

"That's not possible, at the moment, anyway, at least in the current situation." His tone was wistful.

"And tomorrow at the Temple of Moloch, well, you face – I don't know what."

"The method of killing – burning – has a hidden meaning," Enoch said. "When a person dies a normal death, the immortal spirit leaves the body and returns to the source of its arising higher up Creation. But passing through the fire or any death by burning is a terrible thing. The searing pain breaks the subtle bindings of the spirit into many small pieces and prevents it from entering the realms of immortality. It's cruel, barbaric and anti-life."

"I didn't know." There was a lump in her throat and a knot in her stomach.

"The cult of the Temple of Moloch is a blight on humanity," he went on. "The world is polluted by war, famine, pestilence and corruption, and has been since ancient times. But there are a few realms in life that are free of any stain. One is childhood. Like springtime, childhood is pristine and new every time, every generation. The hidden, sinister purpose of the sacrifice to Moloch is to feed off that power of innocence and use it to control what people think and believe. More than anything else, this has severed the connection to the angels."

She was lost for words.

Enoch wasn't. "Outside South Gate, there's a sign that names Topeth 'The Top' town. It's not anymore. Reverse the letters of 'top' and you get 'pot'. Anyone in Topeth today is living in 'The Pot' of a humdrum life, a life drifting on the currents of everyday trends. No one who aims to be true to themselves wants that. No one who aims to fully exercise their free will wants that."

"If, and when, we get out of this mess, will you let me serve the angels with you?"

"Well, it's difficult to say at the moment," he said. He scratched his chin and frowned. For once, he struggled to frame an answer to her question. After a pause, he went on, "But you're not ready for that yet and there are other things to take into account which I can't tell you about, not in here anyway. And I can sense that Ruth is unwell. She needs my help. I have to get out of here. I can't be the next sacrifice to that bronze monstrosity."

"Amen to that," she said.

CHAPTER 19

The Freedom of Prison

Evening was a special time in Topeth. As the pall of dusk fell upon the rooftops, the birdsong quietened to a hush. For the moment, though, prison bars prevented Tula from enjoying it.

From what Enoch had said, mankind's ignorance and cruelty had unduly restrained the angels. Humans were granted the freedom to spark warmth into the freezing cold of the Universe. Angels and humans were partners in a grand dance, in which the ballroom was the Universe, and the orchestra was the Creator. That sacred dance was meant to be a thrilling voyage of discovery, and most important of all, of mutual benefit. Angels were the keepers of the next step for mankind. In passing it on to humanity, they, the angels, through a spiritual osmosis or transference, could learn about the great human qualities such as wisdom, benevolence and compassion.

While they waited for humanity to make the full and final retreat from barbarism, the angels were custodians of that noble purpose. She had no idea if, or when, that would ever happen. But while she lived, she would die trying. What else was more honourable to do with the great gift of life? Angels could learn nothing from people who danced to the tune of the merchant or who bowed before the altar of self-gratification. Ignoring the Covenant, humanity had fallen from its state of grace, not because of some wicked snake, but because they consciously chose to.

In the inner reaches of her soul grew a dull ache, a sense of loss and halted opportunity. Not only was humanity ignorant of this shameful state of affairs, but it was also wrapped in a double bind – it was ignorant of its own ignorance.

And angels felt abandoned by humans. Their life must be unbearable. What anxiety, what pain was theirs, when humans savaged their own kind and destroyed for fun or profit other forms of life with cruel and merciless arrogance? This was not where she had expected to end up after a few days in Topeth; facing the brutal truth of humanity's abdication from its purpose from within the confines of a prison cell.

Despite her own predicament, Tula felt awful for Enoch. They were going to condemn the man for rescuing Opal from being passed through the fire. If it weren't so tragic, it would be absurd. Throughout their ordeal, the man seemed to keep his own peace. She assumed he was engrossed with his own predicament, planning his escape, or preparing to meet his maker. She wished she could do more but did not know what to do or say to him.

Huddled together in the cell with Enoch were Abel and that brute Taurus. There was no separation of men and women inmates, but Enoch and Abel would protect her. The confinement pressed on her chest. Tears of sadness welled in her eyes. She did not know if they were for herself, Enoch, the human condition or all three.

The long evening twilight simmered through the barred window high on the wall of the cell, the only source of fresh air. Taurus's solitary candle had burnt out, so the only source of light was the bright full moon shining in the east. The prison smelled of sweat and body fluids and, most of all, of fear. If only she could turn off her acute sense of smell.

Footsteps echoed along the corridor. The prison warder was coming, his keys clanging in his hands. There was a second pair of footsteps; these were lighter, softer, those of a boy or woman.

The warden's keys clanked in the outer lock.

"You, what's ya' name? Tula is it?" Cyrus asked.

She nodded.

"There's someone ta' see ya'," Cyrus grumbled.

A veiled woman stepped up to the jail grille.

"Amina," Tula said. "What are you doing here?"

"I came to see how you are," Amina said.

"I'm as well as can be expected," Tula said with a heavy sigh.

"I don't know how they can put you in here with all the criminals and rioters," Amina said, her forehead scrunched into a frown.

"Well, they have."

"Geb is furious with you about the key to the bridge gate."

"I guessed he would be," Tula said. "But if only I could explain to him, tell him it was an accident, it wasn't deliberate. If you ask him for me, do you think he'll come here?"

"Yes, I do," Amina replied. "Especially if I tell him his son is here."

"He doesn't know?"

"Not yet, he doesn't."

"Perhaps he'll forgive me about the key."

"Perhaps," Amina said. "Geb can be compassionate, which is more than I can say for Damien. But before I go, Enoch and I have some unfinished business."

"What's that?" Enoch asked.

"You said you had something of Kalim's to show me."

"Yes, I did," he replied. Delving into his pocket, he closed his long fingers around an object, keeping it from her sight. "Open your hand."

She put her hand through the bars of the cell. He placed it on her palm.

"There," he said. "It's a lightning rod sigil."

Amina ran her finger up and down its jagged lines, like broken arrows. "This must be the sigil Wincorn gave him. How did you get hold of it?"

"When Kalim came and joined me and Ruth," Enoch said, "he gave it to me."

"Why?" Amina frowned. "This is a death sentence for my Kalim. Without its protection, if ever he returns to Topeth, Wincorn will make *him* pass through the fire."

"There's no need to pass anyone through the fire," Enoch replied. "There are no devils and it's quite safe to cross the bridge with no protection or blessing. Look at me, I'm quite sane, aren't I? You must believe me."

Amina shook her head. "It doesn't matter what you or I believe. What matters is the Holy Book of COIL because that's all Wincorn believes," she said and grabbed the cell bars until her knuckles went the colour of the whitewash on the prison walls.

"Wincorn's the prime mover, Damien's his executioner," Enoch replied.

"Soon enough, we'll see once and for all," Amina said.

"Why? What's happening?" Tula asked.

"Now Wincorn has refused to bless him, Damien can't cross the bridge," Amina said. "The Commander will lead a search party to find Kalim."

"Release me and I'll take him to Kalim," Enoch murmured. "I'm worried about Ruth; this is the first time in years we've spent a night apart."

"I'll pass on your message to the Commander. I have to go now." Amina turned and left.

Enoch and Abel were quiet. Even Taurus said nothing. Small mercies. Exhausted, Tula lay back against the prison wall.

As night set in, a clap of thunder crashed over the town. The storm broke. Lightning speared above the roofs of Topeth, splitting the dark

141

air and sending shards of divine brilliance into the skies. The rains came in sheets, wave after wave, smashing into the parched, dry earth, rivulets running through the town, along the ground gutters and filling the old cistern.

Tula was shivering, not only from the damp air but from anxiety about Enoch's fate.

Water trickled down the wall from the cell window and pooled on the floor next to her. The waters ran hard, the lightning cleansing, the thunder, startling. The storm reached a crescendo with a last clap of thunder and gradually passed by. Enoch stood next to the cell bars, gripping them tight, staring along the corridor. The town was eerily quiet, as were the other cells. It was as if the hand of providence had relented and wiped away all noise. It didn't last long.

The corridor cell door opened and in walked Cyrus, bottle in hand. He was singing grotesquely out of tune, something about shooting for the moon and the stars. Almost incoherent, he staggered up to their cell. She could smell the alcohol on his breath and that trouble was afoot.

"You!" Cyrus jabbed a finger through the bars at Enoch.

Enoch glanced at him.

"I just remembered who you are," Cyrus said, slurring his words. "So, I come to have a little chat with my old boss, Master Enoch."

That seemed to wake the ingrates in the other cells, who stood up and rattled the bars.

"You was once the prison warden – in this jail," Cyrus thundered for all the world to hear. He took a swig from the bottle, swayed on his feet and went on, "Me, I was your apprentice. You was my teacher, 'ere at the jail. I trusted you." There was a sad, but distinct, bitterness in his voice. He spat onto the floor. The other inmates cocked their ears some more.

Since Enoch wasn't saying anything, Cyrus continued, "That night, twelve year ago, they brought Opal to the prison, left her with you. Soon after, you came and said, 'Now then, young Cyrus, we got a lot to do in the morning, so you go home. Have the rest of the night off.' Me, I was thinkin' that was real nice of you, Master Enoch. There was my boss, lookin' out for his newbie worker. But then what did you do?"

Cyrus burped and sprayed a delightful mix of alcohol and spittle over the cell. "You took Opal and ran off with 'er. Kept 'er from 'er proper fate, you did. You know that. You let the town down real good, you did. And we've suffered ever since. You're a traitor; to yourself, the town and Moloch."

Cyrus drew his face into a vicious snarl, a gesture in which he seemed well-practised. By now, the other prisoners knew exactly who was in their midst. They clinked their iron leggings and chains against the cell bars, making an irksome racket.

Despite the provocation, Enoch wore an air as though he was agreeing to go on a summer picnic. He said, "I did what any normal human being would do in the circumstances."

"You should have been dug out from the workings like a piece of copper ore," Cyrus said, "taken down to Seliga, shipped to the coast and left to rot in a vast warehouse."

Even the night owls and the colony of bats were eavesdropping.

"I know," Cyrus said, raising a triumphant finger. "We're all dirty sinners and you've come to save us. You're the guardian of the angels. Yeah, that's who you are – Enoch, Topeth's guardian angel."

"Guard the angel. Guard the angel," the inmates yelled in mock tribute. "All hail the guardian angel."

The other prison guard, a bald, toothless ingrate, growled and shook his fist to incite the inmates, who responded with more cheers and lewd remarks.

Cyrus's face turned red with a mix of drink and rage. "I'm coming in to get ya', I am," he yelled and fiddled with his bunch of keys. After a toing and froing between key and lock and an obstacle seemingly only visible to Cyrus himself, he unlocked the cell door. To celebrate his success, he took another long swig from his bottle.

Enoch stood in front of Tula to protect her. The knot in her stomach returned. Abel stood next to him.

The other prison guard leaned on the bars of the cell entrance to watch. Cyrus shoved Enoch in the shoulder, but Enoch stood his ground and gently eased Cyrus's arm away from him. Cyrus responded with a ferocity for which drunks are famous. He wound his arm up and then unleashed a huge punch on Enoch. Cyrus missed the intended target by a distance wider than the ravine and spun himself into a coiled-up ball on the floor. The bottle fell from his hand and smashed into little pieces on the cell floor.

The other warden provided some much-needed common sense and hauled Cyrus out of the cell. Amidst gales of laughter from the inmates, many of whom rolled around on the floor, unable to contain their hilarity, the two warders locked the cell door and beat a hasty retreat to the safety of the corridor.

"Now that was worth getting locked up for," Taurus crowed.

*

Later, in the dead of night, the earlier rain had cooled the fractious air and for once, a balmy, soft wind blew through the town. Her inner voice spoke:

"Hark, the dawn,
Spark, the morn.
Heed the mire,
Bless the fire."

This was a warning or a ray of hope for a new dawn. Tula preferred the latter.

Sat on the floor, Enoch was leaning against the grimy prison wall. He was awake and smiled warmly at her, still apparently unconcerned about the fate that awaited him. He must have made his peace with his Creator and found a way to live that carried no regrets. To Tula, the idea of losing him frightened her, especially since he had explained how important his life was in the grand scheme of things. Besides, if he were to die, or suffer a serious injury, that would surely jeopardise her dream to get to Unity.

She plonked herself next to him and pulled her legs into her chest. Slowly, she tilted her head and rested it on his shoulder.

Just as she was dropping off to sleep, her inner voice repeated the rhyme and woke her up. She was tired and was drifting off to sleep again when the voice repeated the rhyme in a high-pitched sing-songy way.

That got her attention. There was something more in the rhyme than hope. Heed the mire? There was no bog or marshy ground in the vicinity, so what on earth was that referring to? Bless the fire? The fire… that must be a warning for Enoch. Perhaps there was something she could do to save him. Yes, that was it. She would keep her eyes peeled. She was going to be his saviour.

Drowsy, she lifted her head. Everything was peaceful. She rested her head back on Enoch's shoulder, closed her eyes and slept the sleep of Siloam.

Long and deep, she slept. She had no idea for how long.

She woke up. Her eyes stung. The darkness cobwebbed the night. For a moment, she had forgotten where she was. Perhaps hunkered down in a cave to escape the wind and lashing rain.

The smell of urine, fear and anger smacked her nostrils.

Another rain squall beat against the outer prison wall. The noise was deafening. It was more a violent, perpetual lashing. The storm brought with it a cold that chilled her to the bone. Not that Enoch appeared to mind. He was sleeping like a baby.

Enoch served the angels in Unity which must have been an extraordinary experience. And how did a person serve an angel? Or were angels meant to serve humanity? From what he had said, the arrangement was more one of symbiosis, promoting shared advantages and benefits.

On her travels, she had met some odd people – a remorseful man who had murdered his wife in a fit of jealous rage, and who was heading for the nearest police station to hand himself in; a blacksmith searching for the perfect cutting blade; a defrocked priest; and even a beggar who claimed he could remember all his past lives, including one as the Vizier in Ancient Persia when bees – yes, bees – ruled the world.

There was a new entry on the top of her list: Enoch – the man who served angels. She had never heard the like of it. Yet curiously, she found his story credible. From her short dealings with him, he appeared more normal than anyone she had ever met – which made everyone else abnormal, herself included.

In the city, there was a time when she joined a girls' choir at the orphanage where her mother worked. She, Tula, must have been seven or eight, still feisty and already fiercely independent. The choirmaster arranged them in three rows. Being small, she was at one end of the front row. He had waved his baton at them and they rehearsed a jolly nursery rhyme. After a little while, something caught the choirmaster's ear and he stalked the choir, up and down, listening intently to their voices, bending his ear, until he called a halt.

He stood in front of her and announced, "I've got it. I know what the problem is."

The girls gawped at him as though he had lost his staves.

"I have a fine musical ear, one that picks up if someone is singing out of tune," the choirmaster said. "At first, I thought she was out of tune and that everyone else was in tune. Now I've realised that all of you are singing out of tune – and that only one girl is singing in tune."

At that moment, before he revealed who that girl was, Tula's inner voice told her she was the only girl singing in tune.

Perhaps Enoch and Ruth were the only ones in tune with the angels, while the rest of the human race, in the general conduct of their humdrum lives, were discordant. They danced after a mysterious pied piper only to discover, when it was too late and they were falling through the air, that they had all been singing out of tune and that their lives had been based on the pursuit of happiness, power and money and other insecure foundations.

The wind eased and the rain abated until it was a soft thrumming on the prison roof. The storm moved on to pound the next town into submission, akin to some arbitrary hand of justice that struck where and when it pleased and brooked no mercy.

Humanity needed freeing from its self-made prison, constructed, not with hard, brittle, physical bars, but with invisible mental and emotional ones. She wanted to walk in the light of truth, but only powers more vital than hers possessed that kind of grace.

The night mirrored her sense of foreboding. It was echoed by the cries of the owls and the screeching of the bats, their homing instincts loosened and ruptured, so they could no longer find their way home.

Like them, she was homeless but so close to home that it hurt. It was a dull, persistent ache in her soul. This was the eve of the storm; the ethereal storm, conjured by dire entities and devils seeking to extinguish the light of truth.

She had an uncanny feeling in her bones. The second storm had passed, but there was another brewing, something far worse, more terrifying and cataclysmic. She could feel it building. It was gathering above the town for a final vindication and she was part of it.

Even she, who had spent her life in the city, who had gone to school with other girls, diligently learnt needlecraft, cooking and other dainty arts in preparation to build a home and a family of her own. That was fine for some girls, but not for her. She was pursuing a different order of service and dedication. And she had found it. It was in Unity. They were in Unity.

She stood up. Thankfully, Enoch's healing on her ankle had worked and she could plant a little weight on it, which was a definite improvement. She smelled the fresh, moist night air and grabbed a crumpled piece of paper from her pocket. Unable to make out the words, she knew what was written on it. She repeated the lines in the verse to herself:

"That you are the key.
With the angels of Unity."

In the hours of darkness, confined by the dull walls of the prison, she felt some new original thought was about to get squeezed out of her. Because as the hours passed by, she drew closer to understanding who or what she was and who or what was the key to this abiding mystery. Her destiny was entwined amidst these two, short lines.

Her inner voice spoke to her quietly and clearly:

"When two becomes three,
A new epoch there will be."

This was another clue. A gift of understanding. A pearl of wisdom.

A new epoch. That sounded charged with destiny. It meant change, change that mankind desperately needed. Perhaps she was to play a part in that. She felt important but afraid at the same time.

When two becomes three? When did two become three? It made little sense.

Oh, but there was one way it could happen. A man... and a woman; they would be the 'two'. Which meant that she was to find a husband. Was that Musa? He was so brave. He had saved her from that bully, Taurus. He had promised to look after her and his eyes were gorgeous pools of manhood.

And then the 'three'... That must mean... Wait, that must mean she was to conceive. She was to give birth to a baby, a special child who would usher in the new epoch, a saviour.

Surely not? She was still a virgin, unfamiliar with sex and inexperienced with boys. It was not by choice; it was because of a lack of opportunity. As she was growing up, she roamed the city with the other street urchins. But her diminutive stature counted against her. She was always being teased for being small. Tiny Tula they called her. It made the boys think she was a lot younger than her true age and so they had steered clear of her. Yes, she had kissed one boy, but he had tried to stick his tongue in her mouth. She was not having that!

Dreaming of her young prince, she closed her eyes and fell into a deep sleep.

CHAPTER 20

The Three Joys

Tula awoke. It was still dark. She had slept for a few hours. Outside, there was an awful mix of the birds' early morning chorus spoiled by the discordant highs and lows of the inmates' snoring.

As she stirred, the sound of footsteps echoed along the corridor followed by a jangling of the key in the lock. The other prison warder saluted briskly and in walked...

"Commander Geb," she murmured. "And Musa."

She was pleased to see them both. The Commander could get her out of this accursed place. And Musa, well, he was her saviour, her prince.

Cyrus staggered down the corridor. To stop himself falling over, he clung to the cell bars with delirious intent. After a couple of heaves in the corner, he vomited a foul-smelling, yellow-coloured liquid.

"S-sorry Commander, I-I had a drink or two," Cyrus said and then belched.

"I can see and smell that for myself, thank you very much," Geb replied. "Now, where's my son?"

"Over here, Father," Abel said.

"Are you hurt?" Geb asked, approaching the cell.

"No, I'm fine," Abel said.

Geb turned to Cyrus. "Why is he here?"

"He's in the cell," Cyrus answered.

"I can see that, numbskull," Geb said. "I know all about Taurus. I ordered his arrest. But why was my son arrested? Answer me straight or I swear I'll..."

"Taurus and Abel were fightin' like cat and dog," Cyrus said. "And so we slung Master Abel in here to cool off overnight."

"Why were they fighting?" Geb asked.

"Taurus was angry with Abel 'cos Abel showed the guards where he was hidin'," Cyrus said.

"Commander, that ain't right," Musa piped up.

"What do you know about this, Musa?"

"It wasn't Taurus, Commander, it was me."

"What was you?"

"I was passin' the old school and saw Taurus movin' around in the classroom. So, I goes to get 'elp and we arrested 'im. Abel come along with us."

"That's cleared things up," Geb said.

"Anything to 'elp, Commander," Musa said.

"What shall I do?" Cyrus mumbled.

"Release my son," Geb said. "And get on with it."

"If you says so, C-Commander," Cyrus said, unlocking the prison cell and opening the cell door.

Abel stood by the cell entrance. "Father, can Miss Tula come too?"

"I don't know if I'm ready to do that," Geb said.

"Commander," Tula said, "I want you to know that I'm really sorry about the key to the bridge gate. The moment after I found it in the lock, I saw Jevros on the bridge, which confused and terrified me. I accidentally put the key in my pocket. I was wrong to do that. I'm not a thief. I don't believe in taking anything that isn't mine."

"I hear you and I accept your apology. Anyway, I've got it back now," Geb replied with a smile. "The trouble is, Damien put you in here; so normally he would need to sanction your release."

She let out a little whimper and put on her most appealing, puppy face.

Geb adjusted his keffiyeh and brushed an imaginary piece of fluff from his shoulder.

She had to find the key to unlock his sense of fairness. It was there, somewhere, nestling in the deeper recesses of his mentality. "You sure you can't exercise your discretion? And see, even my fellow prisoners are sympathetic to my plight."

Geb glanced around the jail. On cue, all the inmates wore this doleful look.

"Come on then," he said, waving her out of the cell. "But for heaven's sake, promise me you won't get into any more trouble."

She nodded and skipped out of the cell. Musa touched her hand, grasping it between his. The gesture warmed the cockles of her heart and she smiled with her eyes.

"Thank you for saving Abel," she said to him.

"It was nothin'," he said. "All I did was tell the truth."

"What about me?" Taurus said to Geb.

"What about you?" Geb replied.

"Let me outta here," Taurus demanded.

"No, I won't. You're a basket of contradictions," Geb replied. "First, you stirred up a hornet's nest against the mine at the riot and the Grand Fete. You're undermining your own uncle's business. Where's your family loyalty? I mean, whose side are you on? I'm not even sure you know yourself. Then you got my son thrown in prison when he hadn't done anything wrong."

"Bah! You gonna free me or not?"

"No! Don't let him out, whatever you do," Tula butted in. "He's just a nasty bully. He scared me in the alley. He said I was a troublemaker. He wanted me to leave Topeth and threatened me if I didn't."

"Did he?" Geb said, shaking his head.

"It's true, Commander," Musa butted in. "I saw it with me own eyes, I did."

"Then here you stay, Mister Taurus," Geb said.

Taurus folded his arms and scowled, "All right, little cub. I ain't gonna forget this!"

"I told you, leave 'er alone," Musa snapped, pushing Taurus in the chest.

"Don't, Musa," Geb said, pulling him back. "Come on, leave him now."

As Geb made tracks to leave, Tula remembered her promise to help Enoch.

"Commander, what about Enoch?" she asked.

"Enoch, yes, definitely," Geb murmured. "For once, I'm going to repay a kind deed and a long-overdue debt. Enoch, thank you for rescuing Opal. You saved my daughter from a horrific death. You're free to go."

"Commander, thank you, it was my pleasure," he replied.

"And besides," Geb went on, "Amina said you'd take us to Kalim. Out you come."

"I'm gonna tell Damien and Wincorn about this." Cyrus was in Geb's face.

"You just do that," Geb said. "I'm the Commander of Topeth, a title bequeathed on me by none other than Herman himself. I decide what happens in this town. And it's about time I wrenched back control from Damien." With his head high, Geb breezed past the prison warden. Tula followed alongside Abel and Enoch.

The prison yard was swathed in dawn shadows. After the night rain, the early morning air smelled fresh and clean. She stifled a yawn as Cyrus unlocked the prison gates.

"Good riddance," he cried, slamming the gates behind them.

The crushing confinement and that horrible feeling of being locked into someone else's world were what she had hated the most about prison. Unexpectedly, she was liberated from that and the stench of the cells. She was free as a starling dancing a pirouette in the mountain air.

She rubbed the sleep from her eyes. Her ankle took all her weight and she walked with no pain. To her delight, it seemed to have healed completely. That was Enoch's doing. These angels and their agents were powerful because they had, through Enoch, healed her childhood wound, and, for the first time in her life, made her whole. And Musa was by her side. He was her 'two'. Together they would make a third. She would tell him all about the prophecy, but not now.

As they emerged into the street outside the prison, Amina and Sarah were waiting for them.

Sarah gave Abel a warm hug and then said to Geb, "Well done, you've released them all. I never believed you'd do it. I'm impressed." She was glowing with praise.

Geb grinned and murmured, "You should have more confidence in me."

"Well, Commander, from now on, perhaps I will," Sarah said with a smile. "Because now I can see that you can actually make yourself useful if you want to."

Geb widened his eyes. "That's a relief, my dear. All I have ever wanted to do is to please you. You're my life, you're my love. I'm sorry my work takes up so much of my time, but I'll try to improve."

"I hear you, husband of mine," Sarah said and gave Geb a peck of encouragement on his cheek.

Amina was pleading, "Commander, will you go to Unity? It's been days since Kalim's been gone and I miss him. Bring him back safely to me. When you see him, deliver a message for me. Tell him… I'm ready to answer his proposal."

"With pleasure," Geb said.

"Wait," Tula said, turning to Enoch. "I told you I'm desperate to serve the angels. I even showed you the Covenant. Please, take me with you."

Enoch stroked his beard and replied, "I hear you. I see you're willing to serve, but you're not ready yet. We can talk more about it later. For the moment, stay in Topeth with Abel, Sarah and Amina."

As he and Enoch were leaving for Unity, Geb turned and said, "Musa, stay here and make sure Damien doesn't leave with the gold rods."

"A pleasure, sir," Musa said. "You can count on me."

"I know, you're my right-hand man," Geb said. "That's why I'm asking you to do it."

Enoch set off with Geb, accompanied by the early morning rays.

Filaments of mist rose like elongated fingers from the depths of the ravine and drifted over the rooftops. Ethereal-looking clumps hung around the remaining columns in the Acropolis, giving the hill an air of faded imperial grandeur. The nature of the day was one of glowering intensity, of something imminent suspended above the town, poised to burst and overpower them. It gripped her around the neck and she swallowed on her dry throat.

The bad tidings came along in the form of Damien and Wincorn, who rounded the corner. The two of them must have repaired their differences over the gold rods because they were laughing and chatting away like old friends. Behind them were Chimor and Damien's entourage of thugs, Silus and Rufus at their head. The gang of Topeth approached Tula and Sarah as they were about to leave the outer prison gates.

Damien said, "Tula, who let you out of prison? And where's the other culprit, that Topeth saint, Enoch?"

"Thankfully, he's gone," Sarah said, "and as far away from you and your kind as possible."

"We'll see about that." Damien gritted his teeth.

Next thing, the prison gates creaked open and out came Cyrus, waddling like a duck.

Damien cut to the quick. "Why've you freed my prisoners? And where's Enoch?"

"The Commander, sir," Cyrus mumbled. "Followed his orders, didn't I? I just wanted a little boost of confidence before I come and report to you, sir," he added, tapping with one hand the near-empty bottle he held in the other.

"Geb was here?" Damien said.

"Yes, sir, just now," Cyrus explained in his own inimitable way, "right where you are standing, he was there, the big Commander, with that fella' Enoch. Enoch, eh, haven't clapped eyes on him in years. Didn't like him then. Like him even less now."

"Enoch's freed, as well? Where'd they go? Let me guess. To Unity?"

"Reckon you're right about that," Cyrus said. "I listened good. They said they was going to look for that Kalim fella'."

"Ignoring my orders, freeing prisoners; Geb's gone too far," Damien said. "This is another attack on my authority and I'm getting fed up with it."

"And your nephew's still coolin' his heels down below," Cyrus added.

"He's a headstrong boy, that one. It runs in the family," Damien admitted with a chuckle to himself. "But you can let him out."

"Yessir," Cyrus said and scurried back into the prison.

"Enoch must be recaptured. Moloch must not be denied," Wincorn said.

"And I want Geb arrested the moment he returns," Damien added.

Enoch and Geb were Tula's allies. If they both were to fall foul of Damien's schemes... She got an awful sinking feeling in her stomach. But not for long, because Musa was by her side.

Damien said to Tula, "Now, young lady, it's your turn. Silus, tie her up."

"Why? What have I done?"

"Geb released you without my authority," Damien said, tightening his fists. "I run this town, not the Commander, or didn't you know?"

Before she could escape his clutches, Rufus held her hands together while Silus got to work with a rope.

Abel tried to stop them, but Damien barred the way.

"Leave him alone," Tula moaned. "He's done nothing wrong."

Damien ignored her and shoved Abel out of the way. He barely kept his balance.

Silus tied her hands together in front of her. She tried twisting her wrists out of the ropes, but they scored the skin.

"You bullies!" Sarah shouted. "Let her go. She hasn't done anything wrong."

"That's not true, is it?" Damien narrowed his eyes. "Let me remember it all. First, little Tula, you turned up at the copper riot and then at the bridgehead where you stole the bridge key. You want to cross the bridge, a clear infraction of our laws. You broke the Law of Census by leaving the Grand Fete. Now, you've escaped from prison. That makes you a rebel, a thief, and an anarchist, for which you'll pay a heavy penalty."

"What's that?" She glared at Damien.

"You don't belong here, so it's exile," Damien said, swishing her away as if she was a bad smell. She might have known. Taurus had tried to get rid of her and now it was Damien's turn. It was a family effort. Well, she would resist them as much as she could.

"Rufus, got your needles?" Damien asked. He wore a smirk that made her feel uncomfortable.

Rufus patted his knapsack.

"Needles? What are they for?" she asked.

"I hope you don't mind," Damien said. "But we are going to take a few precautions to make sure you don't come back here."

She hated it when Damien used that patronising tone.

"Precautions?" she asked.

"Yes. You know what to do, Rufus," Damien said.

"Oh, yeah, I sure do." Wearing a look of mischievous delight, Rufus unfurled a leather pouch containing needles and another containing small bottles of coloured liquid.

Tula did not like the smell of this. No, not at all. She yanked on the ropes, but they burnt into her wrists. "What are the needles for?"

"Rufus is an artist. It'll be perfect. He's going to pretty your face."

"You what?"

"No, you can't do that," Sarah cried, hiding her face with her hands.

"What? I still don't get it," Tula said.

"Let me explain," Damien said. Running his index finger across her forehead, he added, "He's going to tattoo your face."

"Get off me. No. You can't! My face... They'll mock me. I'll be a spinster all my life."

"You should have thought of that before," Rufus said, and then asked Damien, "Etched on her forehead, the usual words for an exile?"

Damien nodded and said, "Fallen in 'The Pot'."

"I've not fallen in anything. I'll be an outcast, everywhere," Tula cried.

"Exactly!" Damien said, rubbing his hands with unabashed glee. "You're not wanted here. We need to cleanse our streets of debris like you."

She struggled to get free from Silus's clutches, but he held her tight. Rufus pricked one of his needles against the tip of his forefinger and then licked the small red blotch of blood that oozed from it.

Amina and Abel stared at him, frozen.

Sarah hurled herself at Rufus, but Chimor grabbed her arm and pulled her back.

"Let go of me, you bastard!" Sarah shouted at Chimor.

Kebel reared up at Sarah, his jaws snapping at her forearm.

Sarah backed off, yelling in their faces, "You can't do this. This is barbaric."

"Leave her alone!" Tula bellowed, still restrained by Silus.

"This is wrong. You gonna stop this." A familiar voice spoke up. It was Musa. *Oh, Musa.*

"Did I hear you right? Do my ears deceive me?" Damien asked.

"You did. I said... leave her be. She ain't done nothin' wrong. Undo them ties. Let her go." His voice was firm and strong making her heart swell with pride.

"Well, you are full of surprises, Master Musa," Damien said, gritting his teeth. "You're actually opposing me. Damien. I *am* this town. My family's copper mine has funded it for centuries. You are nothing."

Before Musa could reply, the prison gates burst open. Cyrus stumbled out, followed by Taurus and Luca.

"Cyrus, for once in your miserable life, you've come at just the right moment," Damien said.

"I have?" Cyrus was as astonished as everyone else.

"Yes, escort this piece of nothing to the cells."

"What you sayin', sir?" Cyrus asked.

"I'm saying," Damien replied, laying on the sarcasm, "that the best guard in Topeth, Master Musa here, is under arrest. Take him away. Oh, and while you're at it you can put him in leg irons."

Cyrus grabbed Musa and tried to push him through the prison gates, but Musa resisted him, shoved back, and Cyrus landed in a muddy pool.

Musa moved towards her, saying, "Miss Tula, you come with me."

She felt so strong at that moment. She had another ally.

"I'll come with you, Musa," she said.

But Rufus grabbed her, freeing Silus who moved like a young baboon, drew his curved dagger, and held it against Musa's neck.

"No! Please!" Tula cried. "Spare him."

The tip of Silus's dagger ripped the skin of Musa's neck.

"You," Damien said, "are a nobody."

Cyrus hauled himself up and, trying to clean the mud, only smeared it down his robe.

"When you've finished," Damien said to him, "take this man to the cells."

"Yes sir," Cyrus said.

Before he was led away, Musa said to her, "Wait for me."

She felt two things at the same time: joy and sadness. Profound joy at his request and a hollow emptiness at losing his safe presence. Something had been wrenched from her soul and she was left with an uncanny sense that they were destined to be together.

"Now, Rufus, where were we?" Damien said. "Hurry up, I can't wait to see your handiwork. I know my brother taught you well. He was the best tattooist, was our Vitus."

Vitus… that name jogged a memory. As Rufus was about to apply the first needle, Tula had an idea. "Wait. My pocket. There's something in my pocket. It'll save me. You'll see."

Rufus raised the needle to her forehead and pricked it.

Tula winced and appealed to Abel, "Please, look inside my pocket."

Abel tried to get near her, but Kebel hurled himself at him. Chimor struggled to hold him by the leash. But Sarah was free. She rummaged around in Tula's pocket and pulled out a metal coin and held it up.

"Is that what you wanted?" Sarah asked her.

"Yes, that's it."

"What is it?" Damien asked.

"It's a sigil. Well, actually, it's half a sigil," Tula said.

"Let me see that." Abel snatched it from Sarah.

"Look," Tula said. "The sigil was in my pocket the whole time. Ask Vitus. I showed it to him when I arrived. It means… It means I have a connection to Topeth. I'm not an outsider. This proves it. You can't send me into exile. Now, get these ropes off me."

"Someone could have given you that half-sigil in the city," Wincorn said. "Or you stole it like you did the key to the bridge gate."

"I agree," Damien said. "Take her away, it means nothing."

"Wait, it may mean a lot." Abel delved into his own pocket. "Here, let me try something…"

While still holding Tula's half-sigil, Abel pulled out of his pocket another half-sigil. Holding his hands out in front of him and, with everyone watching, he slowly moved his hands towards each other. He stopped… only when they slotted together to make a whole. The amazing thing was that the break marks in the two sigils exactly matched.

"I'm confused. What does this mean?" Tula asked.

"They join together to make a whole," Abel said.

"How did *you* come by the other half of *my* sigil?" Tula gasped.

With a fierce passion etched on the lines of her face, Sarah examined the half-coins for herself and stared at Tula as if she had grown angel wings. "My son's right. These two are a perfect match. They are a unity. That means you must be…"

"… Opal," Abel finished the sentence.

As Abel spoke the name, it released into the moment a great ethereal energy that swirled around its participants, seeking entry into the very being of their lives. It felt like the warmth of the hearth and so bore the hallmarks of a homecoming. It seemed to herald a new permission for what was to come and to dismiss from the past what no longer fitted. It was both a cleansing and a renewal, a pervasive sense that everything would change and that nothing would ever be the same again.

"Opal? You think *I'm* Opal? No, I'm not. I can't be."

"But you are Opal." After that statement, Abel's eyes seemed to become altogether sharper and brighter. He stood tall and his posture appeared more erect. It was as if he had shed a skin that he had outgrown long ago, but only now, amidst this turning moment, had been able to cast off.

"What? You've said it again. That's not possible. There must be some mistake. I-I'm Tula…"

"There's no mistake," Abel said, his voice full of an unusual certainty. "I remember it all now. It's so clear I can see it as if it was yesterday. Twelve years ago, we were together. I found a sigil near the entrance to the bridge. We were playing with it. You dropped it and it split in two. The pattern of the break is unique. You gave me one half; I kept the other. Don't you know who I am? Don't you know who you are?"

"What are you saying? Wh-who am I?"

"You're my sister. My big sister."

"I'm…" It couldn't be true, it wasn't true. Was it? Was she?

"Yes, you're Opal." Tears welled up in Abel's eyes.

No, no, no! I'm Tula. T. U. L. A. Tula. Plain and simple. Opal is someone else, not me. I might have a half-sigil, but as they say, I could have got that from anywhere. Though it's uncanny that it matches Abel's. I've never been to Topeth before. For as long as I can remember, I've always lived in the city. I've never been able to imagine my earliest childhood. It's as if I shut out those memories. Perhaps they were too painful. I don't know. Lots of people can't remember that far back. If only I could, I'd know who I really am.

Memories, damned memories.

"Sister," Abel said.

"Am I?"

Her mother reached over and wiped away a tear from her face.

Wait, my mother? No, my real mother – the one who wiped away my tears, washed me and tucked me into bed – lived in the city, not in Topeth. Sarah's not my mother. Or is she?

"You've got a half-sigil that exactly matches my son's," Sarah's voice quivered with emotion. "He's had his since the incident on the bridge twelve years ago. Where did you get yours from?"

"I don't remember, but I know I've had it since I was a little girl. It's like a precious keepsake from a long, lost friend. It protects me from bad things."

"Abel's right," Sarah was insistent.

"I-I don't know."

"I do. You're Opal."

"How can I be?"

"Remember what you did on the first night you slept in our house?" Sarah asked, her eyes bright with hope. "Your instinct took you into Opal's bedroom. You knew that was your old room."

157

"So… I… did."

"You're my Opal. You're my missing daughter," Sarah said with utter certainty.

By the Lord, my Keeper. I am here. It is my destiny to be in this place, at this time, with my mother and brother. This is my home. This is my true family. I… am Opal.

"Come here. Let me hug you," Sarah said. Tula, now Opal, melted into her mother's arms. It was a poignant moment, of people, long separated, coming together again. In it, there were the three joys: of renewal, of homecoming and, above all, of reconciliation. Abel joined them in a moment of familial bliss.

"How touching," Damien said, "a family reunion."

CHAPTER 21

The Galling Chamber

Opal had arrived. She had returned to Topeth. She was no longer Tula nor a lost city girl. Sarah was her mother, Abel her brother. She hugged them both. Her father was Geb. And she had found a nice boy, even though he was in the cells. And her limp had healed – she had been made whole again. At that moment, everything had changed, yet nothing had changed, because she still wanted more than anything else to get over that bridge and serve the angels.

"Abel, go quickly and find your father in Unity," Sarah said, choking on her emotion. "Tell him the fantastic news that our lost daughter, I can't believe I'm saying this... has returned."

"Won't I need protection?" Abel asked.

"You've got two halves of a unique sigil," Sarah replied. "Even an evil spirit will keep away from you. Just make sure you come back safely with your father. Show him the two halves. He'll walk on air coming back across that bridge."

As Abel ran off, Wincorn and Damien were deep in conversation, shielding their mouths with their hands.

"What's done is done," Opal said, holding out her hands to be untied.

"No, it's not." Wincorn was a tower of dissent. "Silus, bring her to me."

The guard yanked her by the rope around her wrists.

"Why? What are you doing now?" Opal asked.

"Simple. We're going to hold you to account for your actions." Wincorn's ominous tone sent shivers down her spine.

"Wh-what do you mean?"

"I mean that you are Opal, are you not?"

"Why, yes, I suppose I am. And?"

"And, twelve years ago, you trespassed on the bridge," Wincorn said, as if he was detailing the ingredients of a recipe for a meal. "You've just admitted it. You and Enoch are both fugitives. Although you are not wanted anymore."

"You're not serious, are you?" The knot in Opal's stomach tightened into a ball of heat.

"You're Opal. You don't belong to me, or Topeth. You belong to Moloch." Wincorn instilled his words with icy malice.

"When this happened thirty years ago, you forgave Amina," Sarah pleaded with them. "There are plenty of heifers you can replace Opal with... Let her go, untie her."

"I wish I could," Wincorn said.

"I don't believe you," Sarah murmured.

"There are two vast differences. First, Amina did not trespass onto the bridge. It was Marcus who did that, and he was thrown off the bridge by the devils. We chose Amina as the atonement. But, out of the goodness of my heart, I forgave her and replaced her with a heifer. Opal is an entirely different matter. She trespassed onto the bridge. Damien saw her with his own eyes."

"Yes, yes," Sarah said. "We've heard this rhetoric many times before."

"And second, Amina submitted to Moloch. She didn't run away. Opal did," Wincorn said.

"Enoch abducted her. She had no choice." Sarah's eyes grew wide in fear.

Wincorn dismissed her objections with a wave of his hand, saying, "Chimor, go to the temple. Prepare for the ceremony. And ring the bell; the town must be told of these great tidings. They will want to witness Moloch's retribution."

Opal felt the terror creeping up her legs and closing her throat. She could not face this on her own. Musa was gone, Abel and Geb too. At least she had Sarah for support. Her mother would save her. Opal trusted in her; she had no choice.

Sarah's face shaped into a heavy frown and she demanded, "Wincorn, let her go. Please. Can't you see? She was a child of six years old when this happened. Even now, she's barely a woman."

"It doesn't matter," Wincorn said. "Moloch has endured many years of grudge, resentment and denial."

"No." Opal plunged to her knees. Her throat was as dry as the desert winds. "I beg you. Have mercy." She lifted her tied hands to heaven. And to Wincorn. Neither responded.

If this is providence, it's cruel and unforgiving.

Pulled along by Silus, her bones ached, her blood boiled and her mind recoiled. She feared falling headlong into the sodden earth, so she shuffled along like a child.

"Can't you forgive and forget?" Sarah was saying. "She is contrite, aren't you, Opal? I'm only now reunited with her. I'm pleading with you. Don't take her from me. Release her. Absolve her. You can do it. Show compassion."

"It's out of my hands. It's the Law of Topeth." Wincorn was adamant. "She must be passed through the fire."

"No!" Opal's inner cry was long and soulful.

"After all these years, Moloch will be satisfied," Wincorn said. "I know this is hard, but the sacrifice must be made for the town. It's the only way. Moloch will protect it for all time."

"I won't submit," Opal yelled, on her knees again. "I will not submit."

Life is a unique and precious gift given only once. I hate ignorance and I love the truth. But there are limits. Because if I was given the choice between saving my life and knowing the truth of my identity, I'd choose to remain blissfully ignorant of who I am. Life over truth.

"And I will not let this happen!" Sarah added her steel.

"Enough. Bring her to the temple," Wincorn ordered. "If she won't take her punishment with dignity, pull her along in the mud."

Slowly, Opal heaved her body upright. The lower part of her robe was smeared in mud. Alone and abandoned, the very fabric of her soul was fracturing by the second.

Sarah thrashed her fists against Silus's chest, who used his height and strength to casually swat her away like a mosquito. Her mother got up again and screamed at him, the angst pouring out of her soul. He grunted like a feral animal, shoved his hand in her face and pushed her away.

The solemn tones of the town bell rang out, summoning all to witness her shame. The murder in cold blood of a young woman for an old offence was 'splendid news'.

Without Musa to stand next to her, where were Geb and Abel and Enoch when she needed them?

And Abel had been trying to help me. Yet in revealing my true identity, he's summoned the ghosts of the past and unintentionally sentenced me to an awful death.

"Good," Wincorn said. "Moloch will finally get his due. He was going to savour Enoch this morning, but you are more than an ideal replacement. Because for twelve long years you have caused all our woes in this town. Finally, we will restore justice to the world of men and the world of the spirits."

161

"What are you talking about – restore justice? I'm going to be brutally murdered for stepping onto a bridge as a child! Where's the justice in that?"

"This can't be happening," her mother whimpered. On this summer morn, Sarah was shivering as if it was a cold, winter's night. Fear clawed its fangs over her face. Her mother would not survive this. Piece by little piece, it would shred her.

The thought made Opal's blood run cold and her eyes glazed over. Her heart pounded in her ears. She stumbled across the market square where the townsfolk were gathering to watch the spectacle. Brushed by the dawn shadows, Silus pulled her through the alley towards the Temple of Moloch and her death. The town crier ushered the unruly mob into the arena in front of the bronze temple.

Even in her slender years, she had pondered how her journey on Earth might end. She had hoped to have been surrounded on her death bed at one hundred and five years old by a weeping horde of close friends and family. She had certainly not imagined being cooked like a goose in a bronze oven.

To one side of the arena, next to the temple, was the wooden stable where Zach stalled his donkeys. Just like the day before, a dozen temple servants filed into it and then emerged carrying twigs, branches, logs and other kindling.

Then it was for a heifer.

But this was for her.

All for her.

Her legs gave way. If Sarah had not held her up, she would have fallen again. Waves of nausea washed up on her shoreline. She choked on her vomit. The taste was acidic, burning, as was the fear and loathing.

Another group of temple servants emerged from behind the temple, carrying drums slung around their necks. Chimor sorted out the kinks and got them into a straight line.

As Silus hauled her across the temple courtyard, out of the corner of her eye she spotted Rufus marching into the stable. He was haranguing a bunch of Damien's henchmen who were yoking mules, loading packhorses, and harnessing a horse to a wagon covered in a white cloth.

Silus yanked on her wrists, burning the raw scars still more. The incessant drumbeat pounded in Opal's brain. Her thoughts were a jumble of lost ideas, failed plans and crushed dreams. The people bunched together in the lee of the temple. They chatted with one another, presumably animated at the turn of events that saw Opal brought to justice after all these years. Silus could barely lead her through the crowd. She was the main attraction!

They reached the front of the temple where the drummers beat out a compelling rhythm, like peals of thunder rolling over the mountain village, echoing off the steep, unforgiving walls of the ravine.

Flanked by Chimor and Kebel, Wincorn stood before the altar and announced, "People of Topeth. Today we gather to worship Moloch. We are proud to bring before him an offering that we hope and pray will quench his fury. It is the very child who long ago evaded his fiery embrace."

The crowd raised a cheer. Her body was shaking from head to toe. It was as if the drama was unfolding in front of her and she was separate from it. Then, when Silus yanked on her tied wrists, the sudden surge of pain brought her back to earth and she was part of it again.

Wincorn went on, "Since the distant days of Godal, we have failed to satisfy the Creator or his angels. Our descent into greed and immorality peaked thirty years ago when, with Marcus's death, we knew for certain that the devils had claimed the bridge as their own."

A gust of wind blew across the courtyard. The chill smeared her face, freezing her cheeks. To the east, beyond Unity, dark, ominous thunder clouds rolled in like black, horned devils. Some of them seemed to be in the crowd, who shouted and jeered at her as if Opal was to blame for this.

Wincorn continued, "I will tell you one of life's secrets about how the world endures. Every generation of children is sacrificed on the altar of the future. Every child is taught and moulded into our image as adults. Profundity is dangerous. It scares people. They prefer to feel safe in the shallows. We must quash the profound in our youth at all costs.

"In each child, there is a spiritual flame as bright and mysterious as the burning bush. It is awe for the mere fact of being alive. But for children to conform to the adult way, to the Topeth way, we must extinguish that terrible flame.

"The three fearful attributes of the child are awe, wonder and reverence for life. If carried into adult life, they upset and challenge the delicate balances of compliance and conformity essential to maintain order and for us to keep control. Our continued worship of Moloch will ensure that each generation of children loses these three attributes. It will be for the good of all of us.

"Today, welcome our precious little girl, our missing link, our Opal."

Moloch, COIL and its adherents, Wincorn and Chimor, were the nearest thing to evil she had ever encountered. Despite what the crowd thought, this passing through the fire was indefensible. It was gratuitous violence against children; a vicious, ignorant attack on the precious essence of youth. Childhood was meant to be just that – a sanctuary in which the 'hood' was an assemblage of protections and securities that any town, any country, or any civilisation would naturally place around its youth, allowing them to grow up in safety.

Wincorn's menace and Kebel's barking galvanised the crowd still further.

Two young men pushed to the front. Taurus and Luca... who else?

"I was lookin' forward to runnin' you out of town," Taurus said, his lips curled down in a sneer. "But now you're Opal, this is gonna be a lot more fun!"

"What's gonna happen?" Luca asked. "The temple ain't seen no sacrifices before. Not for no real person."

"Not till now, Luca, not till now," Taurus said. "There she is. Don't she look ripe and ready for it?"

"I'm not a fruit; I'm a human being." Opal refused to be crushed by him. The High Priest's demonic rhetoric, though, had girded the crowd.

"Op-al! Op-al! Welcome home, Op-al!" they bayed like baboons. Possessed by the morals of the caveman, they seemed to have lost all sense of mercy and compassion. Taurus had not possessed either virtue since birth. He lifted his arms and cried out:

"Isn't it true,
For me and you?
Into the mire, into the mire,
She's gonna pass through the fire!"

The crowd sang the rhyme with gusto. The drums rolled alongside the chanting.

Mire, that jogged her memory... *heed the mire*. That was what her inner voice had said. She had thought it was a warning for Enoch to beware. Instead, it was meant for her. If only she had listened properly... too late now. It was always later than she thought.

There was a raucous clap of thunder. In the eastern skies, flashes of lightning speared through dusky clouds. They resembled a throwback to the primordial beginnings of the Earth, full of fire and fury.

The temple servants streamed past her, their robes flapping in the gusts of wind, carrying knots of kindling, bags of twigs and sacks of logs from the stable to the temple. Inside the hearth, the inner sanctum of the bronze effigy of Moloch, Chimor ordered the servants here and there, as the woodpile took shape.

"Don't look," Sarah said and covered Opal's eyes with her hand. Opal's heart thumped in her chest, but not as loud as the drums, beating their mesmeric rhythm. It shattered her hearing. Nauseous with fear, she struggled to stand. Anger burnt in her soul.

Chimor emerged from the inner sanctum and whispered in Wincorn's ear.

"Good, and about time too," Wincorn said to him.

Even though it was mid-morning, the skies were dark with rain menacing the horizon. The air seemed chilled and swathed in thick, invisible, black cobwebs. A ferocious wind gusted through the temple courtyard, hampering Wincorn's preparations.

She tried to slip out of Silus's grasp, her wrists smarting as he hauled her back. "Oh, no you don't. We lost you once. We ain't gonna lose you a second time."

Wincorn barked some more orders. "Chimor, prepare her. Take her to the upper cabinet. Come down, then fire the oven. Make it fast. Moloch is impatient."

Opal kept praying for Geb and Abel to return, or Musa to escape from prison and come to her rescue.

"My darling daughter," Sarah said, tears streaming down her face.

"Dearest mother," Opal said, clinging to her mother's hand. "I love you."

"How I've longed to hear those three little words," Sarah said. "Just not under these awful circumstances."

"Let's go," Chimor snapped at her.

"Don't take her from me," Sarah cried and clung onto her for life.

Silus pulled them apart. "Let her go," he said.

Sarah launched herself at Silus, this time taking him by surprise and knocking him backwards. Silus snarled, picked himself up, and came back at her. He grabbed her ankle and pulled her over, but she kicked and screamed like a banshee. Three temple servants stepped in to restrain her mother, as Silus pushed Opal towards the hearth.

Chimor stepped in front of the altar holding a crimson-red robe, scored with many small black vertical marks – lightning rods. Wincorn took it from him and said to her, "Wear this robe and you can die honourably."

If her hands had been free, she would have thrown the bloody thing on the bonfire.

Wincorn placed it over her shoulders and pulled the tie around the neck to keep it in place. She was short and the robe was long, so its hem trailed in the earth.

"There," Wincorn said, his eyes full of a perverse belief in the righteousness of his deeds. "You're dressed to meet Moloch. You'll be his pride, his special bride."

Silus pulled on the rope and Opal stumbled but kept her balance.

Wincorn stood in front of her and handed Chimor a piece of black cloth.

"What's that? What are you doing?" she asked.

"It's a blindfold," Wincorn said.

"No, I don't want it," she said. "You've kitted me out for the kill. You've taken my freedom and now you're going to take my life. All in the name of an absurd and spurious belief! I won't let you deprive me of my sight in my dying moments! As I pass on to my next life, I want to see my Creator's face. I have questions for him."

Chimor glanced at the High Priest. "Shall I?"

"No, if that's her will, then let her see everything," Wincorn said.

"Perhaps Moloch will derive more pleasure that way?" Chimor asked.

"Maybe. Now, take her to the Galling Chamber," Wincorn ordered.

"Galling Chamber, what's that?" she asked.

"You'll find out soon enough," Silus said and yanked her towards the hearth.

A temple servant gave Chimor a wicker torch. Wherever they were going was a sombre place. The drums started up again, driving the ceremony forward and headlong into bedlam.

The three temple servants struggled to keep hold of Sarah, who scratched at them like a maniac. "Stop this monstrous injustice!" her mother was yelling at the top of her voice.

Opal's heart was as heavy as her legs as she trudged up the steps of the plinth. They took her next to the hearth where the temple servants were dropping thick logs around the outer edge of the bonfire. As she reached the bottom of the ramp leading to the upper cabinets, she smelled something so noxious, she nearly blacked out. It was scalded flesh; the residue of the smell from the heifer sacrificed the day before.

Even though they were taking her to her death, she was desperate to savour every last moment of her remaining life. In defiance, she sat herself down at the bottom of the ramp.

"Bloody hell. I don't have these problems with the heifers. Get up, will you?" Silus yelled at her.

She refused to budge. Silus grabbed her rope and hauled her up the ramp. She splayed her feet, dragging them on the walls. She wriggled her body. She twisted her arms, trying in vain to loosen his grip. Anything to squeeze another second from life. Anything to delay the inevitable.

"Stop struggling!" Silus moaned at her.

She spat at him.

He slapped her cheek. When she snarled back at him, he kicked her in the head, hard. Stunned, she momentarily lost consciousness.

The next thing she knew, they were hauling her like a sack of coal up the ramp. Torches in the cradles along the way sent shadows scudding across the narrow, ramped stairway, the wind gusting alongside them.

They reached the first floor. Three more to go. Inside the bronze womb of death, the lingering smell of scorched animal flesh made her want to vomit.

She was seeing double. The walls were moving back and forth. She fainted again.

The next thing she knew, Silus and Chimor had halted in front of a door. There was no more ramp. This was it. Beyond it, lay her destiny.

On the door was a smoke-stained sign: *The Galling Chamber.*

The chill wind rattled around the upper stairs like a trapped bird, rattling the metal door in its frame and clawing at her skin.

Silus leaned hard against the door. "The bloody thing's locked," he said.

"No, it's not," Chimor replied. "It's the wind. Here, I'll help."

Together, they shoved a shoulder to the door and, bit by bit, it opened, letting the wind rush through. Abruptly, the wild force of the gale smashed through the gap and jarred open the door. In a bizarre, synchronised movement, the two men stumbled and fell flat onto the floor of the Galling Chamber.

She tried to stand up and run away, but her head was spinning like a top and she slumped back down again against the open chamber door. In the background, she thought she could hear laughter.

Laughter?

The two men brushed themselves down before Silus grabbed her rope and pulled her onto the open platform. It resembled a balcony with a small foot-high barrier overlooking the courtyard. Then she realised where the laughter was coming from: the two men had fallen headlong onto the chamber floor, where they were in full view of the onlookers in the courtyard, who were bent double in stitches at their antics.

From there, Wincorn was shaking an angry fist at the two idiots. He yelled something, but whatever he said was snuffed out by the dogged beat of the drums and the inclement winds, which carried the first spots of rain, cooling her face.

A sudden gust of wind across the courtyard whipped off the crowd's sunhats as if they were made of paper. In the drizzly air, the hats drifted up inside a vortex and whirled around, playthings of an invisible, malevolent hand. They were not alone.

"Tie her to the cabinet, you dolt," Chimor snapped.

"Sure he can manage that?" she quipped.

"Shut up," Silus murmured and tethered her to a railing at the back of the cabinet. The vile odours of the heifer butchered the day before stung her nostrils. The odious smell made her dry retch, but she swallowed hard to stop herself from vomiting.

The honeycombed bronze floor was full of small round holes that allowed the waves and vapours of heat from the oven below. Carved lightning rod motifs decorated the ceiling. When she glanced back, Chimor and Silus had gone and the chamber door was closed. That was a quick exit, but she knew why. If they stayed any longer, they would share her fate.

She was truly alone, trussed up like a doll in a crimson fire robe.

She imagined Silus and Chimor edging down the narrow corridors and joking about her impending demise. After a while, Wincorn emerged into her restricted line of sight and stood before the altar. The drums came to a sudden halt and even the wind abated long enough for all to hear his summation.

"Opal was snatched from the fires," he ranted. "But Moloch doesn't forget those who belong to him. Their names are inscribed on his metal heart."

Chimor gave him a flaming torch and the High Priest went on, "I am the servant of Moloch and it is now my honour to light the oven. With this sacrifice, I will save us all from eternal damnation."

The old priest sidled up the plinth steps onto the hearth and moved out of her line of vision. From what she had seen him do the day before, she imagined him brushing the torch against the dry kindling with obsessive correctness, watching the supple flames devour the twigs, the branches and gradually, the logs.

This seemed to enrage the crowd who shouted and yelled at her. Their screams were not for her release. They were not for mercy. They were not for compassion. No, they were for her blood. Poor deluded creatures. With her death, they believed Moloch would drive the devils from their midst. For such a heinous crime, it could conjure more devils to persecute them.

Alongside their yells, the drumbeat smashed the air with wave after wave of sound.

The first filaments of white-grey smoke rose through the vents. She coughed, her throat hot, her eyes stinging, her head reeling.

Spots of rain dotted her face. Despite the plumes of smoke and heat rising from the vents, the chill in the wind was icy. A tempest, full of glowering clouds, was brewing over Unity and beyond Suria in the east.

In a dark mass, the flock of starlings alighted from a couple of nearby trees and headed off away from the gathering storm. Even they had deserted her.

CHAPTER 22

The Temple of Moloch

Wood smoke seeped through the vents. Her lungs filled with the stuff, burning her throat. She was wheezing. Her chest was tightening. Her eyes were watering, but they still stung like mad.

The binding on her wrists smarted as she tugged at them, desperate to evade the smoke billowing into the chamber. Although tied to the door at the back of the chamber, the length of the rope just stretched as far as the front – and gulps of partially fresh air. Helpless, useless, she could not even raise her hands high enough to wipe the tears from her cheeks or cover her mouth. She wished she had taken the blindfold. Too late for regrets. Her pride melted in the stifling heat.

Damn, so this was how her life was destined to end. Hardly the dignified exit she had imagined.

What was she meant to think of life, of being, of death? Life had not given her a manual for living. In her short tenure on Earth, she had been working it out. And now, she was to have that opportunity cruelly and prematurely snatched away from her. Was it her fault? No, it damn well was not. She did not deserve this barbaric end. Enoch had said death by fire was an erasure, negating a person's life record. It was a death for murderers, rapists, and those unfit to be called by the exalted title of human. She was not one of those. She was Opal. She was a fine young woman grateful for every moment life gifted to her. And she would not bend her will to anything lesser than that noble purpose. Even in this, her last moments on earth, she stood for life, for its grandeur and its magnificence.

The cabinet walls were heating up. The floor even more. She lifted her foot. Then the other. Then the first one again. The heat pulled her up and down like a marionette, mumming a dance macabre.

Her mouth wide open, her body stretched forward, pulling on the rope to its uttermost limit, just for one more breath, one more thread of consciousness, one more sensation, however painful.

There was a noisy crack. Like the lash of a whip. And another. It rammed through her body and shook her soul. There it was again. It came from inside this horrific statue. It was the bronze. It was heating up, expanding. The cracks came faster, each one louder than the last. The heat was stifling.

Out of the smoke, Moloch was rising. Out of the fire, Moloch was present.

She had to keep shifting her weight. Dance to Moloch's tune. Her feet were scalding. Steam rose through the vents. Excruciating pain. Flesh burning. Smelling. Scorching. Cooked alive. The smoke, the fumes. Breathe them out. Don't breathe them in. Can't breathe in. Must breathe in.

Every breath, nearer to death.

Her leather sandals smouldering, curling, shrinking. Sticking to the metal floor. She would be too if she did not keep moving.

Smoke plumed through the vents. The cabinet filled up. Steam. Get out. Must get out. Tear the rope. Pull it. Jump over the edge. Can't. Evade the heat, the terrible heat. Can't. Must live another second.

Through aching eyes, the blurred courtyard. Rain on the people. Drums insistent. Sound and fury. Dark thoughts spin in her head. Her mind splinters into random fragments of her paltry life experience. Each moment that passes takes a lifetime... Her birth mother in the city scolding her for being untidy... That first awkward kiss... Leaving the city for the first and only time... Arriving in Topeth... Witnessing the glory of Unity... Embracing her true mother... The moment she realised – and admitted – who she really was.

Her head, throbbing. The nausea, killing. The smoke, suffocating.

She retched again. Her lungs were like molten lava. Her feet burning. Her eyes felt as if something had stung them a thousand times. Her body convulsed. She fell to the floor. Blacked out.

Awoke with the heat on her body, scalding, penetrating every muscle, every patch of skin. She sat up. Her last act on Earth?

Drops of moisture spat against her face.

Wait.

That was not heat. It was water on her face. On the vents. On the hot bronze walls.

It was water. Cold water. Out of the sky.

Rain. It was raining.

It fell from the vaults like thousands of magical dewdrops.

The light was dim. Not long ago, it was morning. The walls of the arena shimmered into view. The courtyard now barely visible through the veil of slanting rain.

The heavens opened.

A flash of lightning lit the world like a candle in a tomb. It forked down from the high heavens through the soot-black clouds, spitting fire and splitting the sky. Moments later, there was a clash of thunder, a huge, sonorous clap, loud enough to rouse the heavenly powers above from their slumber. The noise and the spearing light pierced her senses, awakening her from death's icy embrace.

Rain bucketed out of the sky. The drops scythed into the Galling Chamber, bouncing off the hot metal, leaping into the air like salmon heading for home. It drenched her and everyone in the courtyard. It poured down in torrents, filling the gutters, crevices and ditches. The drops of rain angled against the cabinet floor and bounced up to her waist. She stood there, letting it pummel her face, her body, stinging her bare arms with a thousand tiny pinpricks.

The heat had gone. It was a miracle. She was saved. The heavenly powers had heard her prayer. And she had kept the greatest gift of all – consciousness. How her senses leapt at the sheer wonder of it all. She was vindicated. Alive. The thrill was unforgettable.

The heavy squall passed by as quickly as it had arrived and softened into a light, refreshing drizzle. She wore a huge smile on her face. A few, last fizzles of steam rose out of the oven. The vent grill, walls and ceiling were cooling. She tugged at the rope and a piece fragmented. Yes. Then another. She pulled again, yanking it back and forth, until it shredded some more, but not enough to free her. She was still tethered. She slipped and fell over.

As she grappled her way to stand, the crowd gawped at her. But she had beaten off Moloch and death. She had passed through the fire and come out the other end, still breathing and defiant.

"Thank the Lord," a woman's voice pierced the gloom. "She's alive." It was Sarah.

The dark clouds scudded across the sky leaving a soft drizzle. It was bitterly cold. Down in the depths, the bronze statue was cracking. Moloch was trying to speak to her. She conjured a few choice words she would like to have said to him:

You belong to the barbaric times. They have gone. They are no more. You don't belong anywhere on Earth. Go back to the hole you crawled out from. And let me go.

Through it all, Moloch was silent. Wincorn stood next to Chimor, pensive and as gripped like everyone else by the sudden ferocity of the rain squall. He glanced at her, then at the altar, then at the crowd and then back at the drummers. The silence was imposing its own will on the throng. It sang to them, gently. It whispered to their souls, softly.

Opal heard it.

As did Sarah. She broke from the ranks. "It's a sign from above," she said. "They've quenched the fires of Moloch. We are free of this ogre; free to pursue our destined journey."

A cheer arose from the crowd. Muted at first, others joined in, until at the end, urged on by Sarah and Amina, the people were yelling in unison, "Op-al! Op-al!"

Their voices were like seraphs, a blessing above all others. If only they were ready to confront the evil of Moloch and defy his henchman.

Wincorn lifted his right arm and slowly, painfully, drew it across his forehead, wiping away any remaining raindrops. His gown clung to him like a leech. His shoulders slouched. He coughed heavily into his sleeve and cried, "People of Topeth. Never forget, that the god of sacrifice has cared for us. For many a year, he kept the devils of the bridge at bay and out of our town. Without Moloch, we would all be mad or, like Marcus and Jevros, end our days with our necks twisted round the other way. Always remember, Moloch is the reason we are still here and still safe."

No one moved. Someone needed to stand against Wincorn.

Sarah spoke for the people, "You fired the oven, summoning your Moloch. But the rains doused his flames. It's a miracle, a sign that Moloch's rule is over. Let's end the slaughter of the innocents and the sacrificial killing of any life. Bring my daughter down from the Galling Chamber. Set her free from this monster. Set us all free from the monster."

Wincorn was unmoved. "Opal has a debt to pay to Moloch. After twelve years, she has come back to him. That is the only real sign."

"What... what are you going to do?" Sarah asked.

The crowd waited. The donkeys finished munching their carrots by the stable. A cat and a dog stopped fighting over scraps. The starlings went off to roost. The griffon vulture circled the ravine, searching for carrion.

Wincorn cupped his mouth and spoke into his assistant's ear. Opal prayed with all her might to be freed. Sarah had spoken for her. The crowd had cheered. The moment of freedom arrived.

Chimor spoke to the drummers in a huddle. They put down their drums and followed him to the oven at the base of the temple. He directed some of them into the hearth.

Yes! He's going to climb the steps, cut this damn rope and set me free.

With the other temple servants, Chimor veered off track and headed for the stable. Like well-trained soldiers, they followed him in a straight line, churning up the earth and sloshing through the mud and puddles. They stayed in the stable for a few minutes. Opal breathed the sodden air, any air; she did not care. Her mother waved at her in triumph.

But the wait drew longer. That knot tightened in the pit of her stomach. Her enhanced sense of smell returned, and it smelled of one thing: nauseating betrayal.

Chimor led the men out of the stable. They cradled objects in their arms with tender love. They wore a common expression, one of fear mingled with an obsessive determination. The first man carried a bundle of twigs and kindling, as did the second. The third and fourth held larger branches. The rest embraced logs, which were as dry as the desert sand.

Wincorn was not relenting. He was going ahead. With another attempt. The fire. The heat, the stifling heat. Not again. If she could have, she would have jumped off the cabinet edge and risked a broken bone or two or three or ten. Better by far than an excruciating death by cooking. But she was tethered... the sacrificial lamb.

"No," she cried. The word sprang from her lips. Providence barely spared her a glance. Sarah did though – her mother plunged to her knees, clasping her hands before her chest in prayer.

"Don't do this. I beg you," Sarah pleaded to Damien, to Wincorn, to the heavens, to anyone and anything that would listen. "She's my only daughter. Don't take her from me. I've only just got her back."

The skies were clearing. The stifling smell of the wood smoke was receding. The temple servants climbed into the hearth, disappearing from her view. She imagined them sweeping out the moistened ashes and wet branches from beneath the oven while the others set about building a new fire in the hearth. It took them less time than she had hoped. Soon her mother's furious cries of dissent rose like incense to heaven, but they were quickly drowned out by the drummers.

Opal tugged on the rope. It stretched a tad but again failed to give. That was her fate. From all the pulling, she had a red raw bracelet around her wrists.

The drumbeat galvanised the people in the courtyard. Urged on by Chimor, the drummers spelt out their waves of sound, calling the fires, summoning the god, the killer of children, the dreadful Moloch.

Up above in the skies, the clouds of darkness had shed their load and had swept on to other towns, seeking more victims on which to unleash their wares.

Once more, as filaments of hot steam rose out of the vents, an awful premonition stuck in her mind. This was the end, for her life. She, in an oven. For a second time. Her mother, newly found, was watching her torture, weeping, wailing, rending her soul with trauma.

She could not do this again. She had nothing more to give. She was out of courage. The tempest had washed her defiance down the drains. Her clothes were unkempt and sodden. Her spirit had departed once. It was halfway to heaven, or was it hell, and had returned to her. Perhaps it was as surprised about that as she was.

She was empty. Her mind flashed to Jevros, the doctor. She remembered the moment in his house when his spirit had come to her, occupied her, and she had thought something so terrifying she had recoiled from it. This time, it winged its way into her fractious mind. It was that Jevros was pleased his daughter had died. Why? Because she would not have to suffer the passing through the fire. The thought of being pleased his daughter had died had driven the poor man to distraction. And this consuming guilt culminated in his sad, avoidable end. Now she knew, now she understood why he had done what he had done. Was he mad? No. Was he driven to do what he did by the madness of the culture in which he lived? Definitely.

Opal was frantic. Harder and harder, she pulled the rope taut, then loosened it and then yanked it again. Her wrists, throbbing. The air, hot with steam. She, in her crimson robe, sweating. Her skin, bursting.

Blotches of a crimson fog appeared out of the corner of her eyes, hanging there like bloodied early morning mists rising from the swamp. If she could plunge her hand into it, she could tell if it was real. Her life was ebbing away, and she was seeing red mist.

She tried staring straight at it, but the thick red fog only reappeared when she looked again out of the corner of her eyes.

The red mist wasn't real; it was ethereal.

It smeared the cabinet walls and ceiling. It moved; the mist shifted in shape as if the clouds were dancing on the rays of the sun. Close to death, she was seeing through the veil, the subtle curtain that separated the seen worlds from the unseen.

The cabinet moved. To balance, she reached for the walls. The red mist did not move. She did though. Involuntarily. The cabinet was shuddering; Moloch was angry. The entire statue was trembling. So were her nerves. And her legs. They gave way beneath her like jelly and she fell. Landing on all fours, she scalded her knees, palms and feet. Though that was the least of her problems.

It was not the cabinet that was shaking. It was not the statue of Moloch, nor the town of Topeth. It was the mountain itself.

Her inner voice said:

"The red mist is no fake.

Tis a sign the earth shall quake."

What providence was hers? From being a plaything of Moloch, she was now one of the heavenly powers. Amidst the turmoil, she was tossed around like a child's toy.

"Into the air burning, somersaults turning.

Spinning in steam, miring in fire.

Alive but not alive, dead but not dead.

Hung amid a strange ubiquitous boundary world."

Hurled into the skies. Flying like a wounded starling. She wanted these moments of liberation, of dramatic flight, to last forever. For in them, in the exhilaration of movement, free from the bindings of death, there was a simple, unerring, singular clarity.

She was alive – again.

She had received not just one reprieve, but two.

She landed – not with the expected hard bump, but with a soft splash. It was swishing around her. A thick, brown, slushy puddle of the stuff. She sat up. That was a soft landing.

Of all things to have saved her life – a mud pool.

CHAPTER 23

Fight at South Gate

The world was spinning in Opal's head. Her vision was one huge blur. Her temples ached. Her body felt like a single giant scald. Was she in heaven, or hell – or still on Earth? It did not matter, because she was alive. Someone was by her side. How Opal recognised the woman's body odour, she did not know. The smell evoked the qualities of quiet firmness, kindly care, and defiant protection. It was her mother.

With Sarah's help, she hauled herself out of the mud pool. Every bone ached. Her heart was racing; her nerves were jangled. She was shivering from the cold. Fear gripped her round the throat. But every breath was one more away from death. Small mercies, then.

Opal's crimson robe, her hands and face, were soaking wet and splashed with streaks of mud. Sarah helped her remove the robe. That felt good. When her mother clasped her to her chest, that was even better. It warmed the frozen, petrified ice of her soul. Sarah swabbed her down with her keffiyeh and Amina wrapped her scarf over Opal's shoulders. Opal was back on the path to being human again, but only just.

As she returned to the world of life and living, Amina was speaking to her mother.

"She's scalded badly… on the feet."

"Remember the saying," her mother said.

"*Treat the scald,*
With water cold."

"Well, there's plenty of that around," Amina replied.

"Opal," Sarah said. "Here, step this way. Just stand in the puddle. You'll heal up in no time."

She leaned on Amina and stood in a muddy puddle, its cooling waters so soothing to her scalded feet. She could have stayed there forever. Next to her was the altar. Realising she had landed inches away from it, she whispered another prayer of thanksgiving.

As her senses returned, the scene before her came into focus. Other than a gash in the stable wall and the severe damage to Moloch, the quake did not seem to have wrecked any of the other buildings. The people in the courtyard seemed as stunned as she was by her extraordinary release. Mud had splashed everywhere; the pair of bull's horns had fallen off the altar whose surface glistened with raindrops.

Wincorn's face was as gaunt as a grave. Shoulders slumped, he gazed with weary defeat at the sodden kindling and the huge vertical crack in the bronze statue. The temple servants scrubbed and cleaned the altar with a strange frenzy. The drummers wiped the moisture from the surface of their drums and the expressions of gleeful anticipation from their faces.

"I don't believe it," Wincorn murmured and coughed heavily into his hand. "What am I to do? What are we to do? Moloch has abandoned us. The devils will have the town."

If the man had not been so brittle and cruel, Opal could almost have felt pity for him.

In the midst of this havoc, Damien emerged on horseback from the stable leading a covered wagon, together with other horses, carts and mules. She recognised the wagon – it was the one covered with the white cloth that contained the gold rods. His pistol tucked into his belt, Rufus sat astride the wagon seat, reins firmly in his hands.

Damien was making his escape. Sodden, scalded and half-dead, she was too weak to stop him and too weary to raise a clamour.

She did not need to, because Chimor, arms crossed, feet astride, blocked the temple courtyard gate and Damien's route to freedom. Kebel in tow, Wincorn stumbled over to join them. His own normally pristine robe was covered in mud and the old priest smelled like the rubbish tip on Acropolis Hill. Along with the rest of the crowd, Opal, Sarah and Amina made their way to the gate. This confrontation, between Damien and Wincorn, she had not expected.

"I thought we had agreed about the gold rods," the High Priest said. His voice sounded weak and hoarse as if he had shouted himself out. "I should have known your word would count for less than nothing."

"Get out of my way, you old fool," Damien said.

"I will not." Wincorn's voice seemed to rise from the depths of his being, as if he too was shredded of every purpose in his life. "You can leave, but you're not taking the rods. I warn you, if you steal them, I'll bring down a curse on you that'll crack your life in two."

"Your religion is worthless. Your dead god is the one that's cracked in two," Damien said. His horse neighed and rocked its head up and down as if mocking the priest. "Do you think your idle threats are going to stop me?"

"The gold stays here," Wincorn said. "It's our future, the future of the town. That's all we've got left."

"Not so, you could raise some funds by selling the bronze in your precious Moloch."

"Don't disrespect the old gods, lest they come back and bite you," Wincorn said.

Kebel added a long, low growl.

"Say what you like, I'm taking all the gold rods. I found them. They're mine. I'm going to start a new life, away from this old, worked-out pit. Topeth is finished."

"What do you mean, finished? Topeth is an icon in the world, the place where mankind first engaged with the gift of free will."

"Those dreams are hollow, they don't inspire anyone," Damien replied. "The worlds of Herman and Godal don't exist anymore."

"So, you're running away with the riches of Unity," Wincorn said. He paused for a moment, clutching his chest as if he was in pain. He glared at Damien. "You've been looking for a way out of Topeth for years. Your contacts in the city, the bankers and the merchants are waiting for you. Your ill-gotten gains are already deposited there. But it wasn't enough, was it? You needed one last big killing. When you stumbled into Unity and found the gold rods, you couldn't believe your luck. The funds from their sale would make you a very rich man. Oh, don't look so surprised. I've known of your secret exit plan for some time."

"And what about you!" Damien shook his fist at the High Priest. "You'd sell the rods for your own gain. I'll gladly trumpet every sordid detail of your nefarious ways to the good citizens of Topeth. Your precious reputation would go up in flames. You wouldn't want to see that, would you? No, I didn't think so. Now, get out of my way."

"You're wrong. You don't understand me. You never have." Wincorn spoke slowly as if someone was forcing the words out of him.

"How's that then?" Damien said. "Because you're stopping me from taking the gold rods?"

"Yes, and you hate me for it. Just like the people I protected from the devils on the bridge. Just like Amina here, who I reprieved all those years ago. Did she thank me? No, she never did."

"What did you say?" Amina asked, screwing up her face.

"You've never thanked me, ever." Wincorn rubbed his chest with his hand as if to ease some discomfort.

"Here's my thanks." Amina gritted her teeth, raised her hand and slapped his cheek hard. Kebel growled at her, but that didn't stop her.

He rubbed his cheek and stared at her, his eyes wide in disbelief.

"Yes, I just slapped you. And I enjoyed it. Do your worst. Set your devils onto me. If you think you deserve thanks for showing me mercy, you really are mad."

"I did what I believed in: I followed the Laws of COIL."

"That says it all," Amina replied, her eyes glaring like emeralds. "Me, I believe in family and I believe in the town and people of Topeth; you believe in one thing... yourself. But now the sands of time have run dry for you."

"No, I don't think so." Wincorn was struggling for breath, but added, "I will defend the righteous."

"Defend the righteous?" Amina was riding on the crest of a wave. "You are like a rich, fat shopkeeper handing out wedges of forgiveness, pacifying a morsel of guilt here and giving balm to a bit of shame there. It makes you appear merciful and compassionate, but you and your priestly kind caused the guilt and shame in the first place. COIL is suffocating the town."

Wincorn's eyes opened wide, and he peered at Amina as if she was one of the devils he believed occupied the bridge.

Amina was undaunted. "Thirty years ago, you released me from Moloch's stranglehold. But it traumatised me and the townsfolk. Since then, you and your COIL religion have fed on our fear of the devils and manipulated its laws to force us to comply with your every whim."

Wincorn's mouth dropped open. His eyes glazed over, and he wobbled on his feet. He clutched his own throat with his hand and coughed. He ripped open his robe at the throat and gasped for breath that did not seem to be there for him. His face turned from red to a garish purple. His body seemed to freeze for several seconds until he fell awkwardly into Chimor's arms. A trickle of blood dribbled from the corner of Wincorn's mouth. Chimor struggled to hold him up and leaned his limp body against the wall.

The High Priest's head slumped to one side, his tongue lolling out of his mouth.

"He's... dead." Chimor made the sign of COIL over his corpse. "May he find peace in the afterlife."

Someone in the crowd sang the opening bars of a mourning song. Another joined in, and a solo became a duet. Soon the crowd was humming a gentle lullaby that swayed with the winds, lifted to a moving crescendo and then gradually softened into a reflective silence. Opal's heart melted

179

to see them show compassion for the man, as he breathed his last, despite his terrible ways.

"He won't be needing this anymore," Chimor said, as he removed Wincorn's chain of office with unbidden relish and carefully draped it over his own chest.

"That's better," he said with a contented sigh. "This should have been mine long ago, but now will do. Don't you think it fits me well?"

Some things never changed. Greed and opportunism were the devil's twins.

Kebel pushed his snout against the dead priest's arm and lay down by his side. At least someone close to the old priest had remained loyal to him.

*

Once the temple servants had taken Wincorn's body into the chapel of rest, Damien led his cabal to South Gate.

Opal moved as fast as she could to catch him. Her soul screeched for rest. She stank of dried mud. With Sarah and Amina, she struggled on, ignoring the puddles and the mud pools along the way. Grey clouds were gathering again, and a chill wind blew raindrops into their faces.

By the time they reached South Gate, Damien's entourage had passed through it and were heading towards the Welcome Boulder. Taurus and Vitus were closing the gates. Through the partially open gates, she glimpsed a dozen guards.

"Geb. At last! It's him. They're back from Unity," Sarah cried. "Hopefully Abel's with him."

"And Kalim," Amina added. "It's about time he came back. I have something to tell him."

Vitus and Taurus seemed immune to their pleas to open the gates because they placed the barrier on the gate sleeve. From outside, beyond the gates, came the loud retort of a gunshot, followed rapidly by several more and then by shouts of alarm.

"Let us through," Opal demanded. She shoved Vitus out of the way and tried to lift the barrier from the sleeve. Taurus grabbed her by the shoulders and yanked her back.

"Take your damn hands off me." She shrugged him off her. "Never touch me again," she growled at him, and he took a step back. She particularly enjoyed the look of surprise on his face. But she had had enough of his temper tantrums. And this was too important. From outside the gates came more booming sounds. Shouts of anger were quickly followed by screamed orders and yells of pain. Horses whinnied. The crack of more gunshots punctured the gloom.

The rain pelted down again. Droplets ran down her face.

"I wouldn't go out there if I were you," Vitus said.

"Well, you're not me, are you?" she replied.

"And if I don't come back, at least it'll be for a cause worth dying for."

"You won't die," Amina said. "I know it, I can feel it." At first, it seemed a casual statement, but it hung in the air, suspended, and with each passing moment, it gathered meaning until its portent reverberated beyond the individual words.

Like the murky clouds of a tornado, groans and yells spiralled into the air from the other side of the gates. There were shouts of "Halt!" There were neighs of a horse in distress, followed by a long, pathetic whinny. The gunfire grew sporadic and stopped, leaving only pathetic groans and cries for help.

Taurus peered through a small hole in the gate and grunted with morbid satisfaction.

"What can you see?"

"Wouldn't you like ta' know, little cub?" he smirked.

This young man unnerved her. She had met a few unsavoury characters in her life, but Taurus was vile. He smelled of death and decay.

Waves of fury shook her body. "You have fought against the copper mine, so why are you now protecting your Uncle Damien? The sale of those gold rods will make him a wealthy man. He's abandoning Topeth and going straight to the city. He's leaving you and Vitus. There's nothing for him here. So, open the damned gates."

Taurus's mouth dropped open.

"She's right, son," Vitus said. "I've given my brother the benefit of the doubt once too often. Damien's poison. So, yeah, lift the barrier."

As soon as they opened the gates, Opal rushed through them.

A riderless horse stood forlorn against a backdrop of carnage. A broken cart was overturned and had spilled its cargo of lightning rod sigils into the mud. A dozen bodies lay strewn on the wet earth, the blood of the wounded staining the waters red. Puddles merged into pools, pools into rills, until a crimson stream ran down the slope towards the cemetery.

Damien and the remains of his cabal – the wagon, Rufus and a few mules and horsemen – were escaping down the Seliga road. They had just gone beyond the Welcome Boulder. In the pouring rain, there was little they could do to stop them.

Fearful that Geb and Abel may be amongst them, she and Sarah desperately examined the cache of bodies. First, she found a corpse face down in a ditch. She baulked from touching the man, whose head was haloed by a thick pool of blood. Sarah had no such qualms and turned him over. It was Silus. He had taken a bullet through the neck. No more would he add to his, or the world's, tally of cruelty.

A wounded man dragged himself through the mud and slowly, painfully, propped himself up against the wheel of the overturned cart. Another younger man rushed over to him, bent down and hung his head in sorrow. Sarah dashed towards them and crouched over the bloodied man. Beating her chest, her pitiful cries pierced the vaults of heaven.

The man was Geb. Blood seeped from a gunshot in his belly, draining into a pool next to his body. He moaned and shivered. His face was as white as a mountain glacier. Thank the Lord, he was still alive, but his life hung by a thread.

The younger man was Abel.

Sarah found a discarded coat, folded it into a makeshift pillow and gently tucked it under Geb's head.

"Thank you," Geb said, his voice as soft as the thrumming rain.

Sarah took off her neck scarf and stuffed it against the wound to stem the blood flow. In a voice hoarse with emotion, Sarah asked, "Geb, darling, did… did Abel tell you?"

Geb blinked at her, his eyes blank and seeing nothing. "Tell me? What?"

"He knows, Mama. I showed him the sigil. He nearly fell off the bridge," Abel blurted out.

Geb's face contorted with pain. With sallow cheeks, he looked like an old man.

"Here she is," Sarah said, inviting Opal to his side.

Geb opened his eyes. "Opal," he murmured.

"Father." She wiped his hair from his eyes.

"I-I prayed you would one day come back to us," he said. Each word seemed to take an age to leave his mouth. The sands of time were trickling by for him.

She bent down and hugged him with grace and tenderness. It felt easy and normal to touch her father. His body was flaccid. She could feel the life ebbing from his soul. She swallowed on her tears.

"Abel, come and join us," Sarah said.

"Yes, Mama," Abel said.

"We're reunited." Sarah's chest swelled with pride. "Now, we are a family again."

"I love you," Geb said. His voice was frail, weak and nearly drowned out by the rain slanting out of the glowering skies. The squall was brief but intense. There was nowhere to shelter from it. The sheet rain pitted the mud. Each drop had its own power.

Damien had left his wounded behind. Some of them hobbled after him. Others lay in agony on the ground, crying for help, mercy or deliverance. Damien's wagon train moved slowly through the mud and past the carpet of blue thorns.

From behind them came a distant rumbling. It got louder and louder. It came from inside the mountain. It made a gurgling, swishing sound. A wall of water gushed out of the cistern overflow pipe and smashed into the row of cacti on the other side of the path from where they stood around Geb.

The water wall thundered towards the Welcome Boulder. Faster and faster it ran, water spouting in a thick torrent out of the pipe. Carrying fragments of cacti, stones, rocks and other debris, the wave gushed into the boulder, making it, at least temporarily, an island on a mountain. Edged along by the flow of mud, the pooled water, the driving rain and the incipient avalanche, the boulder shifted.

That first moment the boulder moved was a giant surprise. It had sat there for centuries, deposited long before the town of Topeth was built, enduring the fierce heat of the day and the cold of the night. It had seen people climb the hill, entering and leaving through South Gate. It had witnessed their ghosts drift by on their way from the cemetery. Having sat in one place for such a long time, it was naturally reluctant to escape its moorings.

The sheer wall of water was like a solid, heaving mass that gushed out of the overflow pipe. The waters swirled around the base of the boulder until gradually it creaked and groaned, and then rolled down the path. With more water gushing out of the cistern pipe, the Welcome Boulder slid towards the cemetery. Picking up speed down the mountain slope, it took with it the blue thorns, plus its precious load of mud, rocks and cacti.

The avalanche mowed Damien and his column down like ninepins. The wall of water and stone and debris plunged down the slope, thundered into his entourage and hurled them, flailing, yelling and screaming for their lives, over the edge of the cliff and into their graves in the river at the base of the ravine, rapidly followed by a wagon covered by a white cloth.

Such was the divine justice Amina had predicted; that Damien would perish in a pool of his own wrongdoing.

After the deluge, the silence.

CHAPTER 24

The Portrait

Opal's aches and pains seemed small compared to the shock of the death of her father. And despite his cruelty, Damien's demise and its bizarre manner had stunned the people.

With bowed heads, Opal joined them in prayer.

"There's been a storm passing over Topeth," Abel said, as if he was in the eye of it, "but now it's gone."

Opal thought it was strange that, amidst this death and destruction, a silver lining was that her brother was now in full command of his faculties. Along with her deliverance from the fires of Moloch, it was a second miracle.

At the entrance to South Gate, Irit and Amina sloshed around in the mud as they tended to the wounded on both sides. One by one, the gravedigger and his mate piled the dead in a donkey cart. Soon they were setting off for the morgue, but the cart was so laden with bodies, the wheels got stuck in the mud.

Sarah cradled Geb like a babe in arms. He was weak and his eyes seemed suddenly empty of life. His head lolled onto his shoulder.

Sarah yelled, "Geb! No! Don't go! You can't go now! You will come back. You must…"

"Mama, he's gone. Let him go in peace," Abel said, closing his father's eyelids with the utmost reverence.

Sarah buried her face in her husband's chest and wept.

As the sun sneaked out from behind the clouds, drying the earth and warming all life with its bountiful rays, Opal hugged her mother, hot tears on both their cheeks. That day, Opal's world stopped spinning momentarily, before slowly, painfully, starting up again. It was a day of new beginnings and old friends, a day when she became Opal and gained a mother and a brother. It was a day she embraced a father she never knew she had and then lost him to fate in the next breath. His death, on the same day she discovered her true patronage, was as uncanny as it was cruel. Her inner voice said:

"Life is given and then taken away.
And in between, we live out our lives every day."

Opal's heart ached at the thought of her dead father. She recalled his kind deeds to her; she had enjoyed the hospitality of his house since arriving and he had earlier today secured her release from prison.

She was shivering in her damp clothes. Abel draped his coat over her shoulders. In this dark, confusing time, it was comforting to have a brother.

Sarah insisted on following the gravedigger and his cart to the chapel. After they saw Geb's body in a suitable place of rest, Abel went off to release Musa while Opal went home with her mother to grieve.

In the late afternoon, the air was hot and moist as the two of them walked through a deserted market square and along quiet alleys where large brown rats scavenged for sodden scraps. Topeth, her new home, was the mountain-top village where free will emerged from Unity. Because of that, it was a special place, but now the town's inner fabric, its reason for being, was unravelling.

At the crossroads, she wandered on ahead, lost in thought.

From behind her, Sarah called out something.

Who was her mother calling? Thinking Sarah was talking to someone else, Opal hobbled on for two or three more steps before her mother called again.

"Opal!"

This time Opal heard her name and stopped dead in her tracks.

She turned quickly and said, "Mother. I'm so sorry. I heard you say something the first time, but the name did not register with me. Please, forgive me. I'm still getting used to my new name."

"I understand," Sarah replied. "I-I still can't believe it, that's why I have to keep saying it out loud. I give thanks that providence saw fit to deliver you into my arms. I surrender to it."

"I'm here with you now," Opal said, taking her mother by the hand. Opal promised herself she would get used to her new name. Tula, her old name, had served her well enough, but Opal had a destiny to fulfil.

The name Opal had barely any history associated with it – at least for her. It represented a clean slate, which was precisely what she needed. She would gladly adopt her new name; Opal it was, Opal it shall be. The name had a gentle rhythm to it, an inner pulse, a soft resonance. Like the semi-precious stone, it was a name that spelt mystery and wonder. It was one she knew she could grow into with relish.

Outside their house, Opal stopped.

"Welcome to your new home," Sarah said.

Opal hesitated.

"What's the matter?" Sarah asked.

"This is a new beginning for me. I have to get used to having a proper home and a real mother. My mother in the city wasn't there for me. A few years ago, when the war began, my foster-father enlisted and went to fight on the plains. We were left behind and had to fend for ourselves. My mother worked even longer hours in the orphanage and I hardly saw her. We were poor and I was often hungry."

"I won't let that happen to you."

Opal crossed the threshold and gazed in wonder at her new home. It seemed pristine in its welcome to her. It was because she belonged here. And her old room awaited her. Opal turned around to see her mother stuck on the threshold, her face ashen with anxiety.

"What's wrong?" Opal's heart was racing.

"It's him, it's Geb." Sarah stood on the threshold, her hand resting on the latch, shaking her head. This was a huge emotional effort for them to come home together. Stepping into the house, her mother headed straight for Geb's portrait on the living room wall.

"Look," Sarah said. "Can't you see?"

Geb's portrait, his eyes and the texture of his skin, were glowing with a subtle luminescence.

"He's here," Sarah whispered, "in spirit."

How was that possible? With her own eyes, Opal had seen him bleed out his life into a Topeth mud pool and escorted him to the chapel. Yet Sarah told no lies. His portrait shone as if the paint had yet to dry.

Sarah stared at the portrait. Her face was transformed; the grieving widow was gone. Her mother appeared as if she had been handed the keys to the heavenly vault and her eyes glowed with the fire of the spirit.

"Geb, tell me, are you safe where you are?" Sarah said and crooked her head to one side as if she was listening to a voice calling from afar.

"I'm glad," Sarah whispered. "Thank you for staying and coming to say farewell."

There was a long pause as Sarah gazed at the portrait, nodding occasionally, and closing her eyes for periods of quiet reflection. She mouthed silent words to Geb's spirit, still roaming the air and at large in the house. As the clairvoyant conversation ebbed and flowed, the expression on Sarah's face flitted between sublime joy and heart-rending grief.

Opal could feel a deep, abiding presence in the room and dared not interrupt. She witnessed this spiritual dialogue, a bridge of words between the world of the living and the world of the dead. The dead could speak. They were… alive. They could communicate from their realm to the realm of the living. It was extraordinary and she was witness to it, as were the goosebumps on her arms.

Opal had always been a keen observer of the natural worlds, of the seasons, the lunar cycles and the movement of the stars. She suspected the laws of Creation were bountiful and full of divine purpose. From an unborn child growing in a mother's womb, a plant growing in the spring, to a galaxy spinning in quiet revolution, she had learnt that there was never any wastage in Creation. Nothing was destroyed, only transformed, often in hidden, unseen ways.

Death was relative, not absolute. A sublime spoonful of god – the spirit – energised the physical body. When the person died, the spirit survived and went to its next port of call, its final destination determined according to what it had done during its life on Earth. In death, as in life, there was no waste, only divine purpose and supernatural justice.

While Opal mused on these matters, Sarah was like a statue. Her mother seemed to be waiting for a clear sign of closure. There was a distinct tension in the room as if Geb's spirit was reluctant to set off on his last journey until… of course, she should have thought of it earlier.

There were heavy, deliberate footsteps outside the house. She opened the front door just as Abel arrived on the threshold.

Her brother was not so little anymore. He seemed taller, leaner and slimmer. She smiled, pleased that her brother, her real brother, had finally loosened the shackles of his youthful adolescence and overcome his childhood trauma.

She asked him, "Did you release…"

"Musa? Yes, he's a free man," Abel interrupted with a broad grin. "You like him, don't you? He's got a few rough edges, but he's a good man."

"I know," she replied.

With Abel in the room, there were three of the family physically present in the house. Without saying a word, Sarah invited them to follow her into the back garden. She stooped to pick a bunch of lilies and led them to a now-familiar place: Opal's grotto. Sarah laid the flowers by the seraphic statue, this time, though, as a wreath of happiness and thanksgiving.

Opal had a lump in her throat. The small ceremony was simple, yet full of charm and warmth. For her mother, these moments were bittersweet; her son and daughter were with her, as was her husband, at least in spirit. For the first time in twelve years, her family was together and yet it was not to be.

187

This was a different healing, a reunion and a parting, all in one. There was a rustle in the leaves, a spiralling vortex of air and then… silence.

Holding Abel's hand and Opal's hand, Sarah glanced up into the late afternoon skies, and whispered, "Goodbye, my love."

As the three of them walked back through the garden, Abel let her hand go and halted by the oak tree. He bent down and delved into the undergrowth.

"Look," he said, pointing to a slither of white reptilian skin on the ground.

They waited. There was nothing to see. Then, a leaf moved as if of its own accord, but it was Miriam the chameleon, her markings now a clear green and black.

Abel shook with emotion.

"So timely," Sarah said, "that she shed her skin at the same time that you did. Both have left the past behind; both of you are renewed."

Opal's inner voice said:

"Do you remember what I prompted you to say to Sarah?"

Yes, I do.

"It has come to pass, so perhaps now you will trust me a little more."

Opal said to Sarah, "Three days ago, you showed me this grotto and I told you then that one day your Abel, who is now my Abel too, would walk in this garden, fully restored."

"And for that, I give thanks!" Sarah said, holding back the tears. "What a day, to lose my soul mate, yet to gain both my children. The Lord gives and the Lord takes away. Will we ever understand the mysteries of life?"

They walked together into the house, which was now empty of Geb's abiding presence, yet renewed with Abel's. Their footsteps echoed on the cool stone floor. Sarah gazed into the corners and looked up into the ceiling as if to catch the last glimpse of the departing spirit of her beloved.

"You carry yourself with a new-found sense of responsibility," Opal said, and patted her brother on the back.

"He has to fulfil an important role in the town," Sarah explained.

"Which one's that?" Opal asked.

"The role of Commander," Sarah replied, with an air of deep satisfaction. "Like that of Head of the Topeth Copper Company, the title passes from the father to the firstborn son. The Commander is chosen by birthright. Abel's the next in line."

"I think I'm ready," Abel said, his voice as clear and strong as the Topeth town bell.

"I know you are," Sarah said. "The town is a dilapidated ruin. It's not your fault, nor was it your father's. You'll have to dig deep to heal its wounds."

"I know, Mother," Abel said. "But I can't do it alone. I need help from the townsfolk and the angels. They'll both provide it, you'll see."

Opal went back to her room to change out of her mud-soaked clothes. She borrowed one of her mother's robes, which smelled of home, glorious home. Only thing was, with her wrists swollen red and raw from the rope bindings, and what seemed like a thousand cuts, bruises and scalds on her body, it took her an age to wash and dress herself.

In the kitchen, Sarah prepared a meal.

As she took her place at the family table, Opal felt dizzy and Abel helped her to her seat.

"I feel so bad about today," Abel said to her. "If we'd been able to get back from Unity earlier, we might have saved you from that ordeal with the bronze god."

"What kept you so long?" Sarah asked.

"First, I had to wait for an opportunity to cross the bridge," Abel replied. "Then it took me a while to find father, who was with Enoch and Kalim. They were tending to Ruth, who was resting. When Enoch didn't come home last night, she worried and, as time passed and he didn't return, she grew more anxious until she fell ill."

"That was unfortunate," Sarah said.

"We waited until she felt better before heading back to Topeth," Abel said.

They ate the rest of the meal in silence, alone with thoughts of what might have been.

The sun was sinking into the horizon when Opal excused herself from the table. Exhausted by the day's trials and tribulations, she climbed the stairs to her room – her old bedroom – where she slept and dreamt.

*

Opal was a little girl, only six years old. Her mother had bought her a lovely pink dress. Opal was so proud to wear it for the Grand Fete. Her father had taken her and Abel there, but amidst the crowd, they had become separated from him.

She and Abel wandered down the snake path. They chased their own shadows, which they never seemed to catch. She ran after butterflies, the flagstones cool on her bare feet, yelping with joy and jumping in the air to try and catch a pretty red and gold one. It seemed to tease her, fluttering around her fingers and gently, languidly, heading off to dance on sunbeams near the bridge. She wished she could dance on sunbeams.

She knew the bridge was special. She was not sure how or why, but her parents talked about it in hushed tones. Anytime they spoke quietly, she had learnt that what they were saying was important. Made of old rope, the bridge sagged in the middle and swayed gently in the wind. It hung in the air and the clouds. The starlings performed some amazing aerial theatrics, first rising high above the bridge on the thermals, then swooping down beneath it and back up above it again in an eternal loop. This excited her because, even for a creature with the gift of flight, it seemed such a dangerous, reckless thing to do.

She liked that the ropey bridge reached all the way over to the other side. It extended the hand of friendship to that other special place, called Unity. It was also special, but she did not know in what way. Her brother said it was the devils. She did not know what a devil was although she had an idea that they were horrible, like the nasty rats which ran around in the alleys.

Standing by the wooden guards' hut, Abel called to her, waving excitedly. He was pointing at something he wanted to show to her. It was a casket. Inside it was a hoard of metal coins with unusual markings on them: a straight line with a curious bend in the middle. It looked like a letter 'z', except this one was a lot longer and scrawnier. Abel accidentally dropped one onto the flagstones and it broke in two. Now, they were in trouble.

She was frightened they would find out that she and Abel had broken the coin, but Abel did not seem worried about it. He picked up both pieces and joined them together. They fitted perfectly, but there was nothing to glue them back again, so he gave her one of the broken pieces and kept the other for himself. They had so many others in the casket, Abel said, they would not miss one.

She tucked her half-coin in the pocket of her pink dress and patted it once, just to make sure it was still there.

Her little brother gathered his butterfly net and chased one through the open gate and onto the bridge itself. He was actually on the bridge, that special place. It could transform him into a mysterious being, a being of wonder like a butterfly or a starling.

Abel was quite at ease on the ropey bridge, his balance was steady and his trust complete. He was playing with the wind and the wind was playing with him. He sauntered along the middle, one hand reaching up to grab the rope stays, the other holding the butterfly net. The bridge was swaying gently like a huge swing made for invisible giants.

Wait. They were not allowed on the bridge. Daddy would tell them off. "Abel! Come back," she cried.

Abel was approaching the other side where the angels lived – or was it the devils? He had not heard her, so she went to fetch him. Anyway, it would be fun to go on the bridge, if only for this one time.

She ran onto it and it shimmied from side to side. The flock of starlings wheeled above her and seemed to peer down at her, mystified that a six-year-old could plod along a ropey bridge that was slung so precariously over a gaping ravine.

The other side of the bridge seemed so far away. Her knees were shaking, and a knot tightened in her stomach. The bridge was swaying this way and that, a plaything of the winds. She thought the bridge was her friend, but she did not like it anymore. She wanted to get off it and her head was spinning.

Abel had got to the far end of the bridge and fallen down. He was hurt. He needed her. Hanging on to the rope stays for dear life, she edged across, step by cautious step. When her feet touched land, she felt good.

Abel was still and lay flat on the ground, face-up.

"Abel," she cried. "Get up, will you?"

His body was shivering as if he was cold, but it was a hot, sunny day. The day of the Grand Fete. She shook him by the arm. His eyes were closed. A colourless froth oozed from his mouth.

"Abel, what's the matter with you?"

No response.

"Are you – ill?"

Yes, that was it. Her brother was ill.

"Wake up, will you?"

His eyes opened.

"Yes. Abel. Say something to me."

"I-I feel bad, Opal," he said, rubbing his head.

She helped him to sit up and lean against the zinc pillar.

After a while, the colour returned to his face and he could stand unaided. They walked side by side, her arm around his waist. Slowly, they shuffled across the bridge. The further they went along it, the narrower it seemed to get. In the middle, Opal felt giddy. The world was spinning. She put down her butterfly net. She wanted to sit down, but there was nowhere safe to do so and Abel was still groggy.

"Can we go now, Opal?" he asked her, his big trusting eyes gazing at her.

She nodded and they edged further along the bridge.

By the time they got back to the flagstones at the Topeth end, she felt good that they had met no devils. The big yellow sun was sinking behind Topeth. Abel was feeling better, but she made sure he rested by the open gate.

He was coming around. He put his hands in his pocket and proudly displayed his half-coin.

She reached into her pocket for hers.

"Mine's gone," she said.

"Where is it? You must find it, Opal."

"I must have dropped it on the bridge. Wait here, I'm going to fetch it."

"Can you do it? On your own?"

"Of course I can. You'll see."

She smoothed the ruffles in her pink dress and adjusted her hairband. She was ready. The bridge was like a lot of coils of rope. She was not afraid of it anymore. The sun was glinting on an object in the middle of the bridge. That was her coin. She grabbed the guide ropes and clung to them with every morsel of her courage.

The wind softened and whispered to her kindly. "Come, Opal. Opal, come."

She liked it when the wind spoke to her.

The presence in the ravine had huge wings. It was invisible, like the wind. But she could feel it, draping its enormous wings around her, keeping her safe from danger. She reached the middle of the bridge. There it was – the half coin with the 'z'-shaped lightning rods. She picked it up. And there was her butterfly net too. In triumph, she strode back to her brother. She was the princess of the bridge.

As she reached him, a man was racing down the snake path.

He had those big strides that important men have. His name was Damien. She did not like Mister Damien. He shouted at her father. He should not do that.

Mister Damien saw her too. She was in big trouble. He had a sour face at the best of times, but now he wore what she called his scrunched-up bitter lemon face.

Opal rushed onto the flagstones to tend to Abel, who still lay on the ground by the open gate.

"You're a very, very naughty girl," Damien said. "You've trespassed on the bridge."

"I didn't pass any trees on the bridge, Mister Damien, promise, sir," she said, feeling flushed with confusion.

"You're coming with me," Mister Damien said to her.

CHAPTER 25

Changing Fortunes

The sun's rays danced through the flimsy curtains as the town bell rang out, waking Opal from her dream. It boomed across the white-washed houses, stone walls and deserted streets of Topeth, waking the townsfolk to a new day. Her eyelids seemed stuck in the down position and her body felt as heavy as the Welcome Boulder. Her knees, palms and feet were sore as hell's fire.

"Opal, you awake?" Abel shouted up the stairs.

"Yes, yes," she said as her eyes jerked open. "What's happened?"

"The town bell's ringing. I'm going to see what the emergency is. You coming?"

"Yes, wait for me."

She cast off her aches and pains and threw on the robe she had borrowed from her mother. As she made her way down the stairs, the soles of her scalded feet moaned like hell, but nothing was going to stop her joining her brother. And her heart ached to see Musa again. Sarah stayed behind. She would join them later.

Opal and Abel soon discovered the source of the emergency; it was South Gate – again. Though this time there was no gunfight; instead, it was Zach.

Vitus and Taurus guarded one side of the open gates, Musa the other. Old man Zach, alongside Amina and Irit, limped along at the head of a long column of bedraggled townsfolk. Abel greeted them as he strode to the front of the column. Opal recognised a few of them – the innkeeper, the waterman, the apothecary and the midwife.

Musa came and squeezed her hand until she pulled it away and blushed like a damsel in distress.

"Glad to see you again," he said. His eyes smiled. Her heart melted.

In the column were makeshift carts with wobbly wheels drawn by donkeys. Rickety wagons were loaded high with a giddy range of items from chests to pieces of furniture and from spades to flagons of water.

Under his hat, Zach wore a hang-dog expression. With dark patches under his eyes, sallow cheeks and a heavy jaw, the vibrant old soak Opal had met five days before was no longer there. He was leading a bunch of refugees, handing Abel a real headache. In the early morning shadows, Opal stood shoulder to shoulder with her brother in the middle of the open gates facing a horde of malcontents.

"Let's talk about this," Abel said.

"Too late for that, lad," Zach grunted, his voice as cold and crisp as winter frost.

"But the quake, it was a sign. It shook up the old and the decrepit. There's going to be a new beginning in Topeth."

"I know, but I'm empty, I'm spent," Zach said. "I've no fight left in my marrow. My daughters are in pieces. We're not alone, as you can see. We all want to escape the tyranny."

"What about you others?" Abel asked.

"We feel the same," Irit said. "I've been through more than enough. And after yesterday and Moloch…"

"But you can't leave," Abel said, a deep frown furrowing his brow. "You're the town doctor. We need you. Please stay."

"I can't," Irit said, holding her daughter tight by the hand. "My father's right, we're beaten. Me, I want to take Esther away from here and make a fresh start elsewhere."

"I can promise you that," Abel said. "Listen to me, all of you. This is the first day of the new Topeth. Yesterday changed everything. We're no longer shackled to the ogres of fear and guilt, shame and regret. Leave them behind and walk forward into a bright future."

"Fine words, from a fine young man," Zach said, wiping his nose with his sleeve. "You've already grown into your new role as Commander. Trouble is, there's nothing left here for you to command."

"That's where you're wrong." Abel's voice was imbued with a thrilling new purpose. "We have a great opportunity here. But we can't do this on our own. We need help. Enoch can provide that."

"How's that? You saw him, he's an old fellow like me," Zach murmured.

"We need the support of the angels. I'm hoping he can intercede with them on our behalf," Abel said.

"Well, good luck with that. We're off," Zach said in a huff.

"What about the donkeys? You can't take them. We'll have no water.

We'll have no town." Abel shifted uneasily from one foot to the other.

"Sorry, they're coming with me." Zach stroked Betty. She snorted and tossed her head. He went on, "The town's a ruin. The copper's been a blight on the soul of the land and now it's caused the death of a child and Jevros, bless his soul. What with yesterday's massacre, I've had enough. Betty and Bethany have too. We're leaving."

"The copper's run out. It's no longer a threat. The mine's abandoned," Abel said. "You'll see, things are going to change around here. It's already happening."

Zach furrowed his brow. "Listen, I've seen changes in my years and lots of them. I've heard promises too. A lot of donkey's poo they turned out to be. I don't see a future for the town. You, Abel, are a good example."

"What do you mean?" Abel asked.

"I'll tell you. Let me start with a question: who's the youngest person in Topeth?"

"Well, now Didi has left, that would be little Esther."

"And she's, what, seven years old? After that, who's the next youngest?"

"That would be me, sir," Abel said.

"And you are?"

"Seventeen," Abel said.

"Here's my point; Topeth doesn't have a nursery. Samuel used to be the schoolteacher, but the building's derelict. Penelope was once the midwife, yet there's been no call for her services for years. Remember that children's toy shop near Copper Gate? That went bust too. You'll find most of the toys from the shop on the town rubbish heap. So, what I'm saying is, other than Esther, there are no children in Topeth. And that's why I say there's no future here. That's why we're leaving."

"But... you can't," Abel said, clenching his fists. Passion oozed from his every word. "Damien is no more. Wincorn's gone. The quake split the Temple of Moloch in two. We've wiped the slate clean. And look, my big sister is back in Topeth. See the changes in me. They're because of her. She's a shining light. She's proof the angels and the heavenly powers have not abandoned us, and that, in them, we have mighty friends. It's a start. We're getting our town back. The tide's turning. It's no longer ebbing. It's flowing back in towards us, you'll see. Help me make it happen. Stay and let's work together to rebuild it."

Opal remembered her first encounter with Abel; there he was, cowering in the corner of a shop front, frightened by his own shadow and shrunk by the enormity of life. Now, transformed, he was commanding in his presence and was commending the virtues of his hometown.

"That may be," Zach replied, shaking his head wearily. "I don't want my daughters to stay here anymore. They've endured enough. Irit has lost her husband and her baby. Amina can't wait any longer for Kalim and is coming with us. She's not the only woman refusing suitors; there's Penelope and others. The women fear bringing children into a world only to have them passed through the fire. And we all mourn your father's passing. He was a good Commander and loved by all of us. But after the terrible incident with you on the bridge twelve years ago, he forfeited the leadership of the town to that ogre, Damien."

"An ogre, was he?" a voice cried out.

It was Taurus. Who else?

"What do you want?" Abel snapped and stood face to face with his foe.

"I might ask you the same question," Taurus said.

"What are you talking about?" Abel said.

"You know what I'm talkin' about, *Commander*," Taurus mocked.

"Yes, I am the new Commander," Abel said, puffing out his chest.

"And I'm the boss of the Topeth Copper Company," Taurus said. His voice oozed even more arrogance than usual.

"That may be," Abel said. "But you're inheriting empty workings and a pile of slag heaps."

"We'll see about that, puny little Abel. 'Cos you're gonna do as *I* say, just like your father danced to my uncle's tune."

Abel gritted his teeth.

As did old Zach, who turned to the column of refugees, brandished his walking stick and cried, "I've heard enough. This family feud never ends. We're leaving. Step away from the gates. Let us pass."

"Zach. Wait. I'm in charge now." Abel's voice was firm and unwavering. "As long as I'm Commander, the copper workings will stay shut. More than that, we'll heal the scars on the landscape and renew the slopes. And that's the job for you, Taurus."

"Dunno about that, *Commander* Abel."

"Why not? You incited the riots against the mine. You were a leading voice against the copper workings. Grow up and help us heal the land."

"Yeah, I could do it. But work with you? You're just a weak and stupid boy."

"Not anymore. Listen. This is what I'm going to do. First, we'll bury my father with all the honours due to a loyal and faithful servant of Topeth. Then we'll clean up the town and remove the waste, starting with that bronze monstrosity. Piece by piece, I'll tear it down. We can be normal again. With no fear of child sacrifice, we can have children and hear their excited little voices in the kindergarten. Samuel, Penelope, stay with us, we'll need your services again soon enough. Zach's right: the feud between the two strands of our family stops. Now.

"Once, Topeth was 'The Top' town," Abel continued. "Herman led the people here to exercise the gift of free will. We've abdicated from that vision, but I'll take us back to our original purpose. Our ancestors gave us the means to do that. See, it's there on the hill: the Acropolis. Stone by stone, we'll restore it to its former glory. After that, we'll read the runes and seek guidance from the angels. They'll show us how to align ourselves again to the great universal plan. That's how we employ our free will with responsibility."

This seemed to inspire the crowd of refugees, who bent an interested ear. Even Zach nodded in agreement.

"I knew you'd suggest that," Taurus said. "Your father was always lookin' to the past. You're just the same; you promise lots but deliver nothin'."

Opal stepped in. "You're a bully who hides in dark alleys, picking on the vulnerable. You and Luca and the rest of your group, you're baboons. And Abel's not so weak now, is he?"

"I'm the boss of Topeth," Taurus scoffed.

"My father has gone, bless his soul," Abel said. "But so too have the rest of the old guard, Damien and Wincorn. This is the moment for a fresh start for Topeth. In this new beginning, let's see who the people want in charge, you or me?"

One by one, the crowd chose their leader by standing behind them.

Opal was the first to join Abel. Musa followed her, brushing her hand with his, sending frissons of excitement up and down her arm. Amina was next. Then Samuel and Penelope. Luca and the baboons joined Taurus. As more people stood behind Abel, Taurus's face morphed into an ugly frown. Most of the town joined Abel. A few had stood with Taurus. By the end, only Vitus, Zach and Irit were undecided.

"Who are you supporting, Vitus?" Abel asked.

The old man said nothing but slowly shuffled over towards him.

"Pa, where you goin'?" Taurus asked.

Vitus pointed his walking stick at his son and said, "You... you're a good boy, at least you can be if you want to be. But one thing's for sure, you ain't no leader."

"Ha, my own pa turnin' on me," Taurus scoffed. "Go back to ya' whittlin', you old fool."

"Now, everyone can see the kind of person you really are," Abel said.

"Well done, Vitus." Zach went over and patted him on the back. "Oh, and this showing of support's good enough for me. I've changed my mind. I'm staying."

"Me too," Irit said, joining her father behind Abel. "At last, there's a future worth fighting for. I'll stay for that. I'll be part of the town's healing, in more ways than one."

"These people share my vision," Abel said. "I'm going to remove the gate from the bridge and call it by its original name, Via Angelica, the Angels' Way."

"No!" Taurus said through gritted teeth. "The bridge ain't gonna be renamed. It won't re-open, no, never. It's worse than the mines. It's full of them devils. There's only one thing left to do."

"What's that?" Opal asked.

"Wait here and I'll show you, it'll make a pretty sight," Taurus said, snatching the reins of a horse. He jumped into the saddle and galloped off along the town walls.

"He's heading for Bridge Gate," Opal said.

"What's he going to do?" Abel asked.

"Whatever it is," Opal said, "I don't like the look of it. Get after him. Stop him."

A knot twisted in the pit of her stomach and she bit her bottom lip.

Abel ran after him. Exhausted from the trauma of the day before, Opal plumbed the depths of her soul to find the energy and the will to follow him. She was about to set off when something warm and wet nuzzled into her palm.

"Oh, Bethany, it's you," she cried, stroking the jenny. "Zach was right. You do know me, don't you? And now I remember you. Before, when I was a little girl in Topeth, you were my best friend, my best animal friend."

"Here, Miss, let me help you," Musa said, giving her a leg-up to mount Bethany.

"Dear Beth, though I forgot you, you never forgot me," she said. "That's true loyalty."

"'Tis that," Musa agreed.

Ahead of them, Taurus galloped, whooping and yelling like a demon from Gehenna down the snake path, and was soon leaping off the horse onto the flagstones. He tethered the animal to the copper pillar.

Musa led Bethany and Opal to the top of the snake path. Abel was ahead of them, halfway down.

Frantically, Taurus ran around the flagstones collecting a handful of leaves and dropped them next to the rope bridge in a mound. Then he scooped some more onto the same mound. Backwards and forwards he went like a man possessed, racing around the damp flagstones collecting debris.

Opal and Musa reached the flagstones, directly behind Abel.

"What's Taurus doing?" Opal asked.

"He's mad. He's building a fire," Abel said.

Taurus pulled a thin strand of rope from the bridge itself and adjusted its height so that the end sat above the kindling, to act as a rudimentary fuse. If the rope strand caught fire, it would quickly spread and the whole bridge would go up in flames. A pretty sight for some, but not for her!

Taurus delved into his pocket and drew out his iron and flint.

A stone's throw away, Abel shouted, "Stop!"

Taurus stuck the iron against the flint. The subtle spark arched across the gap towards the tinder, grabbed onto it and hungrily devoured it. The kindling was alight and the lithe, yellow-orange flames kissed the bottom of the rope strand. The flames singed it. He waved his hands back and forth against the kindling, fanning the small flame, which stubbornly refused to travel up the strand.

Abel lunged towards him, like a cat springing on its prey. Taurus turned away from the fire to fight him off. The two young men rolled around, grunting and groaning, pummelling each other, perilously close to the low stone wall protecting the edge of the gorge.

Panting, sweat pouring from his brow, Musa let go the donkey tether, ripped off his shirt and smothered the kindling fire. With his bare hands, he squeezed the life out of the tiny flame on the rope strand. Opal slid off Bethany.

Abel and Taurus were grappling in the wet earth, pawing at each other like a couple of angry bears.

Musa grabbed Taurus and rolled him over on his side. Abel held Taurus down while Musa tied his hands behind his back.

Opal held up the strand of charred, blackened rope. "The fire didn't catch because the rope strand and the tinder were still moist from the storm. Saved by rain in one of the driest places in the area. It's a sign, an omen. It's got to be."

"Superstitious nonsense," Taurus said, clearly unrepentant. "You know why I just tried to burn down your precious bridge? It's a bridge of sighs, that's what it is. You ever stalked a lion in them mountains? No, well, I 'ave. The bridge is like one of them scrawny, old mountain lions. They're tired an' weary of life. They're dyin' for someone to put 'em out of their misery. That's what this bridge is; old and waitin' to die, past its time."

"The bridge stays, it's part of our great heritage," Abel said.

"Nah, that's rubbish." Taurus was indignant.

"Listen to me," Abel said. "For years, your Uncle Damien pushed your father to exploit the mine. Until your father had the accident that cost him his sight. And you've never forgiven your uncle for doing that, have you?"

Taurus puffed out his cheeks. "He's gone, Damien, 'asn't 'e? Besides, what's it got to do with you?"

"Not much. Except, today, you're going to pay for your crimes. Lock him up, will you?"

As he was led away, Taurus delivered his Parthian shot. "I'll see you in hell."

Vitus tapped his stick, and everyone turned to hear him. "This is my town too. I'm fed up with them scars on the land. I can't see 'em, but I sure as hell can feel 'em. They're like an ache in my old bones. But my family caused 'em, so I'm gonna clear 'em up."

"So, you'll take the job? Head of the Topeth Copper Company?" Abel asked.

Vitus nodded. "I done it before and with my son and brother gone, it falls to me."

"Pleased to hear you taking responsibility for your actions and those of your family," Abel said. "The town will help you as much as we can."

Word of her brother's dream of a new Topeth had spread like the wings of a dove of peace around the alleys and byways of the town. The refugees from Zach's column joined the townsfolk at the bridgehead.

Opal stared longingly at the bridge gate. Unity was near, her dream so tantalisingly close. But so was Musa. He was even closer. He sidled over towards her, a big smile on his face and a mischievous glint in his eyes. He pressed his hand in hers. His firm touch gave her a warm glow inside. She blushed from ear to ear. Once again, he had danced into her heart with surprising ease.

"I like you. Do you like me, Miss?" he whispered in her ear.

She looked up at those pools of manhood and took a deep breath. This young man was intruding into her dreams. This was getting serious.

"I-I," she murmured. "I like you and I like how you make me feel. But…"

"But, what?" he asked.

"But the prophecy…"

"What's one of them?"

Before she could tell him, Abel called out, "Musa, put my sister down and come and help us out here. We want to cross the bridge now. Take this gate down, will you?"

With a wistful smile, Musa let go of her hand. To great applause from the crowd, he strode over to the bridge gate and in what seemed like no time at all, removed its hinges and laid it down to one side. Everyone could see the bridge. In the mid-morning sun, it resembled a long, dried-out piece of curved bone.

"There it is," Abel announced. "We're going across to Unity."

"All of us?" Musa asked.

"Well, yes," Abel said. "If you want to."

"After all these years," Irit said, her face screwed into a ball of worry. "How do we know the devils have just gone away? They'll drive us all insane, won't they?"

"I understand your fears," Abel said. "But listen. Yesterday, I went across the bridge and came back. Look at me, I'm sane and I'm unharmed, aren't I?"

"Well, yes, I suppose so," Irit said. "But I'll never forget that the devils killed my Jevros. I'll never cross the bridge and nor will Esther. You go, but don't ask us to join you."

"Irit," Opal said, turning to speak to her. "When I had dinner at your house, your husband's spirit spoke to me. He told me he couldn't face himself for letting your daughter's life slip through his hands. He thought he had failed his daughter, not only as her father but as her doctor. The guilt and shame were driving him mad. Before he did something he regretted, he took himself away and made sure nothing untoward happened to you and Esther. That had nothing to do with the devils."

"I believe you," Irit said. "And in my deepest fears, I suspected as much. I-I can't talk about it… about him. Not yet. It's too close, too raw, too soon."

"Mummy, don't cry," Esther said, nuzzling up to her.

Irit pulled herself together and said, "I-I'll still stay here with Esther, but please go across. You, and all of you, go with my blessing."

"I hate heights," Opal said. "But I simply have to go."

"I'm comin' too," Musa said.

"After the quake, is it safe?" Vitus asked.

"It is, I can vouch for that," Abel said, slapping Vitus on the back. "At least, there are no cracks in the rocks on either side of the ravine that I can see."

"Good enough for me," Vitus admitted.

"And for me," said Sarah, who had just arrived.

The door of the guard's hut swung open and into the poignant moment strolled a bold, feline tabby, her curiosity aroused by the hubbub.

"Tabitha," Opal said.

The shy tabby sidled towards her and veered off to rub her supple body around Sarah's ankle.

"She already knows who's got her meal," her mother replied, extracting a wrapped morsel of paper from her bag and handing it to Opal.

"Here it is, sweetie," Opal said, unwrapping the paper and placing it on the ground in front of the cat. "That's what I said I'd do, and I always keep my promises."

Tabitha did not hear a word; she was too busy eating her fish.

CHAPTER 26

Via Angelica

With a warm smile, Abel invited Opal to lead the procession across the bridge. As she approached, the morning breeze brushed her face and hair. Sarah, Musa and what seemed like the whole of Topeth clustered behind her, chattering away like the dawn chorus about the dramatic events of the day before and the promise of what was to come.

Musa played a tune on his flute, full of clean air and brilliant sunlight, dispelling the dark clouds of doubt and suspicion. It fuelled the passion and the exhilaration that epiphany naturally brought in its wake. People danced spontaneously and hummed along to the jaunty song.

Zach clapped his hands. Irit joined in, keeping time. Ripples of applause spiralled around the bridge. The temple drummers beat out a driving rhythm, filling the ravine with a crescendo of noise, scaring the devils, if they were ever there in the first place.

Just as she steadied herself, her mother tapped her on the shoulder, saying, "You asked me to bring you this."

And handed her a small bag. Opal looked inside the bag and smiled. Tucking the bag in her pocket, she said, "Yes, I did. And thank you for remembering."

Then she turned to face her nemesis, the bridge spanning the yawning chasm, inviting her into a new future. Twelve years before, Opal had crossed it and here she was again; except that now the path was clear and the way ahead, uncluttered. This moment fulfilled her dreams and spawned a few more.

She paused at the difficult first step. Her inner voice reminded her:

"You are not alone."

"You've been my guide, my nurse and my muse. You encouraged me to leave the city. You urged me to come to Unity and seek out the angels. Yet, in all this time, I still don't know your name."

The reply was like the soft wingbeat of a starling. *"My name is Auriga."*

"Auriga, please tell me. When I was alone in that oven, I could have done with your help, but you weren't there for me."

There was a pregnant pause before Auriga replied:

"Never doubt that I was with you at every moment. I didn't speak because I was applying all my powers to ease your pain and lessen your wounds."

"I-I didn't know," Opal said. "Thank you."

With a clear conscience, Opal reached up to grasp the guide ropes with trembling hands. She had a lump in her throat and a tear in her eye. Spanning the abyss, the bridge was before her. All of Topeth was behind her, expectant. It was one hundred steps across – a short distance but a long way.

The entirety of the seraphic members of heaven held their breath. This was when humans and angels, the two great works of the Creator, could take up their rightful union, re-consummate their ethereal marriage and see their future unfold in purpose, peace and harmony.

She took her first tentative step. It was as if the bridge had its own life, its own rules and that she had to respect them, be equal to them, otherwise it would reject her and throw her into the abyss. She feared that the bridge, like some feral, supernatural entity, would secretly read her deepest fears and promptly give way beneath her feet.

Her heart raced. Beneath her foot, the bridge held. Beneath her weight, her ankle held. A wave of relief washed through her.

Auriga said:

"You can do this. Just remember, don't look down."

She took a second step, sliding her foot along the thick main rope cable.

Auriga, why is this so difficult?

"You are entering the mists of the bridge's unfortunate history. They swirl around it like a devil, sowing doubt and confusion in their wake. But devils do not exist in their own right. Devils are inventions of people's imagination, the ill-fated products of anxiety, fear and trauma. You are real, the devils are not. They are ethereal. Only if you give them credence do they have power over you."

A third step. A pressure clamped her chest and she struggled to breathe.

"I can't go on," she said. Her limbs were leaden. Her body was wracked by aches and pains. The soles of her feet were swollen and blistered.

I can go back. Yes, I don't need to do this. I can try again tomorrow. I can go back to the city. I can...

"Remember, you are not a 'Little Tulip Seed'. You are Opal. You must go on. Use the power of your free will to have it so."

I'll… I'll try.

Opal gritted her teeth and took another step. She edged across the bridge, not daring to look down, not daring to look up, clinging for all her worth to the shoulder-high rope stays.

The flock of starlings seemed even larger than before. They seemed to have come out in their thousands to watch her, to be with her, every step of the way. They dived and swirled in and out of the unseen clouds of force that shifted above and below the bridge. Each one enjoyed the freedom of the air, the freedom of the spirit, the freedom of being alive. Their soft whispering aerial dance inspired her to go on. So did Auriga, who said:

"This isn't only for you. You're doing this for all the people."

Guided by the support, she took the fourth step. The pressure on her chest lifted. The knot in her stomach eased.

This crossing joined two pieces of land and two different realms, that of mankind and that of the angels, the realm of 'to do' and the realm of 'to be', both needing the other to grow, both working by a natural mutuality, like a man and a woman. That there was still a bridge between them was one miracle. That she was on the bridge, crossing it, was another.

She went on; a fifth, a sixth step. She was doing it. She was actually doing it.

The bridge could not take everyone's weight, so the rump of the crowd stayed on the flagstones, while at first only her brother and mother followed her at a distance, with Musa behind them.

As well as Auriga's promptings, a huge wave of emotional support from the citizens of Topeth pushed her forward and nearly lifted her off her feet. She glided along to the midpoint, the exact spot where, as a little girl, she had retrieved her half of the sigil.

Grabbing the bag her mother had given her, she emptied its contents – a couple of handfuls of birdseed – onto the ridged matting. She risked a glance up to see the starlings weaving above and below the bridge, exhibiting the natural wonder of their aerial prowess.

"There," she said to them. "This is a thanksgiving for the help you gave me on the ledge."

She gazed along the spectacular ravine, the two cliffs like gigantic walls of water, frozen in time like the parting of the Red Sea, separated by a thin tranche of air. Cradled in the palms of the heavenly powers, a few strands of rope saved her from a fatal fall.

In the morning heat, she pressed on, encouraged by her own defiance. At two-thirds across, she glanced back to the Topeth end. Impatient for her to cross, the crowd shouted and waved at her.

"*Go on. You're nearly there,*" Auriga said.

When Opal reached the Unity end, she was virtually dancing, her feet were so sure. She grasped the rope stays, as thick as a man's thigh, fastened tight to one of the famous zinc pillars.

Enoch and Kalim were waiting to greet her. Next to them was a woman of Enoch's age; her eyes had a warm twinkle as if she was glowing from inside. Her brown, wavy hair rested gently on her shoulders. She carried herself with an easy natural dignity.

Opal knew who it was and blurted out her name, "Ruth!"

"Yes, dear. That's me," Ruth said. "Well done. You've made it across."

Out of respect, Opal bowed her head.

"Welcome to Unity," Enoch said. "I was so sorry to hear about your terrible ordeal yesterday. But here your wounds will be healed."

"Oh, I hope so," she replied. "My ankle has already got better. Thank you so much for that."

"The angels taught me how to heal by touch alone," Enoch replied.

Opal was about to reply when Abel and Sarah arrived.

"And here is another walking miracle," Enoch said. "At last, you've shed that unwanted skin and you're representing the town with your father's honour and dignity."

"Thank you, sir," Abel said. "After my big sister came home, it was as if a dormant part in me came back to life. I feel rejuvenated and now I'm keen to rectify the town's mistakes. That's why I want to apologise; Damien was wrong to steal the gold rods."

"There are many things the people of Topeth should not have done," Enoch said.

"I've already sent a search party down to Seliga to look for the corpses of all the men who lost their lives yesterday," Abel said. "They'll also bring the gold rods back here. We'll make them look like new and put them on the temple roof."

"By all means retrieve the gold rods from the valley, but it won't be necessary to put them back," Enoch said. "Instead, I suggest you use the proceeds from their sale to regenerate the town and rebuild the Acropolis. That's what your father wanted, too."

Abel replied, "Yes, it was. But the rods belong in Unity. I don't understand why you don't want us to return them."

"The gold angels have done their work here and are leaving," Enoch said.

"Gold angels? Leaving? Why's that?" Opal interrupted. "I've come a long way to be here. I want to serve them."

"Everything is timing," Enoch said. "Angels give permission to mankind. The gold angels worked by constraint, confinement and constriction. In response, mankind has populated their world with guilds and institutions, religions and social classes which are all organised in a hierarchical way like a pyramid. To succeed in this world, a person must meet the requirements of that guild or that profession. That's the figurative meaning of the lightning rods; the more a person ascends the rods, the more permission they have, but they must climb the rods in a prescribed way. If they don't, they're excluded and fall back down to the bottom of the lightning rod.

"The gold angels belong to the previous epoch, whose sands have run out," Enoch went on. "Their established ways are no longer fit for purpose. Yesterday's structures are breaking down into their separate parts, ready to be reformed and recombined to meet the needs of tomorrow. Unity is no longer the order of the day. Today is all about multiplicity."

"And that's why? Is that it?" Opal asked. "I've spent a good part of my life dreaming of being near to these angels and when I finally enter their home, their place of residence, you tell me they're leaving." She found it hard to swallow the bitter pill of her disappointment.

"Their service here has come to an end," Enoch said.

"Why? What's brought this about?"

"The gold angels from the old epoch have brought humanity as far as they can," Enoch explained. "Though, if truth be told, mankind has not come as far along that path as the Creator would have wanted or expected, no, nowhere near it."

Before she could ask another question, more townsfolk arrived, interrupting the flow of the conversation. They stepped onto the flagstones with such reverence, it was as if the very earth itself was sacred to them. Musa, Vitus and Zach were at the front of the excited, incredulous crowd.

She touched Musa's hand by way of a greeting and turned back to Enoch to ask, "How did we end up like that?"

"You folk here in Topeth were the first people on Earth granted free will," Enoch said. "But after the exodus, you chose a path with no soul and lost your way down a dead-end. The low point was the desecration of the land in the copper workings. As the metals are torn out, the angels can hear and feel the land cry in pain. It makes them move away. If your hand gets too near the flames, it burns the skin, and the instinctive reaction is to move your hand away. It's the same for them in their realm when people rape the earth."

"I-I wasn't here for the copper mining," she murmured.

207

"I know, you're innocent of that," Enoch said. "But you people of Topeth are not. You became familiar with and contemptuous of the spiritual assistance offered by the gold angels. You stopped treating it with reverence. Despite that, the angels have tried to help."

"You mean the box and the message?" Abel said.

"Yes," Enoch said with a knowing smile. "Abel, when I left the box on the bridge, I saw you on the flagstones at the Topeth end. What were you doing there?"

"I had inched along the ledge from the cemetery," Abel said. "I liked to sneak onto the bridge when no one was looking, just to get nearer to the angels. Ever since meeting them all those years ago, I wanted to get close to them and to requite their love."

"The angels have tried other ways," Enoch went on. "Have you noticed the blue carpet they laid between South Gate and the cemetery?"

"The blue carpet? You mean the blue thorns?" Opal asked. She loved being near those flowers.

Enoch nodded. "As supernatural beings, the angels heal themselves and the land in different ways. They suffered in the face of the people's abdication from the correct path of free will. These tough little thistle flowers are the angels' way of easing that suffering."

"That's extraordinary," Opal said. "It's the same thing Zach was talking about when he said poppies grow where blood's been spilt."

"And see over there," Enoch pointed to the sheer wall of rock on the Topeth side of the ravine. There, high into the cliff, above the ledge between the cemetery and the flagstones, were carved two words:

Thou Mayest.

"Herman and his people were allowed free will," Enoch said, "the permission to choose the way the Creator had selected for them or not. To tread the true path or deviate from it. That is what is implied by these two words – 'Thou Mayest'. Amongst all the other paths, the true path is narrow and hard to find. No one has followed it for a long time. Now, finally, someone has set their feet upon it. And that is you, Opal."

"Me? Are you sure?" she asked. "I'm not perfect."

"You're not meant to be," Ruth said. "That's why you were sent an angel, a messenger."

"A messenger?" Opal asked.

"You didn't know? Her name is Auriga."

"*You* sent her?"

"Well, what happened is that you called for her and so she attends you," Ruth explained. "And she continues to do so because of one thing."

"What's that?"

"Because you listen to her promptings."

Goosebumps ran up and down her arms. When her tongue decided to work again, Opal said, "I didn't know. How did I call for her? I don't remember doing that."

"Words – through song, chant, or poetry – are only one way to summon things," Ruth said. "You can also call by the strength of your emotions, your feelings, your passion."

"I'm so pleased. I just want to make a difference."

"We hope you can too," Enoch said. "Topeth descended into a sickness of mind and superstition, culminating in the establishment of COIL, the heinous Temple of Moloch and in those odious beliefs in devils. Jevros's death was tragic. When a person commits suicide, it erases their astral record, the complete trace of their life history. It's as though they never existed. Suicide is a symptom of a deeper sickness, a sign that the society has departed from its intended path. When its wrath is turned onto its most innocent – its future, namely its children – then that society is wandering in the wilderness. It has abdicated from its endeavour to be human, to be humane and to be wise. After they reprieved Amina and they came for you, Opal, Ruth and I had to intervene."

"You saved my life, and for that I am eternally grateful. I want to show my respect, not to you, but to what you must have done and the disciplines to which you must have adhered, to be who you are."

"We hear you," Enoch said.

"When you rescued me from prison," Opal asked, "why didn't you keep me with you and bring me up yourselves? How did I end up in the city of all places?"

"We couldn't live in Unity," Enoch said. "Because eventually Damien and Wincorn would have spotted us and we would have been found far sooner than we were. We settled in a croft in Suria, close to Unity but well out of sight of prying eyes in Topeth. You were too young for that rugged life and so we thought you would be safer in the city. So, the night we freed you from prison, we trekked into the mountains. There we left you with a shepherd who promised to take you to the city and find you a family."

"I must have a mental block because I don't remember any of that," Opal said. So, she was a foundling, had suffered from a swollen ankle, and had witnessed her father's death; how strange was the nature of her journey through life?

"This visit to Unity," Abel said, "has been most extraordinary. I think everyone can see what we've been missing all these years. We want to recommence our covenant with the angels. We want to rebuild the Acropolis and seek guidance there from the angels about our future."

Enoch cleared his throat and replied, "It will be possible, but not yet."

"Why not?" Abel said, his face a mix of surprise and disappointment.

"Your people have a long way to go before that can happen," Enoch said.

"Tell us what we must do, and we'll do it," Abel said.

"Angels are supremely powerful. To engage with them takes care and preparation," Enoch said. "They are like machines in that they follow rules with no deviation. They lack subtlety and finesse. They yearn for the wisdom and the kindness and consideration that mankind can teach them.

"Angels can be healing and enhancing to be with, but it can also be fraught with danger and even fatal. If you are under-developed or seriously imbalanced, their high angelic force will burn you, like the legend of the man who flew too close to the sun, melting his wings. Or, if you use its potency for selfish ends, that same angelic force can freeze you, close your throat and you'll choke to death. You saw that happen to Wincorn, your High Priest. So, please, for the safety of you all, you must wait."

"This is a fair warning and I understand now," Abel said.

"You must earn their trust," Enoch replied. "There are bridges to build, harmonies to rekindle and love to engender. You can do this and soon you'll commune with them."

Amina shoved her way to the front of the crowd.

"Wait," she said. "No one's going anywhere until I talk to my Kalim."

"I'm here, my beloved," Kalim replied, stepping over towards her.

"I can see that," she murmured, folding her arms. No one dared move or make a sound. "You've been here for days on end. Why haven't you come to see me?"

"I couldn't leave Unity. Besides, I sent you a message, a token of my love," Kalim replied, his voice shot with surprise.

"The sigil," Amina said. "Yes, Enoch gave it to me."

"And?"

"Well, are you staying in Unity forever?"

"No, beloved," Kalim replied, his eyes moist with emotion. "See, Ruth has recovered. Didn't you know I was tending to her while Enoch was in prison? She was so worried about him; I couldn't leave her alone in that state."

"It's true," Ruth confirmed. "Without Kalim, I don't know what I'd have done. He's a good man, a natural healer."

"Listen," Kalim said, his hands clasping his heart. "I'm ready to come back to help rebuild Topeth. Above all, I'm ready to share our love. With Moloch gone, we can bring the little ones into the world. You and I can start a family of our own. I want to do that with all my heart and soul. And I want to spend the rest of my life with you – in Topeth."

Kalim bent his knee and raised his hands in supplication to her. "My beautiful, headstrong Amina, will you marry me?"

There was a pregnant pause, with all eyes on Amina.

"I will," she said. "Now get up and give me a big hug."

She melted into his arms. Kalim's eyes twinkled like the evening star. He lifted her off the ground and twirled her round and round, as she whooped for joy. The happy couple kissed as everyone celebrated their union with a loud cheer before breaking into the Song of Topeth.

"Congratulations," Abel said. "That's the first betrothal on the soil of Unity for over a thousand years!"

"Come, everyone. We need to leave these good people in peace," Abel said and turned to leave.

Opal lingered at the back of the procession. While waiting to cross the bridge, she dreamed of all that had happened to her on her most incredible of journeys. The next thing she knew, only she, Sarah, Abel and Musa remained on the Unity side.

"Remind me please, Miss. What's this thing about a pro-phecy? Is that how you say it? I ain't much good at words and things like that," Musa said.

"Yes," Opal said. "This is it.

That you are the key,
With the angels of Unity.
When two becomes three,
A new epoch there will be."

"I dunno what that means," Musa said.

"I think I do, Musa," she said. "I think it means I'm to be with you."

"You do?" Musa said, his eyes shining like diamonds. "Well, that's good. Listen, I ain't much good at stuff like this," Musa said, bending a knee in front of her. "But I wanna ask for your hand, I really do. Ever since I saw you, I been stricken, stricken good, stricken like I never been before. I'm all nervous around you and I wanna be with you."

"I-I feel the same."

"You do? That's wonderful."

"Will you be mine?"

There was a momentary pause, within which the hands of destiny moved on another notch and in which Enoch, old man Enoch, coughed and cleared his throat, and said, "You're a free person, Opal, and you and Musa will be happy together, but there's more at stake here. When we were in Topeth, you asked me if you could come to Unity and serve the angels. I said you weren't ready."

She glanced hesitantly at Musa, his face ripe with expectancy, then back at Enoch.

"Are you… are you saying that I'm ready now?"

"I am, yes. That's exactly what I'm saying."

"If I'm to stay in Unity, the prophecy talks of two becoming three. Who are the two then?"

"We are, Ruth and me," Enoch said. "We're not as young as we were, and now you're finally here, you can be the third in the trio. The prophecy says you are the key, doesn't it? We can't make you stay, because true service, service to the higher realm, is always voluntary and freely given. Is this still what you want?"

"I did for a long time, but now, with Musa, and everything that's happened, I-I don't know anymore," she said.

"I didn't mean it to come out like this, where you gotta choose, but there it is," Musa said.

"I know you didn't, dearest Musa," Opal said.

This was the most important decision of her life and as she stood there, watching the throng file across the bridge back towards their home in Topeth, she did not know what to do. In such a short time, she had grown fond of Musa and was enraptured by the prospect of raising a family with him, but making a trio with Ruth and Enoch was equally attractive.

Which one should she choose: Musa or Ruth and Enoch? She looked for a sign and, this time, Auriga was quiet. Even the starlings had vacated the skies.

If she went back to Topeth with Musa, she would be with her family – Abel and Sarah. They too needed her help, Abel to rebuild Topeth and Sarah, well, her mother had suffered her absence for twelve years. Opal could be near her and that would be a comfort to her as she grieved for Geb. But what if that was the wrong choice? What if she was destined all along to be in Unity with the angels? The prophecy said that she was the key with the angels in Unity. But she could still serve the angels and be with Musa in Topeth, couldn't she?

The angels were leaving. That was what Enoch had said. And once they had gone, would they come back? Would they leave mankind alone and without protection? If she made the wrong choice now, what of the future? Look at what had happened to Topeth when they had tried to live without the guidance of the angels. The people had descended into the pot of greed, avarice and lust. Without the help of the angels, mankind would spiral into a worse situation than they were in now. The bad days of Topeth would return; Moloch, child sacrifice, with no bulwark against a heady spiral into evil.

She paused. Her mind was like a blank canvas. She went quiet inside, waiting for a sign, the sign. It came as a quiet, almost imperceptible, whisper:

"Without the three in Unity,
Mankind will never be free."
Thank you, thank you Auriga. It's crystal clear.

"Well? You comin'?" Musa asked, offering her his hand. This time, she didn't take it.

"Musa, no, I'm sorry, I'm not coming with you to Topeth. I can't," she said, listening to the words as they came from her mouth.

"You sure about that?"

"As sure as I can be," she said. "It's always been my destiny to be in Unity. Here, I'm going to help in the endeavour to free mankind of its self-imposed shackles."

"I dunno what that means, Miss," Musa said. "But I reckon you're sayin' the angels' need, Enoch and Ruth's need, is greater than mine."

"Oh, my Musa."

He turned to leave, and she raced in front of him, spread her arms out wide, and hugged him. After what seemed like an age, he gently let go of her and stepped cautiously onto the bridge.

"You definitely going then?"

"Gotta," he said. "It's for the best. I can't stay and you can't go. Besides, your brother's gonna need my 'elp."

Abel nodded. "Yes, I do."

With sorrow, she shook her head as he turned and shuffled across the bridge. She watched him traverse it and with each step he took, a droplet of love fell from her heart. She had never felt anything like this loss. A scourge on her soul, her limbs felt as heavy as lead and her heart felt numb with pain. When he got to the Topeth side, he turned and waved to her, and then merged into the crowd waiting on the flagstones.

For her, this was a deeply poignant moment, a decision made, a heart broken, but a destiny fulfilled, and an epoch saved.

With only Abel and Sarah remaining, she now had to face saying goodbye to her close family.

She stood before her brother.

213

"I'm going to say goodbye by giving thanks for a gift received and by returning something that belongs to you," Abel said, holding her hand. His were warm, soft and firm.

"First then, thank you so much for giving me back the gift of my life."

"I didn't do that," she murmured.

"Oh, but you did," he said. "If you hadn't come back to Topeth, if you had not rescued me in that alley, if you had not believed in me, I would still be half-asleep, cocooned in the bindings of that moment on the bridge, twelve years ago. You have done me the greatest favour – you have given me a second chance at life, one that I am going to relish."

She squeezed his hand.

"And here," he said, delving into his pocket, "I am returning something of yours." He pressed into her hand a small half-coin, the lightning rod sigil.

She smiled with her eyes and whispered, "Thank you."

She turned to Sarah. "This is awful, Mother. I hardly know you and I so want to make up for lost time. I'll come and see you at every opportunity, I promise."

"You'll always be in my heart… and in my garden," Sarah said, hugging her.

"And I will come and help you with it. You can teach me about plants and life. I'd like to grow tulips."

"Then I'll look forward to that," Sarah said, wiping away a tear. "Your room will always be there for you."

"I know that," Opal said.

Sarah turned to Ruth and said, "I'm entrusting my daughter, my special Opal, to you. Please, look after her for me?"

"Of course," Ruth said, holding up her hands in a gesture of reconciliation. "I will care for her as if she were my own. As two becomes three, she will be our foster daughter."

Sarah nodded. "Thank you for the reassurance."

Sarah and Abel turned to leave. Once they had passed the halfway point on the bridge, the mists obscured them from view.

Soon after that Enoch said, "They're safe on the Topeth side now."

Opal turned to ask him, "You said the gold angels are leaving, so when is that happening? And what am I going to do here when they've gone? There'll be no angels in Unity. It's unthinkable."

"They're not leaving… because they've already left."

"What? Already left? When was that?"

"The night you saw them with the aid of the black mirror. What you witnessed was the departure of the gold angels. That was their exodus."

"It was? But that was such a significant moment for humanity and yet no one even knew about it."

"Enoch and me, we knew about it," Ruth said, drawing a sigh. "We felt it keenly, particularly me. When the angels are nearby, they bring a natural well-being and keep us away from misfortune. They're like unseen guardians. During the two days that they've been gone, we've had no protection. Because of that, Damien was able to find and arrest my Enoch, something that would never have happened if the angels had been here. And that was why I was so ill, Opal."

"I didn't know," Opal said. She paused and then asked, "And if the gold angels have gone, who or what is there to aid humanity? Are we truly alone? What will become of us?"

"Don't worry. There are new ones," Enoch said.

"New ones?" Opal asked.

"Why yes, can't you see?" Enoch asked.

"See what?"

"The roof of the temple."

"What about it? It's reflecting the sunlight. It's dazzling. All because it's coated in... *silver*," she said.

"They're silver angels," Enoch said.

Opal stared at them in wonder. "They-they're not the same as the others, the gold angels? They have a different shape. They're shaped like a bell, a huge bell. And, wait, I'm seeing them... without the aid of the box!"

"Welcome to the enhancements of Unity," Enoch said. "And please, remember to breathe."

"Oh, yes, of course," Opal said. "I'm just so excited. It's exhilarating. Tell me, please, why are they here, these silver angels?"

"Their ways are expansive," Enoch said. "They quicken and bring a vibrant, novel permission for humanity. They're heralds of a new epoch."

"When two becomes three, a new epoch there will be," she said. "Now I know what it means."

"What does it mean to you?" Enoch asked.

"The prophecy says I am the key," she said. "I'm here because I am going to join you and Ruth. If you'll have me."

"Of course we'll have you," Enoch said. "Ruth and I are growing old. We've got used to looking after the gold angels. The silver angels were ready to come in, bringing the vibrancy and quick-fire intelligence of youth. We'll help you but they need someone like you, someone young and of their kind."

"But why's this change happening now?"

"The time grows ripe for change and the Creator could wait no longer," Enoch said. "So, the gold angels were recalled, and the silver angels sent in their stead. And you are here to serve them, as are we."

Ruth whispered in Enoch's ear, and he turned to Opal and said, "I'm forgetting my duties as a host. Let me show you the beauty and bounty of your new home."

She followed Enoch to the concourse outside the Cathedral, its twin spires reaching upwards to heaven, its windows gleaming in the slanting rays of the morning sunlight.

Their arrival seemed to further entice the angels from their subterranean retreats because, no sooner had Enoch spoken, than there was an ethereal presence around the Cathedral; a bright silver etheric stood out from it by a foot or so, with flashing sequins of purples and lime greens.

Enoch showed her the market, the residences and the Acropolis: the school, the temple and the Amphitheatre. The streets were deserted but clean, the buildings empty but pristine, all amazingly preserved in the glow of the sun. The gardens were filled with gorgeous cyclamen with their long thin stems and elegant purple flowers alongside pink aromatic damask roses and white Madonna lilies.

They entered a circular arena called the Court of the Topaz Visionary. The ambience of the vaulted marble architecture held a suspended silence full of hidden mysteries. Opal mused on its seams of charisma and soaked up its rich quiescence.

She felt so light she could walk on air. Miraculously, the blisters on the soles of her feet had healed. She had never felt so much at ease, with so much well-being, and so quiet within herself that she could sense the presence of Auriga. Opal knew that her whole life had waited for this moment and, now it was here, she was fulfilled. Her senses were enhanced. The smells of the town were rich and subtle and fragrant beyond anything she had ever experienced.

At the Cathedral concourse, she gazed again at the movement of the angels, like magic lanterns with huge ethereal wings, with cascades of pale green and fountains of tiny, sparkling silver balls.

"I'm glad to see," Ruth said, "you're enjoying the natural enhancements that flow from being close to these great entities."

All she could do was nod her head.

"Opal, you have nothing to fear here," Ruth went on. "You have a ruby heart, your love is deep, your compassion is profound, and you have the mental toughness you'll need to survive what's incoming in the future."

"I-I don't know what to say," Opal said. She shrank in the face of the huge unknown of the task ahead of her. Through her own persistence and defiance, she had succeeded in achieving her dream and now she had no idea what it involved.

"I see a shadow of uncertainty in your eyes," Ruth went on. "It's normal. You're about to embark on an incredible journey. You will find you are far more capable than you can ever have imagined. Always have faith in your own abilities and remember that your presence here was written in the stars."

"I never knew that life, that being alive, that being human, and freely electing to be so, could be this exalted."

ACKNOWLEDGEMENTS

For every story, there's a hidden one behind it, and that's the story of its arising. For this novel, I first put pen to paper in April 2019, but the story's genesis was many years before, possibly as long as forty, if not longer. The writing of it was somewhat shorter, and I finished the final draft in December 2020.

My debt of gratitude grows to my long-suffering partner, Irene, for her patience and also to my good friends, James Harries and Nick Deputowski, who continue to tolerate my idiosyncrasies. Thanks go to my old friend, Irit Sarel, for her help with Hebrew mythology and for supplying invaluable local information.

I want to say a heartfelt thank you to Dea Parkin and her editors at Fiction Feedback for their help with the structural edit.

Thanks also to my beta readers for their erudite comments: Vincent Triola, Dani Rei, Sarah Levesque, Tiffany White, AJ Skelly, Mary McGrane, and Sarah Byard. Once again, warm thanks go to Mike, Gavin and the other members of Bristol Writers Group, you know who you are.

Large parts of this novel were written in the peace of Buckfast Abbey, Devon, England, in the company of the Benedictine Monks. They do not know how fortunate they are.